John wondered if Natalie would ask what he was thinking

She didn't. Because she didn't care enough? Because she didn't feel she had the right?

Had she been the same with her husband? Or was he the one who'd taught her that what he didn't choose to tell her was none of her business? The speculation seemed disloyal. Stuart Reed had been his partner.

The silence lengthened. John became aware of the quiet and darkness beyond the kitchen. He grabbed the edge of the counter. "Time to hit the sack."

She did just what he was hoping to avoid. She touched him. "Are you all right?"

He couldn't insult her by backing away. All he could do was wait until her hand dropped to her side. He sounded hoarse when he said, "Nothing a good night's sleep won't cure."

Her expression relaxed. "I'll see you in the morning." Startling him, she brushed the lightest of kisses on his cheek. Then she left the room.

He stood frozen in her wake, conscious of the faint scent she'd left behind, something flowery that suited her.

Voice harsh and low, he said, "Damn, damn, damn."

Dear Reader,

His *Partner's Wife* was born out of the paranoia we all feel.
(Come on, admit it!) One of the worst betrayals to us
individually and as a society is a cop gone bad. Since I've
been writing so much in the past few years about cops, it was
perhaps natural for me to think of a creepy way one of them
could use his power. I coupled his villainy with the story of
a woman who, after her husband's death, has to take a fresh
look at her memories of him, understanding that he wasn't the
man she'd thought him to be. Bad enough to be widowed, but
what if much of your life together had been a lie?

This story is the beginning of a trilogy, born because I had
ideas for a number of stories that all had cops as heroes. If the
cops were brothers, and had *become* cops because of a tragedy
in their past, I had a whole, not just the parts. Interest
sparked, I started to write.

I continue to write about police officers because their work
holds all the drama, mystery, action and pathos so lacking
in the everyday lives of, say, writers. They take unimaginable
risks daily in every car stop, every domestic disturbance call.
They're heroes, and their motivations and emotions the stuff
of novels.

Here's hoping you find these brothers as compelling as I do.

Janice Kay Johnson

P.S. I love to hear from readers. You can reach me via
www.superauthors. com

Books by Janice Kay Johnson

HARLEQUIN SUPERROMANCE
889—WHOSE BABY?
913—JACK MURRAY, SHERIFF
936—PROMISE ME PICKET FENCES
      (in the BORN IN A SMALL TOWN collection)
944—THE DAUGHTER MERGER

His Partner's Wife
Janice Kay Johnson

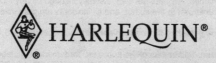

HARLEQUIN®

TORONTO • NEW YORK • LONDON
AMSTERDAM • PARIS • SYDNEY • HAMBURG
STOCKHOLM • ATHENS • TOKYO • MILAN • MADRID
PRAGUE • WARSAW • BUDAPEST • AUCKLAND

ISBN 0-373-70998-6

HIS PARTNER'S WIFE

Copyright © 2001 by Janice Kay Johnson.

This one's for Mom, starting on a new stage of life.
Your strength and independence have always been,
and still are, my inspiration.

CHAPTER ONE

DINNER TABLE CONVERSATIONS about blood-spatter patterns and other minutiae of crime scenes didn't faze Natalie Reed. Her deceased husband had been a homicide detective who talked about his job as if everyone hunted killers for a living.

The abstract, she discovered on the day when she found a dead man in her own house, was not the same as a gory here-and-now.

Nothing had been out of the ordinary at work. Natalie sold advertising space for the *Port Dare Sentinel,* a daily newspaper. The job would be easier, she suspected, in a larger city. Port Dare boasted fifty thousand citizens, but was relatively isolated on Washington's Olympic Peninsula. Tourists from the urban areas around Seattle or Tacoma had a two-hour drive to Port Dare to catch the ferries crossing the Strait of Juan de Fuca for Victoria, British Columbia. Instead of being a suburb to a larger city, Port Dare stood alone, which was why it had a small-town atmosphere. In other words, you constantly tripped over your neighbor's toes.

Today's challenge had been persuading the annoyed owner of a sporting goods store that he'd be making a mistake to quit running his regular advertisement in the *Sentinel* out of ire because the editor had endorsed his opponent for the city council.

"Why the hell should I let you have my advertising dollars?" he'd asked sulkily.

"Because you get more bang for them with the *Sentinel* than you would anywhere else. Our rates are better than good. We're focused—our market is yours. Your customers read the *Sentinel*." She'd smiled wryly at him. "Come on, George. You were a businessman before you were a politician. The editor couldn't make his decision based on advertising dollars, you know that. We would have had an unhappy advertiser whichever one of you we endorsed."

He grunted and grumbled, but in the end grudgingly ran his standard insert in the Sunday edition.

It had been a close call, Natalie knew, so she was still metaphorically patting herself on the back when she parked in the driveway at home and locked the car. Thanks to her good mood, she felt only a tinge of annoyance at the fact that she couldn't pull into the two-car garage. Stuart had filled the garage with so much junk long before she'd married him that not even her compact would fit. She kept meaning to do something about it, but Stuart had never thrown anything away, which meant she would be spending the next five years going through boxes of old magazines or clothes and drawers full of such useless flotsam as old receipts and stamps torn from envelopes. The garage was a low priority.

The house was quiet and fragrant with the smell of freshly baked bread. She had timed the bread machine to finish just about now. A warm slice would taste good with the leftover minestrone soup she planned to have for dinner.

First she intended to get out of her panty hose and suit and into jeans and wool-felt clogs. Dropping her purse on the entry hall table, Natalie headed up the stairs.

The house was a twenty-year-old tri-level: living room, kitchen and dining room on the ground level wing, a family room, unused by her, extra bedroom and the utility room down a few steps in the daylight basement, and above it the master bedroom and bath, her sewing room and Stuart's den. Truthfully, Natalie still thought of the whole house as Stuart's because he'd been so settled in it before their brief marriage. She had been trying very hard these past months to make first small changes and then larger ones that would put her stamp on what was her home until she chose to sell it.

The carpet muffled her footsteps. Taking out her hoop earrings, she started past her sewing room before pausing in exasperation. Darn it, the cat had obviously napped in the middle of the fabric and had torn the tissue pattern pieces she'd laid out and pinned. Clumps of long black fur clung to the material, too. Her fault—she'd meant to shut the door and forgotten.

Or had she? Natalie frowned. Strange. She'd have sworn... She gave her head a small shake and philosophically accepted reality. The door was open. The cat had undeniably napped, leaving plenty of trace evidence. Earrings in hand, she continued down the hall.

Natalie was two steps past the den before a wave of shock hit her. Terror smacked her next. She froze, her own accelerated heartbeat as loud as a snare drum through a thin wall. Had she really seen a man lying in Stuart's den? With his head...

She didn't want to think about his head.

Through the half-open door she could see into her bedroom. It lay still and empty, just as she'd left it. The bed was made, the pinwheel quilt without even a depression left by the cat. The closet doors were closed. What she couldn't see was what lay—or stood—behind the door: her dresser, the second closet that still held some of Stuart's things, the doorway to the master bath. Somebody could be in there, waiting, listening to her heartbeat, her choked breathing.

Somebody could also be hidden in the den with the body or in her sewing room, or downstairs, closing off her escape from the house.

Forward or back? Her mind felt as paralyzed as her legs. *Think!* she told herself fiercely.

The master bedroom door had a lock, if she dashed in.

A dumb little lock that she'd picked herself with a hair pin.

Back, then, she decided.

Natalie eased slowly down the hall, trying to watch the three partially open doorways and the downstairs at the same time. She checked only briefly at the den. Yes, a man lay facedown on the gray carpet, and the back of his head seemed to have...well, imploded. She shuddered.

This door, too, blocked her sight line to part of the room. She did not linger for more than the brief second she needed to be sure she hadn't imagined the horror. Down the stairs. There she clutched the banister, white-knuckled, and scanned the living room and what she could see of the dining room. The familiarity comforted and jarred at the same time. If somebody had been murdered upstairs, why hadn't the downstairs been tossed? If *he* was hiding in the kitchen, why was the morning newspaper open precisely where she'd left it on the table after breakfast? Why was the bread machine beeping as though nothing was wrong?

Natalie recognized that she was on the verge of hysteria. *Now,* she told herself, and ran for the front door. She was sobbing as she struggled with the knob, finally winning the right to stumble out. Slamming the door behind her, she raced to the car, grateful—oh, so grateful—that it *wasn't* parked in the garage. She had the presence of mind to check the back seat before she fell in and locked all the doors. Cell phone…oh, God. It was in her purse, which sat on the hall table. There was no way she was going back in.

On another lurch of terror, she realized that, unfortunately, the car keys were in her purse, too.

She did *not* want to get out of the car. She also had no choice.

Her nearest neighbors on each side didn't get home from work until nearer seven. The new people on the corner, she didn't know. The Porters. She grasped at the thought of the couple, he just past retirement age, she the perpetual housewife. They'd be home. They were always home, nosy and dissatisfied with their neighbors' conduct. Their ranch house with manicured lawn and unnatural edging of bedding plants was across the street and two doors down.

Natalie took slow, deep breaths, made herself unlock the car door with shaking hand and get out. Nothing moved behind the windows of her house. Whoever had been there was surely long gone.

At least, one of them was long gone. The other…

She swallowed dryly. The other would leave in a body bag.

She didn't quite run to her neighbors', but she came close. Their doorbell gonged deep in the recesses of the house. For a moment, the silence made her fear the Porters were, unbelievably, not home. How could that be? Everyone in the neighborhood swore they never went out, even to grocery shop, although Mrs. Porter grumbled about Safeway's produce and Thriftway's service, just as she did about the mail carrier—who threw the mail to the back of the box—and the new people on the corner who didn't mow often enough. Natalie didn't know what the Porters said about her. Right now, she didn't care.

Please be home.

Above her heartbeats she heard a footstep, and then the rattle of a chain. Trust the Porters to bother, in a town that had yet to have a serial killer going door to door.

But there was that dead man in Stuart's den.

The door opened; Mrs. Porter peered around it. The suspicion altered instantly and the door swung wider. "My dear! What's wrong?"

"I..." For all the world, Natalie couldn't seem to get further. Her mouth only worked.

Mrs. Porter, miraculously, drew her in and locked the door behind her. "Come in here and sit down," she said firmly. "There you go." She steered Natalie into the living room, eased her into a wing chair and patted her hand. "Can you tell me now?"

"What is it?" Mr. Porter asked from the doorway. He looked stooped, his hair whiter than Natalie remembered. It seemed as though he'd aged ten years in the one he'd been retired.

"Hush," his wife said. "Give her a minute."

"I…" Stuck again, Natalie closed her eyes. Big mistake. As though her mind had snapped a digital photo available for instant review, there he was. White bits of bone and brown hair matted with blood. Gray tissue. Her stomach heaved and she pressed a hand to her mouth.

"You're ill." Mrs. Porter half rose.

"No." Natalie swallowed. She could not give in to the nausea. Not yet. "I…I just got home from work. And there's somebody in my house." Above their twittering, she finished. "Somebody dead."

They were amazingly kind and efficient. Mr. Porter called the police. Mrs. Porter wrapped an afghan about Natalie's shoulders and vanished briefly to return with a cup of tea. The warm, sweet brew settled her stomach as nothing else could have. Her neighbors waited with her, Mr. Porter stationed at the front window.

A color commentator, he peered through the crack between the drapes, announcing the arrival of a squad car. "No, two," he corrected himself. "They've gotten out and they're circling your house. Going in."

Natalie pictured the uniformed officers, guns drawn. What if she *had* somehow imagined the corpse in Stuart's den? No. She couldn't have. She hadn't known *that* was how a skull would look if bashed in. She wished she could have continued in blissful ignorance.

"There's a plain car now," her neighbor continued.

Sipping her tea, huddled in the afghan, comforted by the delicate, papery touch of Mrs. Porter's hand patting her every few moments, Natalie saw the scene through his eyes: two big men in suits conferring with the patrol officer who had come out of the house. Both disappearing inside briefly, then reappearing. Glancing down the street, spotting the Porter's house. She knew before the knock when they arrived on the doorstep.

Please, please, let them be friends, she prayed. *Not strangers.*

Most of all, she quite fiercely wanted John McLean. He'd told her of Stuart's death, carried one corner of her husband's coffin, scraped out the gutters on her eaves last January, painted the house this July. He was quiet, soft-spoken, solid, her bulwark. He had been Stuart's partner and, she supposed, was watching out for her from a sense of obligation to her husband rather than from real friendship for her. Nonetheless, she couldn't imagine what she would have done without him this past year. She wished she had told Mr. Porter to ask for him.

But Natalie knew that, even if she had thought of it, she wouldn't have asked. She never called John, except a time or two to suggest he bring his children to dinner. Natalie refused to be the stereotype of a lonely widow, the kind of woman who needed a man at her beck and call, or at least wanted one. Her pride barely let her accept his help when he offered it.

The doorbell rang, and Mr. Porter went to let the officers in. On a rush of relief almost painful in its intensity, Natalie recognized the slow, deep voice of Stuart's former partner before he filled the entry to the living room. At about six feet, John McLean wasn't unusually tall, but his shoulders were broad and his build muscular. Mid-thirties, he kept his russet-brown hair short, as befitted a police officer. His face was pure male—not handsome, in fact undistinguished, she had always thought, except for compelling eyes.

"Natalie!" Gaze locking on her, he came straight across the room as if nobody else was here and crouched in front of the chair. Taking her hands, he said roughly, "You're all right."

"Yes." She sounded tremulous and was embarrassed by the weakness her voice gave away. "Is whoever did it gone?"

"Afraid so." His eyes were bluer than she'd realized. "We recognized the address from dispatch and burned rubber getting here. Who the hell got himself dead in your house?"

We. Of course he wasn't alone. She tore her gaze from his to see another friend beyond his shoulder.

"Geoff." She tried a smile. "I'd forgotten you two were working together."

Perhaps ten years older than John McLean, Geoff Baxter was nearly of a height with John and perhaps a little broader, his waistline thickening and his hairline thinning. He and Stuart had been partners back in their patrol days, and had remained friends until her husband dropped dead of an unexpected heart attack at forty years old. Like John, Geoff had stayed in touch since Stuart's death, even going so far as to offer to haul that "crap" out of the garage so she could use it. He'd wanted to install an electric opener, too, so that he wouldn't have to worry about her.

She doubted even his darker worries had included a corpse inside her house. Natalie gave a shiver.

"You're in shock," John said abruptly. "I hate to ask you questions, but I have to."

"I'm okay." This smile was slightly more successful. "Really. I just had the daylights scared out of me."

He squeezed her hands hard and stood, stepping back. Not only physically—he assumed an air of remoteness. "Tell us what happened."

Mrs. Porter, still hovering, suggested they sit and offered coffee, which both accepted. After she'd brought in a tray, John thanked her and asked if they could speak to Natalie alone. With thinly disguised disappointment, the Porters withdrew.

Natalie took another sip of her tea. Both men had taken out the notebooks ubiquitous to police officers and held pens poised. Their expressions were still sympathetic, but also intent, razor sharp. This was their job. Natalie felt a chill at the realization. Suddenly they had ceased being friends and become detectives who, by nature, were suspicious of everyone.

Including her.

"I got home from work, parked in the driveway—"

"What time?" Detective Baxter interrupted.

She remembered looking at her watch. "5:35—I noticed before I got out of the car."

Pens scratched on paper.

She described events: unlocking the front door—yes, she was sure it had been locked—setting down her purse on the hall table and going straight upstairs. The kitchen and living room had looked just as she'd left them that morning. She told of noticing the sewing room door open, then actually making it a couple of feet past the den before her brain accepted what her eyes had seen: a dead man in Stuart's den. The tale of her flight felt ignominious, but she also knew she'd been sensible.

"You didn't set foot in the den?" John McLean asked.

"No. I was afraid..." She clutched the afghan tighter against another shiver and finished softly, "Somebody might still be in the house. Besides, I could see his head. I knew he couldn't be alive. My checking his pulse wouldn't have done any good."

"You didn't recognize him?"

"I couldn't see his face from the doorway. It never occurred to me that I might know him. I thought..." She didn't know what she *had* thought. "That he must be a burglar or something."

"Very likely." John didn't sound satisfied. "Two of them may have had a quarrel."

"But why *my* house?" Was she asking them, or the Fates? "Stuart's stereo is nice, I guess, and a burglar could have that big-screen TV with my compliments, but they're both still there. I don't know if anything was touched."

"The scumbag might have panicked after bashing in his partner's head and fled. Or run when he heard you opening the front door."

"But how did he get in? And out?"

"The side door into the garage was unlocked."

"But..." Disturbed, she looked from face to face. "I always keep it locked. The one from the garage into the house, too. I've hardly set foot into the garage in weeks!"

"Neither door had very good locks." A frown furrowed John's forehead. "I should have replaced them for you."

"You couldn't possibly have predicted that anything like this would happen. Or that anybody would want to break into my house at all. Beyond his stereo system, about all Stuart had was the house and, gosh—'' she waved her hand vaguely ''—treasures like ten years of *Field & Stream* and *Sports Illustrated* packed in boxes. Totally intact, no issues missing.'' Stuart had made a point of telling her that when he caught her about to recycle a copy of *SI*. He'd looked at her as if she were an idiot when she ventured to ask why he was keeping them all. ''Heaven knows the house doesn't exactly shout money,'' she added now.

John grunted. ''It's a decent place in a decent neighborhood. These days, everybody has electronic equipment. Our Port Dare criminals specialize in stuff that's easily turned over. None of them would know a piece of genuine artwork from a reproduction if it was labeled. Jewelry is always good, and I'm sure they would have hunted in your bedroom if everything had gone according to plan.''

''But the den?'' Why was she arguing? She *wanted* murderer and victim to be common burglars, having nothing to do with her. Still… ''Stuart's computer is dated.''

''You might have had a laptop tucked away in there, a pager, an expensive calculator.'' He shrugged.

''Yes. I suppose.'' Now *she* was the one to feel dissatisfied, but it took her a moment to analyze her unhappiness with the scenario.

Why wouldn't two burglars have immediately unplugged and taken the obviously expensive television and stereo equipment before exploring further? Her sewing machine was a fancy, electronic model that did everything but wash the dishes. Wouldn't they have considered it worth taking? Besides… Now the discontent stirred anew.

"The cat had been napping in there."

"What?"

She saw that she'd startled both men.

"It must not have just happened," Natalie explained, thinking it through as she went. "I shut the door to my sewing room last night. When I got home today, that door had been open long enough for the cat to have taken a nap on the fabric I'd laid out in there. And Sasha wouldn't have relaxed enough to take a nap in the open unless strangers were long gone. Which means I didn't scare him away."

Geoff Baxter looked doubtful at her logic.

John frowned thoughtfully. "The coroner hasn't arrived yet. She'll be able to give us a time frame."

"I suppose it doesn't matter what time he was killed."

The two men stirred.

"I know it does to you," Natalie conceded. "To your investigation. But to me... Actually, I'd rather think he *wasn't* still in the house when I got home. The idea that he was standing behind one of the doors, listening to me, maybe even watching..."

John half rose to his feet, then seemed to force himself to sit back down. His face was grim.

Natalie hunched inside the afghan. "*That* gives me the creeps," she concluded simply.

John made a gritty sound and slapped shut his notebook. "Damn it, you're coming home with me tonight."

She wanted nothing more, but her pride, so important to her, insisted she protest. "I have friends I can stay with."

"Yeah, and I'm one of 'em." He stood. "I'll see

if I can bail out your toothbrush and drop you at home right now.''

"But I can drive.''

"No.'' His pointed gaze took in her knotted fists and the shiver she couldn't hide. "You're in shock. Mom's with the kids. She'll enjoy babying you.''

Ridiculous to feel disappointed. Of course he wouldn't stay with her. He had a murder to investigate. She knew the drill: he would probably work for twenty-four straight hours, canvassing neighbors, supervising crime scene technicians, following up on the tiniest leads. The older the trail, the less likely that a murderer would be caught, Stuart always said. Homicide cops did not drop an investigation to take the night off and pat the little woman's shoulder.

"I...that's nice of you, but shouldn't you ask your mother?'' Natalie had only met Ivy McLean a handful of times, the first at Stuart's funeral. John was divorced and his two kids lived with him. His mother must be baby-sitting tonight.

Geoff cleared his throat. "You know Linda will give me hell if I don't bring you home with me.''

Natalie doubted his wife would go that far. The two women were casual friends because of their husbands, but they had so little else in common, they'd never progressed beyond the occasional invitation to dinner.

A tiny spark of bemusement penetrated the numbness she'd wrapped around herself as snugly as the afghan. "I do have women friends who can run me a hot bath and tuck me in. Really, you don't have to...''

John's hard stare silenced her. "Yes. I do. I'd rather know where you are.''

Because she was a suspect in a murder investigation? The thought shook her. John couldn't really believe even for a second that she would do something like that, could he?

"Yes. All right," she said, sounding ungracious but too discombobulated to figure out what woman friend would actually have a spare bedroom without putting a child out. She would have to explain, too, listen to exclamations of horror, perhaps endure avid curiosity. Ivy McLean was the mother of not just one son in law enforcement, but three. She would have heard it often enough before to imagine the scene without wanting the details. Natalie didn't like the idea of putting out a near-stranger, but if she just took a hot bath and went straight to bed, she didn't have to be much trouble.

"What else do you need?" John asked. "Are you on any prescriptions? What about a nightgown or clothes for morning?"

Morning would be Saturday, and she wouldn't have to work, thank heavens.

"My purse," she said, explaining where she'd dropped it. "The middle drawer in my dresser has jeans, and T-shirts are in the one below that. I left a sweater draped over a chair in my bedroom. Nightgowns are in the top drawer."

"Underwear?"

She could rinse out the ones she was wearing. But she'd sound so missish if she suggested that, Natalie tried to match his matter-of-fact tone. "There's a small drawer on top next to the mirror."

"Good enough." John left to go fetch her things. He and Geoff had a brief discussion she couldn't hear at the door. A moment later, Natalie heard Geoff telling the Porters he needed to ask them a few questions.

In the living room, they sat side by side on the couch, Mrs. Porter clutching her husband's hand. She sat very straight, a dignified, tiny woman whose dark hair was whitening in streaks, her husband a tall, thin man whose color was none too good. Her eyes were bright, his dull. Natalie remembered guiltily that she'd heard something about bypass surgery a few months back. Had anybody in the neighborhood brought meals or even just expressed sympathy? Their kindness today made Natalie feel terrible about the way she'd shrugged off the casually mentioned news.

Geoff's questions were routine. Had they seen or heard anything out of the ordinary? Cars they didn't recognize?

Shaking her head, Mrs. Porter said, "We grocery shopped this morning, then had lunch."

So they did actually go out.

"This afternoon Roger mowed the lawn while I deadheaded the roses. I don't believe a car passed the entire while. Did you see one, dear?"

He frowned, giving it careful thought. "No. No, I didn't notice one."

"Then we lay down for a quick nap," his wife continued. "I'd just begun thinking about putting dinner on."

Geoff thanked them gravely and closed his notebook. Natalie carefully folded the afghan and laid it on the arm of the chair.

Standing, she smiled even as she felt the hot spurt of tears. "You've been so kind. I don't know what I would have done if you hadn't been home. Please, let me know if there's ever anything I can do for you."

"Oh, my dear!" Mrs. Porter stood and came to Natalie, taking her hand, hers dry but surprisingly strong. "We've wished we could help you since your husband died! All by yourself in that big house. You come see us anytime." She turned a commanding gaze on the detective. "You will let us know when you catch the man who did such an awful thing, now won't you?"

"It'll be in the newspapers," he promised.

"Assuming you do catch him," she said acerbically, sounding like her sharp self for the first time tonight.

Geoff's expression became wooden. "We'll do our best, ma'am."

"See that you do." She gave Natalie's hand a last squeeze. "Warm milk does help you sleep."

"I'll remember that." Natalie was teary again as Geoff escorted her out. She must still be in shock. She wasn't usually so emotional.

"We will catch him," Geoff promised as they crossed the street. "Count on it."

"I know you will." Natalie paused on the sidewalk in front of her house and gazed at it, wondering if it would ever seem familiar and safe again. She felt again the sense of wrongness, and this time, it raised goose bumps on her skin. She rubbed her forearms. "I only hope you arrest him soon. It's going to give me the creeps to go home, wondering why they were in my house and whether *he* could get in again."

"Maybe you *shouldn't* go home." Frowning, Geoff held open the car door for her. "Until we figure out for sure what they were after."

She liked the way he worried about her. Even if his concern, too, was for Stuart's sake.

"Yeah, but I don't want to develop a phobia about my own house." Natalie sighed and climbed into the passenger seat of the dark blue car. "We'll see how it goes."

He nodded, as kind in his way as the Porters had been. Voice gruff, he said, "Just remember, there's a fine line between bravery and idiocy. Don't push yourself to do something you're uncomfortable with."

"I won't," she promised.

John McLean emerged from the house carrying her overnight bag and purse. Both she and Geoff turned their heads to watch him cut across her lawn. She liked watching him move, with the discipline and grace of an athlete, his stride purposeful and long.

What would she have thought of him if she were a normal citizen who didn't know the investigating officers? Natalie wondered idly. Would his physical bulk and the bulge of the gun he carried in a shoulder holster have intimidated her? She certainly couldn't have known that he had a dry sense of humor or that his eyes often held a twinkle even as his mouth remained unsmiling. Or that this cop in a dark, well-cut suit would go home most days to cook dinner for his children, help them with homework, supervise baths and tuck them in.

Her mind roved further. If she'd never met Detective John McLean, if she weren't a widow of barely a year, could she have been attracted to him?

Jolted, Natalie uttered a small, startled sound that Geoff, mercifully, seemed not to notice. Where in heck had *that* idea come from? For goodness' sake, she'd known John for several years and never once thought of him in those terms! He was Stuart's friend. Period.

No, not period. Of course he'd become her friend,

too. Why else had she needed him so desperately today?

Of course she wasn't attracted to him. She would have noticed before now.

No, Natalie knew perfectly well what she was doing. John was an excuse, that's all. What she was avoiding thinking about was her house, and especially what—who—lay upstairs, or of the cleaning job she'd have afterward. Would she ever be able to go upstairs again without her heart pounding? Would she be able to stroll into the den—stepping just where the body now lay—and sit down to use the computer without a frightened consciousness of where blood had soaked into the carpet?

Natalie was grateful for the distraction John provided when he stopped by the open car door. At the same time she noticed that he carried a brown paper grocery bag in his free arm, she caught the whiff.

"My bread!"

"It seemed a shame to let it go to waste." His rare smile relaxed his face. "I doubt we're going to lift a fingerprint from your bread machine."

"Thank you." Those wretched tears threatened again. If one more person was nice to her, she was going to start sobbing. Natalie took the grocery bag and wrapped her arms around it, the delicious aroma and warmth almost as comforting as a hug. She blinked hard. "John, I almost forgot poor Sasha. She's going to be scared by all the strangers trooping through."

"Actually, I just shut her in your sewing room." John cleared his throat. "She was, uh, somewhat annoyed. I doubt you want her in there, but we can't have her in the den."

"No, that's fine." The fabric could be washed again before she cut it out, the pattern pieces taped. "Her litter box is in the garage." As if they wouldn't find it.

"And her food in the kitchen. I saw it. Don't worry. I'll take care of the cat."

As he'd taken care of her gutters and her Christmas lights and the rotten branch from the maple tree that had splintered a ten-foot stretch of the cedar board fence that enclosed her backyard.

"You're always so nice to me." She sounded watery.

The two men exchanged a look.

Seemingly galvanized, John slapped the roof of the car. "Geoff, you get started here. I'll be back in twenty minutes."

"Then get the hell out of here." Geoff gave her a crooked smile. "Forget the warm milk. Raid the liquor cabinet."

She laughed through her tears as he closed her door and John got in behind the wheel.

CHAPTER TWO

NATALIE FELT John's searching gaze as he started the car.

"You okay?" he asked again, quietly.

"Of course I am!" She wiped wet cheeks. "I don't know what's wrong with me. Well, yes, of course I do. It shook me up, and I suppose I'm in shock, a little."

"More than a little." The car accelerated into traffic on Neah Drive. Speaking deliberately, John said, "The first time I saw a man who'd been murdered, I stayed cool long enough to get outside and around the corner of the warehouse where he'd been gunned down. Threw up everything I'd eaten in the past twenty-four hours. I went back in and did my job, but every so often I'd find myself looking at him and just being hit by it—that's a guy like me, flesh and blood. That's what *my* blood would look like spilling out." He gave his head a shake. "Nothing brings your own mortality home like the sight of violent death."

"I suppose that's part of it," she admitted. "I don't like to think that my head…"

His hand closed briefly on her knee. "Most of us don't walk into a crowbar."

"No. I know." She bit her lip. "But he was in my house. So maybe…"

When she hesitated, he finished for her. "Next time someone will take a swing at your head."

Her nod was tiny and slightly ashamed. Shouldn't she be grieving for the death of even a stranger, feeling—how did it go?—that the loss of any man diminished her? Instead she felt violated because he had bled out his life in *her* house.

And she was afraid.

"Natalie, look at me."

Startled, she realized that they were stopped at a light in the old part of town. An enormous Queen Anne style turn-of-the-century house on one corner was now a bed-and-breakfast; across the street, an antique shop spilled onto the sidewalk from what had probably once been a carriage house. She had been blind to the view of the bay during the drive here, to the arrival of a ferry that had disembarked the long line of cars waiting to race up the hill toward the highway. John lived here in Old Town, just a few blocks away, in a more modest restored Victorian.

She turned her head to meet his frowning gaze.

"I will not let you be hurt." His words had the power of a vow. "I promise."

The idea panicked her. Natalie shook her head hard. "No. Don't promise. How can you? At some point, I'll have to go home even if you don't make an arrest. What if he did come back? Are you going to abandon your children to hover in my shrubbery every night? No," she said with finality. "I don't want to be a weight on your conscience."

A horn sounded behind them, then another one. For a moment John still didn't move, his electric, brooding eyes holding hers. Then he blinked, shuttering the intensity, and flung an irritated glance at the mirror.

"Yeah, yeah, hold your horses," he growled, stepping on the gas. He drove the remaining blocks in silence, but her stolen look saw the deep lines carved in his forehead. In front of his house, he set the emergency brake and turned off the engine. Turning a near-scowl on her, he said, "All right. How's this instead? I'll do my damnedest to keep you safe."

"That," she said, smiling shakily, "I can accept. Gratefully."

SHE WAS GOING TO ACCEPT his help gratefully?

Driving away from his house, John gave a grunt of wry amusement. Oh, yeah. Sure.

The next moment, his brows drew together. No, he wasn't being fair. Natalie would be grateful, all right.

She would just hate having to be.

Actually, he liked that about her. His mother excepted, the women John had known well had tended to be dependent on the men in their lives. They assumed a man would fix anything that was wrong.

Not that Natalie was the prickly type; far from it. She was warm, gentle, relaxed, a comfortable voice on the phone when he felt like talking out a day's problems. But she was also determined—sometimes infuriatingly so—not to lean on anyone, even if she was a new widow.

No matter what he did for Natalie, no matter how trivial, she'd thank him gravely but with a troubled expression puckering her brow. Then he could count on her bringing a plate of cookies to the station, or sending a casserole home with him, or buying gifts for Evan and Maddie. She had to balance the scales. Always.

In John's book, friends did each other favors. Natalie was on her own now, and he didn't mind picking up some of the slack. He liked working with his hands, and if painting her house meant dumping the kids at their friends' homes, heck, they'd have a better time with their buddies than they would if he took them out to the spit anyway. It wasn't as if his five-year-old son and eight-year-old daughter didn't get plenty of his attention. Except for work, he was with them most of the time.

He knew Stuart Reed hadn't left any life insurance, and he was pretty sure Natalie didn't make enough to be able to afford to put out fifteen hundred dollars or so to have her house painted. The very fact that she bit her lip, let him do the work and thanked him prettily told John that he was right: she needed him.

She just wished like hell that she didn't.

Did she feel guilty at putting him out? Hate any hint of dependence? He didn't know, hadn't asked. John would have been over there cleaning out her gutters no matter what. She was his partner's widow. Stuart would have done the same for John's children, if he'd been the one to go.

Natalie seemed to understand and accept that. She'd let John hold her when he brought the news of Stuart's death. He had stood beside her at her husband's funeral, kept an arm around her as Stuart's casket was lowered into the ground and the first, symbolic chunk of earth was flung down onto its shining surface. That was John's place, and she hadn't tried to keep him from it.

Huge dark circles under her eyes, she'd gone back to work a week after the funeral. She hadn't asked to be held again, and wouldn't. Admiring her strength,

John had found himself talking to her as if she was another man.

He knew she was a woman, of course. Her ripe curves and leggy walk might have fueled a few fantasies under other circumstances. But that wasn't how he thought of her. It was her laugh and her wisdom and her grave dignity that characterized her. He'd never been friends with a woman before, but somehow it had happened with her, perhaps because he'd known her for several years as his partner's wife. That was another page out of John's book: you didn't lust after a friend's wife.

The end result was that he'd quit noticing her looks. He liked talking to her. He'd call just to see how things were going, stop by casually to do small jobs around the house he figured she wouldn't get to. She seemed to enjoy his kids. As far as he knew, she hadn't begun to date. No possessive man had taken to hanging around questioning John's presence. He and Natalie had an easy relationship that he savored. He didn't know when—if ever—he'd been able to relax around a woman.

But she wasn't going to like having new reason to be grateful, he reflected.

The damn ferry traffic was still bumper-to-bumper up the main drag. Drumming his fingers on the steering wheel, John strove for patience.

His mother had been just the right medicine tonight, he decided. Strong herself, Ivy McLean expected everyone else to be as well.

He'd left Natalie in his mother's competent but not tender hands. Her brand of coddling, he suspected, would suit Natalie Reed fine.

Ivy McLean hadn't been the most sympathetic of

mothers when her three sons took turns being heart-broken by high school femmes fatales or suffering knee injuries on the football field. *Get over it* was her sometimes impatient message. *Stand up tall, focus on what's important.* Football was not. Neither were teenage romances.

Swearing when he didn't make it through an inter-section before the light turned red, John grimaced. Come to think of it, not much that had mattered to seventeen-year-old boys had been truly important in Ivy MacLean's eyes. Grades, she cared about. Living honestly and with integrity. Accepting the duty their father's murder had laid on all three boys.

In Natalie Reed's case, Mom would understand a degree of shock and would respect outrage. She would be kind in her brisk way, without encouraging an excess of tears or self-pity or fear. Hell, John thought ruefully, most likely Mom would buck Nat-alie up and have her ready to rip down the crime scene tape and move home tomorrow morning, to hell with the murderer on the loose.

Maybe this hadn't been such a good idea.

Earlier, when Ivy had seen her son out, they'd left Natalie listening to Maddie chatter about a roller-skating party.

"You'll find out what happened and why," Mom said, chin set and gaze steady. It wasn't a question. *This* was what counted. She'd raised her sons to be-lieve that any one man could make the world a safer place and now she was expecting him to get on with it.

She hadn't said, *Make an arrest tonight,* but she might as well have.

A frown stayed on his brow until he reached Natalie Reed's tri-level house. The crime scene techs were here, he was glad to see. A flash popped upstairs. The coroner hadn't yet arrived. She was probably stuck in ferry traffic. Every time one of the giant ferries docked, hundreds of cars poured out, clogging Port Dare's narrow streets.

After parking behind the Investigations unit van, John got out of his car and stood on the sidewalk, making no move to go up to the door. He tried to put himself in the shoes of a stranger and see her house and this neighborhood with fresh eyes.

The paint job—forest-green with cream trim, his doing—didn't look half-bad. All the same, 2308 Meadow Drive was not a showplace. It was an average house in an average neighborhood, one of many developments that had sprung up around the nineteenth-century port town. In this middle-income neighborhood, yards were generally well cared for but standard issue. Most of these were single family homes, owner occupied, not rentals. Bikes with pink tassels on the handlebars lay on their sides in driveways. Gardening was carried out in traditional flower beds mulched with bark, edging lawns that varied from the Porters' velvet green to the shaggy, brown-spotted grass surrounding the corner house. The Porters, John was willing to bet, wouldn't like those fluffy dandelion heads. Or the neighborhood eyesore that sat out in front of the same house, a rusting junker resting on blocks instead of wheels. Nonetheless, even at that house, a tricycle listed half off the driveway, and in the backyard a swing set shared pride of place with a barbecue grill. The lawn got mowed, just not often enough.

Ordinary people.

A neighborhood like this wouldn't have crack houses or marijuana-growing operations in the spare bedroom. Nor did these houses suggest real wealth. The cops would get called here when a mountain bike was stolen out of an open garage. Teenagers committed the few break-ins. Maybe a car prowl from time to time. Serious burglaries would be few and far between. Murder? Never.

So why was there a dead man in Stuart's den? Why had two people broken in, and why had one of them been killed? A quarrel mid-crime was the obvious answer, but then again, why Natalie's house? Why hadn't two burglars carried the obviously expensive electronic equipment out before they risked taking the time to check out the upstairs? Had they parked right in the driveway, a truck backed up to receive stolen goods?

Or were they after something else? Something small?

What? he wondered in frustration. He'd have to ask Natalie whether Stuart had any collections that might be valuable. Coins? Stamps? Hell, he'd collected enough junk to have lucked out and hit on something worth taking. Or did Natalie have jewelry? She hadn't said, and John thought she would have. He remembered seeing her at the Policeman's Ball, drop-dead gorgeous in a simple green velvet sheath, but the only jewelry he could picture were sparkly earrings. Diamond, maybe, but tiny, not ones worth killing over.

Figure out why murderer and victim were in this house and not the neighbor's, and he could as good as snap those handcuffs on. Unfortunately, the *why* was the true mystery here. Murders happened all the time, even in Port Dare. Just not this kind.

He sighed. Better find out what the neighborhood canvass had turned up. Too bad the Porters hadn't seen anything. According to Natalie, they were the only near neighbors who were stay-at-homes and nosy to boot.

Geoff shook his head when John tracked him down a block away.

"Nada. Zip. Nobody was home. Not even latchkey kids."

"Why am I not surprised?" John rocked on his heels and looked back. Meadow Drive curved, and this was the last house from which anyone could have seen Natalie's. "You get everybody?"

"A few haven't come home yet." Geoff glanced down at his notebook. "Four. No, three. The place down there is for sale, and empty right now."

"What about the houses behind hers?"

"I sent Jackson. But what are the odds?"

Nada. Zip. Of course. But they had to try.

"Looks like the coroner is here. Shall we go hear what she thinks?"

Elected in this rural county, Dr. Jennifer Koltes was a pathologist at St. Mary's, serving in addition as part-time public servant. Hereabouts they didn't need a full-time coroner yet. John was counting on it staying that way.

A tall skinny redhead, Dr. Koltes was in her mid-thirties, married to a cardiologist. Currently, she was pregnant, easily six or seven months along. Maybe John was old-fashioned—okay, he undoubtedly was—but the sight of a pregnant woman checking the body temp of a corpse with a smashed skull struck him as jarring.

Hearing their arrival, she glanced up with a pleasant smile also at odds with the scene. "Detectives. Haven't seen either of you for a whole day or two."

The last body had been the result of a bar shoot-out. Neither victim nor shooter, both tattooed, black-leather-garbed motorcyclists, had been locals.

"Busy days," John said laconically.

"Well." She was already closing her bag. "Cause of death looks obvious from here, although you never know. We might be surprised when we get him on the table."

"Weapon?"

"Something darned heavy. Probably smooth and rounded." She pursed her lips. "A metal pipe, maybe. There are a few flakes caught in his hair that might be rust."

"Time of death?"

"I'm guessing morning." She groaned and pressed a hand to her lower back as she straightened from her crouch over the body. "Say, ten, eleven o'clock."

Both men had both taken involuntary steps forward when she began to heave herself to her feet. Now they exchanged a glance.

"That's consistent with what the home owner says."

"Which is?"

Geoff told her about the cat that had napped on the fabric. "And the old couple down the street, the neighborhood snoops, would have been grocery shopping about then."

"I wonder," John said thoughtfully, "whether the Porters go grocery shopping every morning. Or the same morning every week."

Geoff made a note. "Easy to ask."

Dr. Koltes left after conferring with the uniforms

who had been delegated to bag the body. "I can do the autopsy tonight," she said, promising. "You'll have my report tomorrow."

Gazing with distaste at the corpse, John said, "Time to have a look."

He checked back pockets—no wallet. Ditto for the pockets of the crumpled linen jacket. The jacket interested him. Men in Port Dare leaned more to denim or heavy flannel, maybe a dark suit if you worked in a bank or law office. This looked...hell, like *Miami Vice.*

He called for the paramedics, who put a collar on the neck to protect the bashed skull for Dr. Koltes's benefit, and then rolled the body onto a gurney. Face-up, a man who could have been mid-thirties to forty tops stared sightlessly at the ceiling. Longish brown hair, brown eyes, a stubble of beard—this guy had stumbled out of TV land, John thought again. On a wrist that had been under the body was an obviously expensive watch, the kind that probably told you the time in Paris, the altitude and your heart rate.

Sinking back on his heels, John contemplated the face.

"Damn it, Baxter, he looks familiar."

His partner nodded. "I was thinking the same."

"If we know him, he's probably not a realtor or the manager of the Rite Aid pharmacy."

Geoff gestured toward the watch. "Drugs?"

"Could be."

They stood back and let the photographer get full frontal pictures as well as close-ups of the face.

"I want those as soon as possible," John said, and was answered with brisk nods.

"Fingerprints?" he asked.

"The victim's," he was told. "Half a dozen others. Mrs. Reed's, presumably. We'll need to get hers tomorrow."

Feeling uncomfortable admitting it for reasons he didn't like to examine, John said, "Mine will be here, too. I used that bathroom just last week when I was treating the back deck."

To his relief, nobody gave sly or knowing glances. Nobody made an off-color joke about widows—one that would have been deeply regretted.

It helped when Baxter said, "Hell, mine'll be here, too. Natalie had Linda and me to dinner Friday night."

He and Baxter took their time studying the den once the body was carted out. It was a room that could have used Natalie's lighter touch. John guessed that she stayed out of it.

Stuart had smoked cigars, or at least liked to have one clenched between his teeth curling noxious smoke into the air. The smell, faded with time, nonetheless still lingered in here. Walls were papered in a masculine navy-and-tan-striped paper. Bookshelves held Stuart's favorite bedtime reading: Ken Follett, John Le Carré and the ilk.

A monster, the desk was one of those huge oak ones that had probably graced the office of a CEO in the 1920s. The finish was yellowing, the top covered with a blotter. In its own way, the computer that sat atop it was as much an antique, a 385, maybe a 485. Forget Pentium. No telephone line to it, which meant no internet access. No CD drive. In fact, the floppy drives were for the outmoded bigger disks. The keyboard was covered, the monitor screen a little dusty.

Using a handkerchief, John carefully opened drawers. The top one held nothing but paper clips, pencils that needed sharpening, a staple remover, markers and packing tape. The big drawer was set up with hanging files, all labeled: 1986 tax return. Ditto '87, '88, and so on through the year before last. MasterCard statements. Appliance warranties. Household receipts.

On the face of it, nothing of any interest to anyone but the IRS doing a back audit. And, damn, was Stuart ready. No midnight scrabbling for torn receipts for him. It was almost a shame the IRS had never, to the best of John's knowledge, chosen to audit Reed.

The closet held boxes and plastic-wrapped clothes on hangers. A cracked leather aviator jacket, ski pants and parka, a high school letterman's jacket. Some of the boxes were labeled: check stubs, photo albums, records. His turntable had probably given up the ghost, but he wouldn't have given up the records. A faint musty odor lingered in here.

Baxter muttered a profanity. "Did Reed ever throw anything away?"

"Not so's I can tell." John eased the closet door shut again. "Nothing unusual in here, though. We all have crap like this."

"We'd better look in those boxes."

He grunted agreement, however much he disliked the idea. Mining every detail was their job, but usually what he learned about people's lives was of academic interest. He made a mental jigsaw puzzle, slotting pieces in until every one fit. This time was different. Stuart Reed had been not just a fellow cop but John's partner and friend. Even more, he hated the idea of intruding on Natalie's privacy. "Tomorrow," he said.

They tried the remaining houses on the street. One

was still dark; at the two places where someone came to the door, shakes of the head were their answers. They'd been gone all day. Neither knew Natalie or, quite frankly, would have noticed a truck in her driveway if they had been home.

"I say we go back to the station and look for that face," John said at last. "Even odds we have his picture in our books."

"No point in waiting for fingerprint ID," his partner agreed. "Tomorrow is soon enough to look hard at the house."

Mug shots were arranged into books by theme: drug arrests, rape, B and E, and so on. That way, if a store owner was held up, say, he didn't have to gaze at the face of every rapist or marijuana grower who had ever been arrested. He could concentrate on likely perps. This worked fine normally. In this case, however, the face could have been familiar for dozens of reasons.

John's money was on drugs.

The next hour and a half was punctuated only by the slap of a cover closing, the abrupt departure of one man or the other for another cup of coffee, and a couple of trips down memory lane.

"Ha!" Baxter crowed once. "Remember our friend Jerry Canfield? Sending him to the pen in Walla Walla was one of the greater pleasures of this job."

It was Geoff Baxter who found their victim. "Bingo," he said softly. "I knew we'd met."

John rotated his shoulders and waited until his partner shoved the book across the table. From the rows of mug shots, the sullen face jumped out at him.

"He was better looking alive," Baxter said.

"Who isn't? No, don't answer that."

Ronald Floyd had a lengthy rap sheet, starting with possession of cocaine when he was seventeen in Tacoma. Thirty-four the day he died, Floyd had stuck to his chosen career of dealing drugs and slowly risen on the ladder. The part that always amazed John was how little time a guy like Floyd ever served despite multiple arrests. The system was overwhelmed; he'd walked a couple of times because prosecutors had shrugged and decided he wasn't worth the bother. John knew how the arresting officers had felt; after all, *they'd* bothered.

Memory nudged by the photo, he recalled being involved in Ronald Floyd's last arrest, which had led to four years in the Monroe State Penitentiary. Acting on a tip, officers had been waiting when a cabin cruiser docked at the marina. The hold had been packed with plastic bags full of white powder. It had been a pretty good haul, by Port Dare standards.

Unfortunately, those standards were rising by the day. Half the border between Washington State and Canada was water: the Strait of Juan de Fuca and the Puget Sound. The rocky, wooded Canadian Gulf Islands and American San Juan Islands made the waters a maze of spectacular channels and inlets. Pods of orcas tried to elude the ubiquitous whale-watching ships. Sailors and boaters were in paradise, with every island offering hidden coves. Green-and-white Washington State ferries plied the waters between islands and Canada and the USA, while the blue-and-white Canadian ferries carried traffic between Vancouver Island and the mainland.

Paradise for sailors was a nightmare for Coast Guard and law enforcement. Boaters didn't respect customs laws or international boundaries. Smuggling was a breeze—literally, as it filled gaudy sails on blue waters. Officers couldn't search every boat that docked at one of the marinas or anchored in the bay, even when they knew damn well some of them were here on business. Luck and tips led to the few big busts.

Ronald Floyd must have made an enemy, because a muffled voice on the telephone had set him up. Officers had waited in the nighttime shadows at the marina while the pretty white boat eased slowly in, water lapping against the pilings. Floyd himself had bounded from the bow to the dock with the first line. The Port Dare P.D. waited until the boat was tied bow and stern and the engine snuffed. Two other men joined Floyd, all wearing jeans, deck shoes and windbreakers. They'd talked briefly, laughed. Then the spotlight froze them as a dozen police officers packing guns and a warrant surrounded them.

"Stuart cuffed Floyd," John said slowly, remembering. "I got one of the others."

"I didn't make any of the arrests, but I was there." Baxter ran a hand over his thinning hair. "So Stuart booked the guy. That's not much of a connection."

"But it's something. I've been asking myself, why Natalie Reed's house? Why not the one two doors down with the new sunroom?"

Baxter shrugged. "Chance."

"Or maybe not." Suddenly energized, John shoved back his chair. "What do you say we have a chat with some of our stiff's buddies?"

CHAPTER THREE

NATALIE CAME DOWNSTAIRS in the morning to the sound of a girl's laugh and a man's deep voice.

She felt like the walking dead. She'd been able to snatch only bits and pieces of sleep from endless wide-eyed hours. She supposed she'd dreamed, but it was hard to separate unsettling scenes supplied by her unconscious mind from the gruesome images that played behind closed eyelids when she was awake. Last night, sleepless and still in shock, she had wished that today was a working day so that she would have something to *do*. This morning she was intensely grateful that she didn't have to go into the office. Coaxing bad-tempered advertisers into agreeing that a check written to the *Sentinel* was money worth spending was beyond her in her current exhausted state. Maybe she could take Evan and Maddie down to the spit. If she found a warm, sandy spot, she could lean against a log and watch them build castles or splash in the water.

Or fall asleep at last, which wouldn't make her much of a baby-sitter.

In the dining room, she found John and his children seated at their places at the table, which had been nicely set as if for company, with quilted place mats and cloth napkins. As a centerpiece, asters in bright colors made a casual bouquet in a cream-colored pitcher. French doors were closed against a gray, misty day.

She stood in the doorway unnoticed for a moment, feeling as if she were outside, nose pressed to the glass, looking in at a perfect family tableau. Father and children were laughing together, the affection, humor and patience so obvious she felt a pang of envy. For what, Natalie knew quite well. Stuart had squelched her first tentative suggestion that they think about having children. On their wedding day, she had just assumed...

It hurt still, remembering Stuart's quick, thoughtless, "What the hell would we want brats for?"

She must have made a sound, a movement, because John's head turned sharply, his grin fading.

"Good morning." He searched her face with grave, intent eyes even as he gestured at an empty chair. "Mom's making bacon and eggs. She wouldn't let us help." A faint smile pulled at his mouth. "We've been complaining about how slow the service is. My tip isn't going to be big."

"Daddy!" His son giggled. "Grandma doesn't want money!"

Evan McLean was a miniature of his father: russet, wavy hair, vivid blue eyes and big feet that suggested someday he'd match Dad's size as well. Natalie wondered if John had had freckles, too, at five years old.

From the lines in his face, she doubted he'd slept any more than she had, if at all, but he had obviously just showered and shaved. His wet hair was slicked back, the auburn darkened by water. Despite the tiredness that creased his brow and added years, he crackled with energy and the grin he gave his son came readily.

"You don't think Grandma would scoop up a buck if I left one?"

Evan looked crafty. "I bet she'd give it to me. Why don't you leave a dollar and we'll find out. Okay?"

"Greedy," his sister scoffed. Maddie McLean had her mom's blond hair and blue eyes of a softer hue than her father's. Gawky and skinny at this age, she wasn't pretty in a dimpled little-girl way, but Natalie was willing to bet Maddie would be a beauty by the time she was sixteen.

"Just to see," Evan insisted.

"Uh-huh." She rolled her eyes. "Like you'd give it back to Dad."

Her brother bounced indignantly. "I would!" He stole a glance at his father. "If he said I had to."

John laughed, although he still watched Natalie. "Let's not put Grandma to the test, shall we?" The door from the kitchen swung open and he said, "Ah. Looks like breakfast is going to be served."

"At last!" Evan said.

Carrying a plate of toast in one hand and a heaping bowl of scrambled eggs in the other, his grandmother bent a look on him. "Young man, that didn't sound very polite."

Even at five, he had the grace to blush. "I'm just awful hungry, Grandma."

"Ah." Still sounding severe, she said, "You need to learn to *think* 'at last,' not say it. That's the secret to good manners."

His forehead crinkled. "You mean, I can be really rude, just to myself?"

"That's right." A tall woman with beautiful bone structure and gray-streaked red hair cut very short, his grandmother headed back to the kitchen. Just before disappearing through the swinging door, she added, "Truly nice people, however, don't think rude things, either."

"Oh." Looking very small, Evan beseeched his father. "Is that true?"

"Here's a secret, bud." John lowered his voice. "I can't imagine a single person so saintly that he or she doesn't think rude things once in a while. Just so you keep 'em to yourself, you can be a nice person."

Maddie sat with a very straight back and head held regally high. "But you're boys. Girls are *lots* nicer. Aren't they, Natalie?"

Weary as she was, Natalie had to laugh. "Let's see, what grade are you in? Third?"

Maddie nodded. "*He's* only in kindergarten."

So much for the illusion of family harmony she had seen like a shimmering mirage before she stepped into the dining room.

"Right. My point is, girls *are* lots nicer than boys at your age. I'm pretty sure boys reach their peak of awfulness in about fourth grade. But then they do start getting better."

"Really?" both kids said simultaneously.

"I can be *awful?*" Evan sounded delighted at the prospect.

"You mean, they get *worse?*" his sister asked in horror.

"'Fraid so," Natalie said sympathetically. "Or, at least, that's my recollection."

John was laughing as his mother returned with a plate of bacon and another with sausage.

"In case anyone would prefer it to bacon," she said, slapping down the plate. "If that's funny."

The laugh still lingering on his mouth, John said,

"Sit down, Mom. This looks fabulous. No, we were talking about the horrors boys are capable of. Fourth grade was definitely my peak of awfulness."

Mrs. McLean didn't hesitate. "For all of you. No," she corrected herself, handing Natalie the bowl of scrambled eggs to dish up. "Hugh was slow maturing. Fifth or sixth grade was his worst. Do you remember that poor girl who had a terrible crush on him and sent him a poem she'd written?"

John paused with the plate of toast in one hand. A grin deepened the creases in his cheeks. "Oh, yeah. He wrote *her* a poem in return. Rhymed pretty well, too, as I recall. Actually—" he cleared his throat "—I helped. Just with the rhyming. Which, come to think of it, would suggest that I was *still* awful in…what would I have been?"

"A freshman in high school." His mother sounded acerbic. "I can't believe you helped him."

"What did it *say?*" Evan demanded.

"Something about her stink and, um, why she had to pad her bra and her laugh sounding like…" He stopped. "Never mind."

"Awesome," Evan breathed. "Uncle Hugh?"

"It was *not* awesome," his grandmother snapped. "It was cruel. Hugh was unable to play Little League that year in consequence."

Evan's eyes grew big. "Oh."

"What did *you* do, Daddy?" Maddie asked. "When you were in fourth grade?"

He layered jam on his toast and waved the bread knife dismissively. "Oh, I was just repulsive. My idea of falling-down-funny was a fart joke or tripping another kid or somebody making a dumb mistake in an oral presentation."

"That's what *all* the boys in my class are like!" Maddie exclaimed. "My own *dad* was like that?"

"Yup." He tousled her hair. "I don't have a single excuse, kiddo."

"Gol," she muttered.

"If your father had been here," Mrs. McLean began, with a sniff.

A shadow crossed John's face and was gone before Natalie was quite sure she'd seen it. "He was here, Mom. I was in fifth grade when he died."

"Grandad was shot, right?" Enjoying the gory idea that *he* had a relative who had died a bloody death, Evan shoveled in a huge mouthful of scrambled eggs and chewed enthusiastically while he waited for the familiar answer.

That same snap in her voice, his grandmother said, "You know perfectly well that he was, young man, and it's not something we discuss in that tone."

He immediately seemed to shrink. "I didn't mean…" he mumbled around his food.

His father laid a big hand on his shoulder. "It's okay. We know." The gaze he turned on his mother was cold. "Evan is five years old. Death is very academic to him. And he never knew his grandfather."

Her nostrils flared, and her stare didn't back away from his. "Hugh was barely older than Evan when he lost his father."

Tension fairly crackled between them. "And he had to deal with it. My son doesn't." Deliberately he turned his head, dismissing her. "Natalie, once you've eaten, we should probably talk."

Aware out of the corner of her eye that his mother had flushed, Natalie nodded. "Whenever you're ready." She looked apologetically at Mrs. McLean.

"I'm not very hungry, I'm afraid. Although this is delicious."

"A decent breakfast will make you feel better."

"Yes," she said meekly. "I'm sure. It's just that I keep thinking…" She had to swallow on a bout of nausea.

Mrs. McLean's face softened marginally. "Perhaps a cup of tea. With honey?" She stood, surveying everyone's plates. "Children, please eat. Evan, smaller bites." She swept out.

"I…" Natalie tried to think of something tactful to say. "She's being very kind."

"In her own way," John said dryly.

John brought a cup of coffee and Natalie her tea when they left the children with their grandmother and retired to his home office.

Family obviously wasn't checked at the door to this room with warm woodwork, white walls and floor-to-ceiling bookcases. Childish drawings filled a bulletin board, and some action figures lay on the hardwood floor in positions that suggested they had died rather like their grandfather. A one-legged Barbie lay among them.

John nudged at the doll with his foot. "My son is bloodthirsty," he remarked ruefully.

"Aren't most little boys? I know my nephew is."

He sat rather heavily in his leather office chair, his tiredness suddenly visible. "Having known the reality, my mother isn't very comfortable with that fact."

"How could she be?" Natalie said with quick sympathy. "It must have been horrible to lose her husband that way, and to have to raise three kids by herself."

He made a rough sound. "I only wish she could

have let us forget, just now and again, how Dad died.''

Startled, Natalie asked, ''What do you mean?''

John rotated his head as though his neck was stiff. Sounding impatient with himself, he said almost brusquely, ''Never mind. It's nothing. History.'' He sighed. ''Natalie, we identified the dead guy.''

In an instant forgetting his unusual sharpness toward his mother, she locked her hands together. Her voice came out breathless with the anxiety that suddenly gripped her. ''Really? So fast?''

''Geoff and I both recognized him. We had to hunt through mug shots to come up with a name, but we'd been in on his arrest four years ago. Stuart was the arresting officer.''

Natalie sat silent for a moment, absorbing the news that her husband had once arrested the man who yesterday had died in her house, in Stuart's den.

''What did he do?'' she finally asked tentatively. ''Was it burglary?''

''His name was Ronald Floyd. He was a midlevel drug dealer.''

A drug dealer? She groped for understanding. ''But why would he have been in my house? Did he think Stuart was still alive and he was, well, looking for revenge or something?''

John reached out and covered her knotted hands with his for a brief, reassuring moment. ''I doubt it. This guy has been arrested half a dozen times before. Yeah, he got put away this time for a decent prison term, but it wasn't because Stuart had hunted him down. We got a tip. A whole crowd of us was waiting when Floyd docked at the marina with a boat hold full of coke. The fact that Stuart cuffed and booked him was just chance.''

Perhaps it was lack of sleep that made her feel so stupid. "Then...what *do* you think?''

He shook his head. "I've got to tell you, I don't know what to think. The fact that there's a connection between Stuart and the dead man makes me curious. I don't believe in coincidences, and it would be one hell of a coincidence if our guy, fresh out of prison for dealing, had just happened to decide to break into your house of all others. And, oh yeah, instead of walking back out, happy, with your TV and stereo, he instead gets himself killed in your husband's office.''

During this speech, her anxiety had sharpened into a knife blade of fear. She dampened her lips. "Then he must have been looking for something.''

"That's one possibility,'' John agreed.

"But what?''

To her dismay, he shook his head again. "I wish I knew, Natalie. Any ideas would be appreciated. Stuart didn't brag about collecting anything valuable, did he? Stamps, coins? He didn't tell the whole world that he had his life savings stored as gold bullion in his house?''

She was shaking her head the whole time he talked. "He played golf. He liked old car shows. He did tear stamps off envelopes if he thought they were curiosities—there are a bunch of German ones somewhere because he had a cousin in Munich, but he didn't know anything about stamps. Or coins or...'' She couldn't even think of what else he might reasonably have collected. "And his life savings, which weren't all that much, were in a mutual fund and a twelve-month CD.''

So casually she knew he'd been waiting to slip the question in, John asked, ''What about you? Antique jewelry Stuart might have bragged to someone else about?''

Again she shook her head hopelessly. ''The closest thing to a valuable antique that I have is a set of early Nancy Drew mysteries. I can't imagine that your drug dealer wanted *The Secret of the Old Clock*.''

''That does seem unlikely,'' he admitted.

''Besides,'' she pointed out, ''Stuart and I hadn't even met five years ago. So they couldn't have chatted about my collection of Nancy Drew. And how would they have run into each other since, if this guy didn't get out of prison until after Stuart was dead?''

''True enough.'' He rubbed the back of his neck. ''I'm groping here, Natalie.''

She nodded, understanding. It was a form of brainstorming, like sessions they had at the paper.

''What will you do next?'' she asked.

''Talk to Floyd's friends or relatives. I'm heading for Tacoma this morning to tell his parents about his death and find out whether they knew a damn thing about what he was up to. Hell, maybe he wrote them letters about how he intended to rifle Det. Stuart Reed's house when he was released. And, oh, yeah, his buddy Bill Doe wanted to help. We should be so lucky.''

She nodded.

''Then we'll wait for fingerprint ID,'' he continued. ''Take a harder look at your house.'' His tone changed, his eyes softened. ''I'm sorry, Natalie. We need to see if we can find something Floyd might have been looking for.''

"I understand.'' Strangely, the idea of him searching her possessions wasn't all that disturbing. She had always found him a *comfortable* man.

If she had been more self-conscious around him yesterday and today, it was hardly surprising. Their roles had shifted; his job required him to consider even her as a suspect.

And somehow here in John's home, she was discovering tensions she hadn't known existed. He clearly harbored some resentment concerning his mother, for example. His protectiveness toward his children had seemed both natural and misplaced— except that she didn't know why he was still angry at his mother. Once she would have said she could ask him anything, but the guard he'd snapped into place when she asked made her realize their friendship had been more superficial than she'd realized. There was so much about the inner man she didn't know. And so much about herself she had never told him, including a biggie, considering he had been Stuart's friend first. He had assumed her marriage was completely happy, Natalie knew, and she had never disabused him.

She came back to the present to realize that he was looking at her strangely. Had she been staring? Had he said something?

Rushing into speech to fill what must have been a peculiar silence, she argued, "But mightn't the murderer have taken whatever it was?''

He grimaced. "Unfortunately, that's a possibility, too. But what the hell could it have been?'' Now he sounded frustrated. "You've surely looked through the records Stuart left. The files in the desk seemed orderly and totally uninteresting to anyone else. None of the boxes in the closet had been ripped open. Your place wasn't ransacked. Had *anything* been disturbed that you noticed?''

"No." She pressed her lips together. "It was strange, wasn't it? The house seemed so normal. Untouched. Only, there was this dead man upstairs. It would almost have been easier if the house *had* been tossed. You know?"

"Violence should spread ripples," he said unexpectedly.

She blinked. "Yes. Exactly."

"I need to be on my way." He didn't move. "What are your plans today?"

"I hadn't thought yet." She hesitated. "I could watch your kids if that would free your mom to go home."

His dark brows drew together. "I'm not going to use you. You're a guest."

Puzzled by the edge in his voice, Natalie said, "It's nice of you to have me here, John, but it won't hurt me to help out a little."

"You always want to pay your way, don't you?"

"Is that so bad?" she asked quietly.

He got to his feet and looked down at her. "Just this once," he said, almost harshly, "do me a favor. Accept my help without baby-sitting my kids, bringing me cookies or knitting me a sweater. Okay?"

"I don't—"

"Yeah. You do." He reached out, touched her cheek, the most fleeting of contacts but enough like a caress to steal her breath. "Friends don't have to be repaid."

She found herself nodding dumbly. "Yes. Okay."

"Do something self-indulgent today. Get a massage. Go to a movie. Hey, go back to bed."

"I'm going horseback riding." She hadn't known she'd decided.

His quick, warm smile erased the harshness on a face made more angular by lack of sleep. "Good girl. Sounds like the right medicine. You probably don't get enough chances."

"I go two or three times a week."

The one gift from Stuart that she truly loved was Foxfire, the bloodred Arabian stallion she kept stabled at a ranch just outside of town. He was probably too much of a handful for her. He wasn't mean, but he danced and twisted and fussed over the smallest leaf blowing across the path. Despite his value, she'd considered having him gelded, but everyone who saw him thought she should put him up for stud. She'd pried out of Stuart the fact that he'd paid an outrageous twenty-five thousand dollars for the horse, and she was told she could maybe charge five hundred for each live birth. But to do that, she'd have to move him to a different farm where workers knew how to handle breeding, and she guessed if he was being regularly bred, with his blood fired up he might be even harder to handle. Since she did so love riding her elegant Arabian, it seemed more bother than it would be worth. She didn't really need the money. Except that it made sense, of course, to geld him if she *wasn't* going to breed him.

"You should come with me someday," she suggested impulsively. "Have you ever ridden?"

"I seem to remember a pony ride at the Woodland

Park Zoo when I was five.'' He shook his head. ''No, thanks.''

''Coward.''

A smile in his blue eyes, John said, ''Haven't you heard that discretion is the better part of valor?''

''That from a man who risks his life day in and day out.''

''We all choose our poison.''

''I'm sure we could rent a placid horse that wouldn't break out of a walk,'' Natalie coaxed. ''Maddie and Evan could go, too.''

He groaned. ''Maybe. And don't you dare go behind my back and prime them.''

''Wouldn't dream of it,'' she promised, crossing her fingers in her pocket.

''I've got to get out of here.'' In passing her, he gripped her shoulder briefly. ''Go ride. Then take a nap. I'll try to be home for dinner.''

By the time she followed him out of the office, he had already disappeared toward the front of the house. She heard his voice, then the slam of the front door.

''Drive carefully,'' she murmured.

THE WOMAN WITH SOFT, flyaway gray hair gazed at him with bewilderment and the beginnings of horrified understanding. ''Ronnie is dead?''

This was the moment John hated most. There was no kind way to tell parents that they would have to bury the son or daughter who was supposed to long outlive them. Ronald Floyd might have been a scumbag, but he was still their son, a baby born in hope.

''I'm afraid so,'' he said gently.

He stood on the front porch of the small frame house in south Tacoma, his vision of Marvella Floyd obscured by a screen door. She had briefly opened it, but when he told her why he had come, it had slipped out of her nerveless hand and snapped shut between them.

Now she clutched at the door frame, bewilderment still predominating. "But…what happened? Was it a car accident?" Hope made her sound eager. She wanted it to have been a tragic accident, the kind that could have happened to anyone. "He'd gone straight, you know. He said so. And even in his bad days, he never hurt anybody, not Ronnie."

No, he just helped hook the youth of America on a relentlessly addictive white powder that replaced jobs, family, loved ones as the very reason for existence. And, oh, yeah, damaged hearts, destroyed nasal passages, and was generally a fun party favor.

"When you deal drugs, you're coming in contact with some brutal people." Understatement. "Ma'am, may I come in?"

"What?" She stared at him with dazed eyes. "Oh. Yes. Of course. I'm sorry." She backed slowly inside the living room of the small frame house, leaving him to open the screen door and follow. When he did, she looked over her shoulder with apparent confusion, as if she'd forgotten where she was or who ought to be here.

"Is your husband home?" John asked. When she swayed, he reached for her elbow, expecting her to crumple.

Her worn brow crinkled. "I don't know where he is." She raised a voice that quavered. "Ralph!" Both she and John listened to the silence. "He was here a minute ago," she fretted, completely focused on her husband's absence rather than her son's death. Denial was something John knew well. "Ralph?" she called again.

"Could he have stepped outside?"

"Oh!" Relief infused her voice. "I think he did. Tomorrow is garbage day, you know. That's it. He was taking the garbage out, he said."

"Why don't you sit down," he suggested, steering her to the couch. "Let me get your husband."

"Oh, but…" She tried to rise again. "The kitchen is such a mess! We haven't cleaned up from breakfast yet."

"Don't worry." He smiled reassurance. "I'm a single father. You should see mine."

She sat again but quivered with worry as he cut through the old-fashioned kitchen to the back door. It swung open before he reached it. A heavyset, balding man entered, mind on other things until he saw John and came to an abrupt stop.

"I'm Detective McLean," John said, holding out his shield. "Port Dare P.D. Your wife let me in. Sorry to startle you."

Worry settled on him, stooping his shoulders. "It's Ronnie again, isn't it?"

"I'm afraid your son has been killed, Mr. Floyd."

He caught the implication immediately. "How?"

John told him.

Mr. Floyd shook his head. "His mother has always believed every word that boy said, but the last time he was here I knew he was going right back to the low road. That was Ronnie—always spoiled. If he could get it for nothing, that's what he wanted."

What child didn't? John thought. Wasn't it a parent's job to teach the virtues of hard work and charity?

"He was our only boy. We have two girls. Good girls. They both have families now. One works for the county assessor's office. I don't know, maybe we're the ones who spoiled Ronnie. But that boy. He was in trouble with the law by the time he was twelve. Shoplifting. It's just been one thing after the other."

"Ralph?" From the living room came his wife's shaky voice. "Ralph, are you talking to that policeman?"

Moving wearily, feet shuffling, Ralph Floyd passed John and went to his wife. He sat beside her on the couch, patting her restless hands on her lap, and they both gazed with deep sadness and anxiety at John, who sat in an armchair facing them.

He explained again how Ronald Floyd had died. "I'm hoping you can tell me something that might help find his killer," he said. "Can you give me names of friends? Was he working? Do you have his address?"

They did have that. His father gave the names of some friends from high school but shook his head when pressed for others. "He'd mention people in prison—Joe or Buzz Saw or some such nonsense, but I have no idea whether they're still locked up or not. He wouldn't have brought a cell mate home. He knew better than that."

"Job?"

"Ronnie was working at a marina," Mrs. Floyd said timidly. "He was good with boats, you know."

Her husband nodded. "He always liked boats. He did say he had a job. I think he was taking out those whale-watching trips."

John made a note.

"Was he angry about his arrest? Did he ever mention the officer who arrested him?"

Both shook their heads. "He said somebody had set him up, but a couple of years ago he mentioned that the fellow was dead. Said he would have liked to have punched his nose, and he guessed he wouldn't get the chance now."

"Did he give a name?"

They didn't remember if he had. Pretty obviously, they didn't know this son who mystified them. To his credit, he'd stayed in touch, but it came down to a few letters and phone calls a year, and one fleeting visit when he got out of the pen. The job was likely a fantasy. John only hoped the address wasn't.

He promised to call them once he'd checked out the apartment, and to send any effects. They'd be in touch about the body, he told them.

"You'll let us know?" Mr. Floyd asked at least three times. "When you find out why someone killed him?"

"I'll keep you informed as the investigation progresses," he agreed. After offering his regrets again, he left the couple standing on their front porch, their body language expressing the inertia, disbelief and grief he so vividly remembered his mother showing when his father was gunned down. But, because the Floyds knew in their hearts that their son had brought on his own end, they wouldn't find relief in anger as John's mother had.

As he crossed a sparkling blue neck of Puget Sound on the high span of the Tacoma Narrows Bridge, John brooded about the visit. Forget the easy answers. Ronald Floyd had not spent his years in the clink planning how he could wreak revenge on Officer Stuart Reed.

On the other hand, he had left Monroe and gone right back to Port Dare. Less than a month later, he was killed in Natalie Reed's house, which wasn't tossed. There had to be a reason he was there, and a reason he died.

But what the hell was it?

And how safe was Natalie while they hunted for hard answers?

CHAPTER FOUR

ONE HOOF PAWED and the stallion's wiry tail snapped viciously across Natalie's face as she checked the girth. Cross-tied in the barn aisle, Foxfire had been in one of his twitchier moods from the minute she'd slung the saddle blanket across his back.

When she led him outside to the mounting block, however, he followed like a lamb and stood obligingly still for her to swing her leg over his back.

"You're setting me up, aren't you?" she muttered. Taking a deep breath, she sprang.

He might have caught her by surprise if he'd been just a tiny bit less docile. As it was, she was forewarned. The wretched animal bucked before her butt even hit the saddle.

She grabbed at the horn and her dignity, slapping his neck with her reins as she inelegantly shoved her toes into the stirrups. All the while he whirled and tossed his head and shivered his skin.

Pam Reynolds, the stable owner, shook her head as she watched. A once-pretty woman with a weathered face and a grip as callused and strong as a construction worker's, she leaned against the white board fence, hands shoved into the pockets of the down vest she wore over dusty jeans and a denim shirt.

"That horse is going to come back without you one of these days."

Natalie gave the stallion one more reproving whack on the neck. "Probably," she admitted.

Pam continued critically, "That horse was not bred for trail riding."

The stallion flattened his ears and hunched his back.

"No," Natalie agreed, forcing him to tuck his chin and go into reverse.

He scrambled back so quickly he sank onto his haunches, then danced in place.

"I'd advise you to sell him."

"I know you would."

Pam's grin gave her the look of an aging elf. "Of course, then I'd have to snap him up and risk my own life and limb, so maybe it's just as well you keep him."

Natalie laughed. "You know, you're welcome to ride him anytime."

The stable owner shook her head. "The damn horse is worth too much. I don't want him breaking a leg on my watch."

Foxfire spun in a circle.

Ruefully feeling as if she'd be seeing a chiropractor for whiplash, Natalie said over her shoulder, "I wouldn't sue you. I'd know he had it coming."

"You better get before he decides not to wait for you." Pam jerked her head toward the gate. "But do stick to the trail so someone can find your body if you break your neck."

Wincing at the idea of a body, even her own, sprawled on the mist-dampened ground, Natalie simply nodded. "I'll be good." She eased the reins and sat back only a minute amount, feeling the horse's eagerness as he bounded forward. "Hey, guy," she murmured, "this isn't a race."

He didn't want to trot and, to punish her, managed a stiff gait that jarred her teeth as if she were driving a road that was wall-to-wall potholes.

Nonetheless, she held him to it, and as they left the gates of the ranch behind, Foxfire's ears flicked forward and the ride smoothed. At best, Arabians had a bouncy trot, showy in the ring but not comfortable. They had been bred for endurance, for traveling all day in the arid desert without rest or water.

Once the trail intersected the broader one used by horsemen, runners and bicyclists, Natalie let the stallion stretch into an easy lope. The gray mist clung to treetops and hid the mountains from her, beading on long, autumn-gold grasses in the fields that sloped toward the Strait of Juan de Fuca. Foxfire's hooves thudded on the damp earth in a rhythm, a mantra. The cool, moist air cleansed her; the power gathered beneath her gave Natalie an intoxicating sense of control and invincibility.

Illusory, of course, she was reminded when a small bird exploded from the underbrush to chase a hawk above, and the stallion shied, shaking his head and kicking his heels, twisting beneath her in momentary rebellion. She loosed the reins, urged him with tightened legs to go faster and, in his eagerness, he forgot his pique. The adrenaline rush made Natalie feel gloriously alive.

Best of all, she couldn't afford for even a second to let her mind wander, to picture the body in the study, to wonder when she could go home or if she wanted to. The chestnut stallion demanded that every grain of her attention be on him. She needed to read his every quivering signal and search the glistening Oregon grape and brown fronds of ferns beneath hemlock and cedar for any creature or oddity that might spook him. Her body had to flow with his. Too much tension, and the next time he leaped sideways she'd be flat on her back on the trail, hard packed despite today's mist, breath knocked out of her.

Oh, yes, her difficult horse and a damp day and the deserted trail had been exactly what she needed.

IT'S 11:02 p.m., do you know where your daddy is?

Weary to the bone, John pulled into the detached one-car garage off the alley and headed for the back door. The kids would be long since asleep, he hoped. Hell, even his mother rarely stayed up past ten. Natalie, he didn't know about. Wondering heightened his senses slightly as he inserted the key in the lock. He didn't hear voices, real or canned from the TV, and from the street he'd seen no light on in the living room.

He tried to be home for meals and to tuck his children into bed at night. Their mother's diagnosis of multiple sclerosis was tough enough for them, since it meant losing her as a part of their daily lives, having to visit her in a place where illness couldn't be forgotten and they were reduced to awkward kisses on her cheek and polite responses to her questions about school and friends. They needed to be able to count on Daddy.

But his job wasn't nine-to-five, not in the first throes of an investigation. Some of the lowlifes he'd needed to talk to didn't come out from under their rocks until after dark. He was lucky to be home this early.

His mother's sporty Chevrolet was parked to one side of the driveway. Even as irritated as he'd been at her this morning, John was grateful that his kids had her and their uncles, that he wasn't their only close family. But he was damned if he'd let her use chilly judgments and icy disapproval to hammer his son into the avenging angel she'd wanted her own sons to be. Hell, wasn't that what they were, cleansing the streets of the devil's spawn?

The house was quiet when he stepped in, one light left on in the kitchen, a note taped to the microwave. He crossed quietly. Even Natalie must be asleep.

Tidy block print read, "Leftover casserole in the refrigerator. Heat for five minutes. I don't want to find it uneaten in the morning."

He gave a rusty laugh. That was his mother all over. Caring but stern.

He should be hungry and wasn't, but he obediently took out the plastic container, noted that it was one his mother made with cashews and Chinese noodles that he liked, and stuck it in the microwave. Five minutes.

Listening to the hum, he thought how idiotic it was at his age to have fleeting, wistful memories of the mother she'd been Before Dad Died. He always thought of it that way, in capital letters. She had changed in one horrific day, bewildering and terrifying her three boys. Instead of progressing through all the stages of grief, emerging at the end as the mother they knew, she'd seemed to get stuck part way, consumed by anger she still carried. More of an optimist then, he'd actually hoped, back when Debbie was pregnant, that in starting over with grandchildren his mother too could begin again. Better than Hugh and

Connor, he remembered her as a woman who had patiently bandaged skinned knees and run breathlessly down the sidewalk holding up two-wheelers, and not cared if paint happily slapped onto butcher paper dripped off the edges onto the kitchen floor or table-top. Those memories of laughter and tenderness and easy hugs were fading these days.

But he was still lucky she was here for Maddie and Evan. They loved her, as much as she would allow.

Trouble was, he could foresee her getting harder and harder on Evan. Opening the refrigerator again to look for something to drink, John scowled. He'd been old enough when his father died to have some inner defenses. His brothers, especially Hugh, hadn't been. His mother had messed with Hugh's psyche but good, and he couldn't let her do the same to Evan. He didn't want to hurt her by cutting her off from the kids, but the day was coming when he'd have to find alterna-tive baby-sitting—and either a tactful explanation of why he had made the change, or the guts to be blunt.

"Is something spoiling in there?"

He jerked and dropped the milk carton. Milk sloshed at his feet. Swearing, he bent to pick it up.

Natalie stayed in the doorway, eyes huge, dark curly hair tousled over her shoulders. "I'm sorry. I didn't mean to startle you."

"No, no." He grabbed a glass from the cupboard and poured the milk before it could all leak out the bottom.

"Do you have a pitcher you could put that in?" She came shyly into the kitchen.

"Uh, yeah. Somewhere." He left the milk carton in the sink and banged cupboard doors until he found a plastic pitcher. He salvaged a pint or so, enough for breakfast cereal, anyway.

Natalie had taken paper towels and was mopping up the mess on the floor.

"I can do that," he said, frowning again as he looked down at the top of her head and realized she wore a robe. She had probably been in bed when she heard him come in.

"It was my fault." She didn't even glance up. "Besides, the microwave beeped. I think your dinner must be ready."

John hesitated for a moment, then opted for the casserole. What was he going to do, hand-wrestle Natalie for a soggy paper towel?

"Come sit with me?" he asked.

Now she did look up, that same unexpected shyness in her dark eyes. "Are you sure you wouldn't rather be alone?"

"Positive." He hooked a stool at the tiled breakfast bar with one foot and pulled it out. "Are you hungry?"

"Heavens, no! Your mother made me eat every bite at dinner."

He gave the same rueful chuckle. "That's my mom."

Natalie wiped the floor again with a damp, soapy towel and then tossed it into the garbage under the sink. Straightening, she hesitated, pulled her robe more snugly around herself and then came to the bar.

John pushed a second stool out. "Join me."

"I couldn't sleep." She scooted her rump onto the stool, keeping both hands on her robe so that it didn't gape above or below the belt.

Of course, nothing was so calculated to make him

wonder what she wore under it. He hastily turned his attention to his dinner. Damn it, he did *not* want to have sexual fantasies, however fleeting, about Natalie Reed.

"Did you nap this afternoon?" Maybe not a smart question, as it made him picture that curly hair spread on her pillow, her cheeks flushed like Maddie's on the rare occasions when she would still lie down during the daytime.

Natalie shook her head. "I never do, you see. Going so against habit would have just made me think."

He chewed and swallowed, washing the bite down with a slug of milk. "What did you do, then?"

"Rode." The hand possessively clutching the robe at her bosom began to relax, as if she forgot she had to. "Then, believe it or not, I went shopping at the mall. A woman's refuge."

"Ah." Debbie had shopped, too, whether the credit cards were maxed out or not.

"I wasn't sure you could let me into my house. I bought some clothes for the next day or so."

"You didn't have to do that," he said roughly. "I could have gotten what you needed."

"No, that's okay." She bent her head and fingered the shawl collar of the robe, which he realized belatedly was his mother's. "I hardly ever take the time to shop, and I can use some new jeans and…things."

Panties? Bras? Another irritating, unsettling image of her lush body in dainty, lacy lingerie flitted through his mind. His brows drew together and he shoved another bite in, although the damn casserole seemed tasteless tonight.

She said quietly, "You looked angry earlier. And now you do again. Did something happen today?"

"What?" He realized he was glowering at her and wiped the expression from his face. "Sorry. No. Nothing happened. In fact, too little happened."

She didn't say anything. She never did probe. What he didn't offer, she didn't ask. Because she didn't care enough? Because she didn't think she had the right?

Had she been the same with Stuart? Or was Stuart the one who had taught her that what he didn't choose to tell her was none of her damned business?

The speculation felt disloyal. Stuart Reed and he had been partners. Friends. Yeah, there had been moments when John hadn't much liked him, but that was water under the bridge. Stuart was dead and buried. This was no time to question his character.

"I was thinking about my mother," John said abruptly, as much because he wasn't yet ready to admit he hadn't made an arrest today, that Natalie couldn't go home, that he didn't have a damned clue. "Like I said, she's too hard on Evan especially. I'm just not sure what to do about it."

"Have you talked to her?"

"I said something this morning."

"Did you?" Her voice was soft, uncritical, but he got the point.

Okay. So what he'd really done was snap at his mother.

"Talking to her isn't going to do any good."

"I don't understand." Tiny crinkles formed in her brow. "I always thought you were close to her."

John shoved his plate away on a sigh. "Yes and no. I stayed in town, I see her often. I appreciate what she did, somehow keeping us all together when she had no job skills and Dad hadn't left any life insurance." He didn't usually talk like this. What he felt toward Stuart's memory was nothing when compared to his fierce loyalty to family. But Natalie listened with those wide, compassionate eyes and no hint of judgment. He could use a sounding board.

"What did your mom do?"

"Worked two jobs. Apparently she'd learned to type in high school, and she managed to get a secretarial job even though she had no experience. Nights she cleaned office buildings."

"But when did she sleep?"

The question took him by surprise. "I don't know." He grimaced. "No, that's not true, of course. Whenever she got home in the middle of the night, maybe three o'clock to seven in the morning. A couple of hours after work in the afternoon." Somehow he hadn't thought about how sleep deprived his mother must have been all those years.

"What about you and your brothers? Did somebody take care of you when she was working?"

He shook his head. "I guess we were the original latchkey kids. We were all school age when Dad died. I watched Hugh and Connor after school until I started playing high school sports, and by then Con was old enough. Nighttimes she left us alone." He frowned, trying to remember. "I'm not sure she had the janitorial job the first year after Dad was killed. I was probably in middle school by the time she started that. Old enough to be in charge."

Still with puckered brow, Natalie studied his face. "Did you *feel* old enough?"

No. Hell, no.

The explosive quality of his realization startled him. Perhaps to disguise his quiet shock, John rubbed a hand over his chin, which felt bristly.

"You didn't, did you?" She was too damned perceptive.

"I went through a stretch when I was scared to death at night. The cops never arrested the guy who shot my dad. Did I ever tell you that? Every night I'd imagine he was breaking into that crummy apartment we rented. The building creaked and whimpered all night long. I was old enough to know the locks were flimsy. If he'd been able to kill my dad, who seemed huge and strong to me, what could I do?" He shook his head. "I never told my mother how scared I was. What could she have done? She had to work. As it was, she went without anything for herself to make sure three boys growing by half-foot leaps had enough on the table, decent clothes and the chance to play sports like our friends."

Now he felt like a son of a bitch, resenting the way his mother had brought him up. No, what he felt was childish, for forgetting how hard it had been for her.

"I must sound petty," he said.

"You mean, worrying about how she treats Evan?" She abandoned the collar of the robe, which gaped enough for him to glimpse flowered T-shirt fabric. So much for those visions of satin and lace. "It's your *job* to worry about your son."

John grunted. "Mom didn't have time to be soft with us. I think she forgot how to be soft."

"Was she different? Before?"

"Yeah." He stretched. "Dad was the one who was too busy to throw the ball or help me learn to ride my two-wheeler. I remember that especially, for some reason. I wasn't kidding about those half-foot leaps, by the way. I think I must have grown six inches that year. I was incredibly clumsy. My buddies were all racing up and down the sidewalk on their two-wheelers, and me, I was stuck with training wheels and humiliated. Mom would go out with me after dark, when no one would see us, and she'd run up and down the street holding me up. When she said she wouldn't let me fall, I believed her. One day, I just knew I could do it. I yelled for her to let go.'' A bittersweet smile tugged at his mouth. ''I rode up to the end of the street, got off and turned the bike around, then got started all by myself. I can still see Mom, clapping and jumping up and down and laughing like crazy.''

When he fell silent, Natalie said softly, ''Maybe she could learn again.''

John shook his head. ''Mom's spent plenty of time with the kids since they were born. If she was going to, she would have by now.''

''Hey. Don't give up on her.''

He shrugged and said nothing for a moment. Time to change the subject.

Probably too abruptly, he said, ''Ronald Floyd's parents didn't know anything. They saw their son a couple of times a year. He told them he was going straight, working at a marina.''

Tension minutely tightened the muscles in her jaw and around her eyes. Her hand, lying on the counter, knotted. ''Was he?''

''He did pilot whale-watching tours. He'd only been out of the joint a month, got the job two weeks ago. Mom and Dad didn't know why he had come straight back to Port Dare. We found some of his old acquaintances. Some admitted seeing him, some not. Nobody knew anything about him dealing, or taking up a new trade like B and E. He liked boats, they all agreed.''

She thought about that. ''Stuart got seasick. He didn't even like to take the ferry.''

''What about you?''

''Me?'' She stiffened slightly, making him realize he'd sounded like a cop. ''They're okay, I guess. I do enjoy taking the ferry to Canada. I haven't even done that since…oh, in May, I went up to see Butchart Gardens, when the rhododendrons were in bloom.''

''No whale-watching trips?''

She shook her head.

He sighed. ''I'm reaching here. I thought he might have seen you, maybe flirted. I don't know.''

''You mean, that he was looking for *me?*'' The thought obviously horrified her.

Sorry he'd raised it but knowing he'd needed to, John said, ''I didn't really think he was. You work every day. If he'd done any checking, he'd have known that. And we can't forget that he wasn't alone. So who was with him and why?''

Tiny, worried lines crimped her forehead. ''You really don't think they were there to burglarize, do you?''

''I can't say that. I'm eliminating other possibilities.'' John spread his hands. ''According to Floyd's parents, the only grudge he harbored was against whoever tipped the cops off the night we arrested him. He never mentioned Stuart to them.''

''Could that person have killed him?''

''Apparently he died a couple of years ago, while Floyd was still locked up. Or so he told his parents.''

John's mouth twisted. "Unless he lied. And why would he have?"

Natalie brushed her hair back from her face, pulling it into a ponytail with one hand and twisting it into a sort of rough chignon. The movement parted the collar of the robe, and he saw both the swell of her breasts and the cartoon cats on her T-shirt nightgown. She left the heavy knot at her nape and tugged her robe together. Hell, had she seen him staring?

If so, she didn't show it. "What will you do now?" she asked.

"Search your house more carefully. Focus on fingerprints, trace evidence. Keep hoping we can find a neighbor, a delivery truck driver—*somebody*—who saw a vehicle parked in front of your house or in the driveway. In other words, boring police work."

She nodded. The knot slipped and tendrils curled against her neck. "When can I go home again?"

His gut instincts rebelled violently at the idea. Logic didn't support his unhappiness, however. Whatever had happened in Stuart's study had nothing to do with Natalie. The killer had had time to do whatever he'd gone there to do. Why would he come back?

"A couple of days, maybe," he said reluctantly. "Then, if you're comfortable going home, I don't see why you can't."

She nodded. "What else can I do? Drift around town taking turns being a guest at all my friends' houses? Put the house on the market? Even if I were going to do that, I'd have to go through Stuart's things first, have a garage sale—" she made a face "—probably a huge bonfire. Of course I have to go home."

His brows drew together.

Natalie laughed. "You don't like admitting I'm right, do you?"

"You know you can stay here as long as you need to."

"Yeah." She smiled. "But *you* know I can't."

He did. A few days here would be okay in the court of public opinion; people would figure he was helping her out for Stuart's sake. Any longer than that, whispers would start. John remembered his own brief discomfiture when he'd had to admit that his fingerprints would be all over Natalie's house. For her sake, he didn't want any whispers or lewd jokes.

"We'll get done with the house in the next couple of days," he promised. "In the meantime, I can take you over tomorrow to get clothes and anything else you need."

She nodded.

A moment of silence developed. John became newly conscious of the quiet and darkness beyond the lighted kitchen. Knowing everyone else was asleep made this conversation feel more intimate, as if they were married or something. If he moved his leg, his knee would bump hers. Their shoulders almost touched. Her hair was loose, her face scrubbed clean, the toes curled around the rungs of the stool bare. She was wearing a nightgown and robe, for Pete's sake. Here he was, smelling of beer and tobacco smoke from the bars he'd prowled, his jaw scratchy from a day's growth, his eyes likely bloodshot and his tiredness acute enough to have him swaying as he abruptly swiveled and stood.

He grabbed the edge of the counter. "Time to hit the sack."

She did just what he was hoping to avoid. She slid from the bar stool and touched him. "Are you all right?"

Her hand felt good on his bare forearm, below his rolled-up shirtsleeve. Warm, soft and, in some indefinable way, womanly. He despised himself for the shot of heat that steadying touch sent through him.

He couldn't insult her by backing away. All he could do was wait until her hand dropped to her side. He sounded a little hoarse to his own ears when he said, "Just light-headed for a minute. A good night's sleep will cure me."

Natalie's fingers curled into fists at her side. "Yes." This smile looked forced and her gaze slipped from his. "Of course. I'm sorry. I shouldn't have kept you up talking."

"No apologies. I'm the one who dumped my troubles on you. Actually, talking helped me unwind." He managed a crooked imitation of a smile. "Maybe that's why I'm so tired now. I talked so damn much."

To his relief, her expression relaxed. "I'll have to try it sometime. But not," she said with a breath of laughter, when he started to open his mouth, "tonight. I'll see you in the morning, John. Thank you for...well, everything." Startling him, she rose on tiptoe and brushed the lightest of kisses on his cheek. Then, with a whisk of the robe, she passed him and left the kitchen, her bare feet silent on the tiled floor.

He stood frozen in her wake, conscious of the faint scent she'd left behind, something flowery that suited her.

Voice harsh and low, he said, "Damn, damn, damn."

CHAPTER FIVE

"THIS IS A BAD IDEA." Geoff Baxter reluctantly backed onto Natalie's porch, broad face set in a scowl. He had expressed the same sentiment a dozen times already. He didn't think it was safe for her to move back into the house, he had said. More than once. What if the killer returned? Aside from which, she'd be sullying a crime scene. She was in the way. She...

Mercifully, John had interrupted at that point.

Right now, if Geoff hadn't been standing with his head thrust pugnaciously forward, Natalie would have been tempted to thank him one more time—briskly— and shut the door in his face. As it was, the door would break his nose.

John stood a step behind his partner, expressionless. Except when he was talking to his children, his face had pretty much looked like that for the past three days. Which was one reason Natalie had been determined to go home. Obviously, that evening when she impulsively kissed his cheek, she had stepped over some boundary that defined their friendship. She'd felt the constraint ever since.

The two men had insisted on accompanying her, hovering like nervous parents over a reckless toddler as she put away fresh milk and eggs and carried her own bag upstairs just to prove to them and herself that she could walk past the study door without flinching.

It was closed, sealed with yellow ''Do Not Cross'' tape. As was the door to the garage.

''We think we're done with the study,'' John had explained, ''but let's give it another day or two to be sure.''

At which point, Geoff had shaken his head morosely. ''Damn it, you shouldn't be back in the house until we're finished with it.''

With eroding patience, Natalie had said flippantly, ''You guessed! I did plan to peel that tape back and sneak in there tonight. You know, I always shake out the floor mats from my car in the study. And then, of course, I have to vacuum and wipe every single surface clean. Gracious, why don't I just get the shampooer out of the garage and do the carpet in there while I'm at it?''

Geoff had flushed dangerously, while John had given her a look he most likely reserved for one of his kids when they misbehaved in public.

She'd thrown up her hands and exhaled in a rush. ''I'm sorry! But you've said yourself there are no fingerprints in the kitchen or my bedroom or bathroom. Nobody laid a hand on the remote control or the toaster. You're done with the main part of the house.''

Geoff had opened his mouth.

She swept on. ''You've told me what not to do. Ask my fifth-grade teacher. I've always been obedient.''

John had looked as if he was trying not to smile.

''So don't fuss!'' she said now.

''Fuss!'' Sweat beaded Geoff Baxter's receding

forehead. ''We're friends! Aren't friends supposed to worry?''

John laid an arm across his partner's shoulder and firmly turned him toward the street.

He gave Natalie one last, rivetingly intense look. ''Call if you need me,'' he said, and steered his cursing partner from the porch and across the lawn—which really needed mowing now—to their dark blue sedan at the curb.

Natalie took a deep breath, closed the door and locked it. Alone at last.

''Thank goodness,'' she said aloud, but without quite the fervency she'd tried to tell herself she felt. Hastily she raised her voice again. ''Sasha! Kitty, kitty. Those noisy men are gone. Come here, kitty, kitty. I'll open you a nice can of Fancy Feast.''

No sign of the cat until Natalie reached the kitchen, when Sasha materialized by her food bowl.

''Oh, sweetie.'' Natalie plopped onto the kitchen floor and gathered the long-haired black cat into her arms. Sasha wasn't a particularly cuddly cat, preferring to choose her own time and place, but this time she submitted with good grace, even purring in her quiet, restrained way.

''You missed me,'' Natalie mumbled, gaining a mouthful of hair. Absurdly, tears pricked at her eyes and she gave the cat a squeeze.

Sasha looked up, round eyes molten copper, and abruptly butted her nose against Natalie's.

''You did!'' She gave a sniff. ''I'm so sorry I haven't been here, sweetie. It must have been scary.''

Her half-Persian refugee from the animal shelter agreed in her tiny chirp that yes, she was scared of all those big, bad men. Leaping from Natalie's lap, she indicated that a particularly tasty treat would make her feel ever so much better.

Natalie laughed and blinked away the dampness. Ridiculous to cry just because she was glad to be home and glad she'd been missed. As she opened the can and served trout to the cat, she almost wished she hadn't paid for a housecleaning service to take care of the fingerprint powder and the dirty footprints on the carpet. It might have been good for her mental health to have something vigorous to do.

She'd make dinner, she decided on an upsurge of energy. Not the scrambled eggs and toast she'd planned, but a real, honest-to-goodness meal, the kind that usually seemed like too much trouble. Hungarian goulash.

A chuck steak she'd put in the fridge would work, and she unearthed the other ingredients. While the meat browned, she diced green pepper and onion and took spices from the cupboard.

Once the goulash was simmering, Natalie turned on the television news. *Her* murder—not a good way to put it, she thought queasily—had been covered by the Seattle stations on the local news, even though Seattle should have had enough murders of its own to keep journalists busy. But, just her luck, this one had seemed to appeal to them. A woman who worked for a newspaper—never mind that she sold ads instead of writing hard-hitting features—had come home after work to find a dead body in her house.

"Although the police deny they've reached conclusions, we're told that there is no sign that murderer or victim were attempting burglary," they had avidly reported. "How and why did a stranger end up dead on the upstairs floor of this newspaperwoman's home?''

After half an hour, she could relax. None of the networks had anything new to work with. Local news was followed by national, focused on an earthquake in China, Mid-East peace talks, which never seemed to bring peace, and the president's veto of controversial gun-control legislation. Maybe feeling so cynical was a sign of impending middle age, Natalie feared, sighing as she turned off the television.

She put noodles on and wondered what she would do with the remainder of her evening. Usually weekday evenings were filled with a scramble to keep the house clean and her clothes ready to wear. But she'd done all her laundry at John's house, and the maid service had taken care of the parts of the house she was allowed in. She could have mowed earlier and put dinner back, but it was too late to think of that now.

During dinner, Natalie gave herself a stern lecture. For heaven's sake, she was a woman of many interests! She wasn't such a wimp that she was going to let that…that invasion of her home turn her into a nervous wreck.

After putting leftovers away and loading the dishwasher, Natalie marched right upstairs to her sewing room to see how much damage Sasha had done to the fabric and pattern pieces that had been laid out. The yellow crime scene tape stretched across the door frame checked her briefly. It was jarring, even bizarre, an image from TV cop shows transplanted to her upstairs hall. Never mind that it reminded her of what lay beyond the closed door—of what *had* lain beyond that door.

With a shiver, Natalie hurried into her sewing room. She pulled this door closed just far enough to shut out her view across the hall, leaving it ajar in case the phone rang, or…

Admit it, she thought ruefully. What she really wanted was to be sure she would hear footsteps, or a creak from down below, that she'd have some warning. Somehow up here she felt more vulnerable.

"Don't be silly," she said aloud.

Somebody—presumably John—had thought to fold the fabric carefully with the pattern pieces pinned inside. When she spread it back out, she found the delicate tissue no more torn than when she first noticed that Sasha had napped in here.

She unpinned and put the fabric in the hamper to wash. Using tape she'd brought upstairs, she mended the brand-new pattern. The project was to be a dress with pinafore for her five-year-old niece. Natalie's sister, Maryke, didn't sew at all, and her daughter was to be the flower girl in an outdoor wedding in Golden Gate Park in San Francisco, where they lived. The bride had chosen the powder-blue fabric and pattern. Fortunately, Natalie still had several weeks.

She laid out the pinafore pattern on filmy white cotton with a delicate pattern woven in, and cut it out, even getting a start on the sewing. Pleasantly tired, she scooped Sasha's litter, checked that doors and windows were locked and started up the stairs to bed with a book in hand. Feeling like a coward, she nonetheless turned back around and grabbed a sturdy maple chair from the kitchen, which she braced under the bedroom doorknob after she'd pushed in the flimsy lock.

IT WAS ENOUGH to allow her a good night's sleep. After her morning shower, Natalie set the chair aside, a little embarrassed at last night's fears. For goodness' sake, nobody was going to break into her house in the middle of the night! With police having crawled all over the place and left their yellow crime scene tape plastered everywhere, no burglar—or murderer—in his right mind would come near her house. She was probably safer than any home owner in Port Dare right this minute. She wouldn't have moved home again if there was any real danger.

"I blame you, Detective Baxter," she muttered, although in all fairness that darned yellow tape gave her the creeps this morning, too, on her way downstairs.

The phone rang while her coffee was brewing. She picked it up cautiously. Unless the press had really and truly lost interest, they'd still be trying to reach her.

"Hello?"

"You okay?" John said.

"If somebody had murdered me in the middle of the night, wouldn't it be a little late to ask if I'm okay?" Phone between her shoulder and ear, she poured the coffee. "I'm fine, of course. Why wouldn't I be?"

"I thought you might not sleep well."

"You were wrong. I slept like a baby. Which," she said thoughtfully, "is one of those odd sayings. I stayed with my sister for two weeks after she had her second child, and I swear he screamed all night long. If he slept at all, it was in half-hour snatches. I, on the other hand, didn't stir for eight hours."

"I'm glad to hear it." His voice had a rumble of amusement. "Geoff was sure you'd be petrified."

"What did you think?" She couldn't resist asking.

"I think you wouldn't admit it if you had been."

He was right. Which meant he knew her all too well. "Is that all you called for?"

"Yup." He paused. "And to let you know we may be in and out today."

"Surely you've searched this place top to bottom."

"Not even close, and frankly, at this point, I can't justify the hours it would take to winnow through every box in that damned garage. Baxter doesn't agree. You know him, he's worried about you."

"I noticed," she said dryly.

He gave a grunt of amusement. "He was a little heavy-handed yesterday, wasn't he?"

"I was ready to slam the door in his face."

"I did drag him away."

Natalie popped bread into the toaster, one eye on the clock. "I duly offer thanks."

"The truth is, Floyd and some buddy of his probably broke in to steal everything portable. They went to check out the study, started to argue, and things escalated. The buddy panicked and ran."

The toast popped up. Natalie didn't move. "Except that he just happened to have a pipe in his hand for bashing in his friend's head."

Damn it, why couldn't she just accept the easy answer? The one that made this crime random, having nothing to do with her?

She wanted to. Oh, how she wanted to. But her mind stubbornly poked at the facts. Could the choice of her house truly *be* random, when there was a connection between Stuart and the murdered man? And

burglars hardly ever killed each other in the middle
of a job. She would have guessed they worked
quickly and silently. If you'd broken into somebody's
house, it would be the height of foolishness to start a
loud argument when a neighbor might be home to
hear.

"Maybe the buddy always carried a length of pipe
in case the home owner strolled in the door unexpectedly," John suggested.

Comforted by the logical if unpleasant explanation—what if *she* had strolled in her front door that
morning?—Natalie reached for the butter knife.

"That makes sense," she admitted. "But what a
time to argue."

"Crooks are, by definition, dumb. We wouldn't
catch them otherwise."

This reminder, too, was comforting. She'd read
about a would-be bank robber who wrote his demand
for money on the back of one of his own deposit slips.
Or the one who tried to rob the bank via the drive-
up window with bullet-proof glass—and then politely
waited for the teller to package money until the police
arrived.

"Okay," she said. "I feel better. And—" her gaze
fell on the clock "—I'd better get moving or I'll be
late for work."

Yesterday she'd told John about today's meeting
with a representative from a major chain of hardware
stores, during which she intended to persuade him to
advertise in the *Sentinel*. So far, despite opening a big
new store in Port Dare, the company had declined to
include their weekly ad in the *Sentinel*. Most residents
also took at least the Sunday *Seattle Times,* the manager of the local store had said with a shrug. Today

Natalie was armed with figures showing how many of the *Sentinel*'s subscribers did not, in fact, also subscribe to any metropolitan newspaper.

"You go bag 'em, girl," John said now.

She laughed and hung up, feeling cheered by the conversation. It was nice that somebody cared. And John had sounded looser, friendlier, more like his usual self than he had these past few days. She hoped he'd just been tired or nursing a headache, that his mood hadn't had anything to do with her waylaying him for a midnight chat in her bathrobe, or—heaven forbid!—that impulsive kiss.

Armored in her best suit, charcoal-gray wool that looked businesslike while being formfitting enough to also be feminine, Natalie went forth to battle. The district manager was more cordial than her previous contact. He explained their reasoning, looked at her proposal, which outlined costs and subscriber numbers—including those who *wouldn't* see his weekly ad—and the full-color circular that his major competitor ran weekly. The meeting ended with him noncommittal.

Two hours later he called to buy space. Her success softened the usual daily annoyances, including a grocery store insert printed with a huge error and intended to go into the morning paper.

She had dinner with a friend at a small waterfront seafood restaurant, where she kept finding her gaze wandering to the marina below. Regina had excused herself to visit the ladies' room, so that for a moment Natalie didn't have to hide her distraction.

The sun hadn't yet set, although the light was gradually deepening, the water taking on a lavender tint that would become almost purple as dusk settled.

Snow-white, clean-lined powerboats and sharp-masted sailboats bobbed at the crisscrossed docks. A teak sailboat that must have been forty feet long was slowly motoring in, the sails wrapped and figures bustling on deck.

At the edge of the parking lot, Natalie could just see the corner of a building topped with a bold black-and-white sign that promised "Island Whale Watching." Was that where Ronald Floyd had worked? Was this the marina where Stuart had arrested him? She tried to imagine the boat easing in, the cops stepping from the darkness with guns drawn, and came up with something like the gory scene at the end of *The Big Easy*, when the Port Dare version had probably been far more mundane.

And it might not have taken place here at all, she reminded herself. Another good-sized marina was tucked behind the arm of the spit to the west. She'd caught a glimpse of tips of the masts from horseback the other day. And it might even have been a cooperative sting with another police force. John hadn't said.

Natalie had never asked to see a photograph of Ronald Floyd. She tried not to think about him. When she did, he was...faceless. It was like one of those investigative TV show interviews, where someone's face had been blacked out and his voice distorted. The anonymity stole some of the humanity from the person being interviewed. He was everybody and nobody at the same time. So long as she didn't see his picture, she didn't have to know whether he'd had a nice face or if sadness or fear lurked in his eyes. She didn't have to care about him.

"Deep thoughts?" Regina asked, dropping her

purse onto the empty chair and sitting back down across from Natalie.

Feeling distaste at her own selfishness, Natalie lied. "Not a one. Actually, I was gloating. Let me tell you about today's triumph."

An emergency room nurse, Regina Gresch in return told a hushed story about a prominent but nameless local citizen who had come into the ER with broken glass in an orifice on her body where it didn't belong.

"Eew," Natalie pronounced. "Did she wear a brown paper bag over her head?"

"Wouldn't have done any good." Straight-faced, Regina shook her head. "We require proof of insurance."

They both laughed. Later, driving home, Natalie thought about how uncomfortable it would be to have a job where you found out things about people that you didn't want to know and that you couldn't tell anyone, at least with names attached.

Cops were the same, of course. Stuart had sometimes been indiscreet with his wife, while at other times he had been grim and silent, shaking his head when she asked what was bothering him. Neither police nor hospital workers had the luxury of not seeing the victims.

She didn't envy John, who had had to tell Ronald Floyd's parents their son was dead. Natalie wondered if they'd told stories about the boy they remembered, whether they'd had grade-school photographs of him displayed, if they'd insisted on bringing out an album to show John.

Trying to shake off the morbid thoughts, Natalie parked in the driveway in front of her house. She'd have left lights on if she'd known Regina would call suggesting they have dinner.

The windows were blank and dark. She mentally traveled inside, up the stairs, where the yellow police tape draped the doorway like a cobweb. The door would push silently open. Inside gray fingerprint powder lay on every surface like an ancient gathering of dust. There, in front of the desk, was the rust-red stain of spilled blood.

She shuddered and wished suddenly, violently, that the study had been gutted by fire. Damaged irreparably, so that she could start all over with it.

Maybe she would. Instead of cleaning the carpet at all, she could have it ripped out, Natalie thought on a rising bubble of hope, or relief. She could paint and paper afresh, install filmy white pleated blinds, have warm, shining hardwood floors installed. She hated that huge, ugly desk and metal file cabinets. She'd sell the desk, carry the boxes to the garage until she had time to go through them. Or, better yet, *make* the time. Would Regina and some of her other friends help? Maybe, in a weekend, they could make some inroads. If they priced everything as they weeded, she could have a garage sale the next weekend, before the weather turned too rainy for the year.

New optimism accompanied Natalie, a shimmery surface on the well of disquiet as she unlocked the front door and groped for light switches. The living room looked as it always did, the kitchen clean except for her cereal bowl in the sink and a note on the counter. John's scrawl said, "Done with study. You can get carpet cleaners out tomorrow."

Determined not to let fear get the better of her, Natalie walked through the house, looking in closets and under the bed. At last, she stood in front of the study with her heart drumming. The yellow tape was gone. Still, as she made herself push open the door she had a disquieting feeling of déjà vu. She had stepped into her waking nightmare.

Thank heavens, the reality was different from her fears. The fingerprint powder was smudged and tracked on the carpet. The bloodstain was smaller than she'd anticipated. Otherwise, the study hadn't changed. If a spirit lingered here, it was Stuart's, not faceless Ronald Floyd's.

Standing in the doorway, Natalie churned with uncomfortable emotions. The truth was, she'd avoided this room ever since Stuart had died. She hated it, the masculine beiges and heavy furniture, the labeled cartons full of the residue of his life before her, separate from her. This study symbolized for her an unhappy facet of her marriage: the realization that Stuart had acquired her much as he had the big-screen TV. He wanted her, he liked her, perhaps he even thought he loved her, but she belonged only in certain parts of the house, in certain parts of his life. Her secret dreams of someone who would let her inside as he would let no one else, who would want to know *her* as no one else ever had, had been trampled by the Stuart who would look at her with vague irritation if she intruded in here when he was paying bills or talking to some buddy on the phone, cigar smoke drifting upward. In the three years of their marriage, Natalie had learned that much of what Stuart had been or would be was closed to her. He was still the sexy man she'd married, who could exert enormous charm when he cared to. But, beneath the charm and his occasional, careless cruelty, she didn't really know him.

Every widow had moments when she forgot her husband was dead, she'd been told. For some, it was when waking in the morning and reaching for him, or hearing a joke or an intriguing bit of news and thinking, *I'll tell Bill.* For Natalie, those moments had invariably come when she was passing the study. She'd *feel* him inside, a palpable presence. But when she turned her head, of course, his desk chair was empty, the radio he liked to listen to silent and gathering dust.

This room was the secretive part of him. Unless she gutted it, it would always be his, would always rebuff her, would haunt her with what would never be.

The desk would definitely go, she decided defiantly. And the oak office chair that went with it. She'd make it a study for herself, airy and pretty. Maryke and her husband and children were coming for Christmas this year, which gave her incentive to get started. With the room remodeled, a roll-away could go in here for the kids, and Maryke and Reeve could have the guest room downstairs. Work on the house would reassure Maryke that Natalie was recovering from Stuart's death.

Her gaze stole to that unexpectedly small but dark stain on the beige carpet. Perhaps she *would* have carpet cleaners come after all, since she'd have to spend time in here as she decided what of Stuart's to keep and what to throw out. Stepping around a man's lifeblood seemed unbearably macabre.

Downstairs again, she found that John had left a phone message, too, telling her to call if she wanted to talk. He'd done the same a couple of times a week since Stuart died. Often she did return his call. They were the best friends then, his voice on the phone not the same as a living, breathing, powerfully built man in person. Maybe he was relieved, too, to be able to forget his buddy was a woman. Their phone relationship was like having a pen pal, Natalie guessed. There was a kind of anonymity in a telephone or e-mail friendship.

Every time John had been here a good deal, like when he was rebuilding her fence or this summer when he painted her house, she'd begun to feel uncomfortable in some way she had never wanted to analyze.

Natalie made a face. *Oh, come on,* she jeered herself. *Why lie to me, myself and I?* Face it, his sheer physical presence was what unsettled her. When he painted her house, he'd worn faded jeans and, in the heat of the sun, stripped off his T-shirt, baring rippling muscles and sweat-slick tanned skin. He was pure male, and she didn't want to think of him that way. She wanted him to be genderless, unthreatening. She didn't want to feel…

Natalie swallowed, the telephone still in her hand. Slowly she hung it on the cradle and finished her own sentence.

She didn't want to feel *aware.* Tingling, warm, excited, alive. And she couldn't help it when she was with him.

Maybe he hadn't acted different after that night they'd talked at his house. Maybe *she* was the one who'd frozen in panic after she'd sat there in her bathrobe, conscious of the intimacy and her relative state of undress, of the tiredness and discouragement that made him seem so approachable, of the fact that they were the only people in the house awake. She'd sat close enough to see his spiky eyelashes and the bristle on his unshaven jaw, the lines that fanned from the corners of his eyes, the easing of his hard mouth as he smiled, the bluntness of his fingers, the…

Humiliated, Natalie moaned and buried her face in her hands. That night, she had not *once* consciously thought, *This man arouses me,* but she had gone back to bed aching and restless and thinking about him, if not in that way.

Wonderful. She was attracted to Det. John McLean and was admitting that fact just when she needed him most and when he felt his honor required that he take care of her. How horrible if he ever suspected, even for a moment, how she felt!

Lifting her head, dry-eyed, Natalie thought, *We are friends. We can be just friends.*

But not tonight. Tonight she wouldn't call him back.

Perhaps it was time she started dating. Maybe that was the trouble. She'd been alone for a year now. Her emotions and body both had thawed, and John was the nearest unmarried man. What she would do was let her friends know she was ready to date. They were always suggesting somebody. Far better to take that route than to turn her loneliness into a crush on John.

She went about her evening chores more absent-mindedly than last night. Sasha decided to sleep with her again, and Natalie thought maybe she'd leave the litter box up here for good rather than putting it back in the garage when the police were done. Especially if she was going to keep the bedroom door closed and locked at night.

She read for a few minutes, then turned out the light. She hadn't lain there in the dark for more than a minute before, feeling silly, she switched the light back on and got out of bed to brace the darned chair under the bedroom doorknob.

"Who's to know?" she asked the cat, and went back to bed.

When she awakened with a start hours later, her first, grumbling thought was that Sasha had walked on her. Feeling disoriented, she rolled over to see the digital clock. The glowing green numerals told her it was 12:51.

Mind less foggy, eyes adjusting to the dark, Natalie saw Sasha on the floor halfway to the door. She seemed to be frozen, staring at the door.

Natalie was reaching for the lamp when she heard an audible thump. Pure terror shivered over her skin and stopped her breath.

Not moving a muscle, she strained her ears. Her lungs were ready to explode when another sound came. A bump. As if somebody in the next room, in Stuart's study, had knocked against the closet door or the desk.

She was not alone in the house.

CHAPTER SIX

JOHN LIKED KICKING BACK with his brothers. Connor was his closest friend, Hugh next best, maybe just because he was the youngest, but they were still close. Since John was tied down by the kids, the brothers tended to hang out here, at his place.

Tonight Hugh had cooked spaghetti, his specialty, with Maddie's earnest help. She softened him up. As a cop and a man, he was too hard-assed for John's taste—come to think of it, maybe *that* was why he was John's second-favorite brother. Having listened too closely to his mother, Hugh's mission in life was to get the scumbags off the street. Problem was, Hugh was far too quick to decide someone was a scumbag. Excuses left him unmoved, and the word *sympathy* was not in his vocabulary. If someone didn't have his sense of morality, he didn't bother trying to understand why not or see their viewpoint. John and Connor worried about shades of gray; Hugh apparently wore glasses that made the world clear-cut black-and-white.

But with Maddie and Evan, Hugh laughed often, made ridiculous jokes, and even seemed to feel occasional twinges of tenderness. John had hopes that fatherhood would one day seriously change his outlook on human nature.

The brothers didn't talk shop until John had tucked

the kids into bed. Hugh was the only one of them still in uniform; John was a detective in Major Crimes, while Connor had gotten sucked into the child abuse unit, where he saw some of the ugliest human behavior of all. John didn't envy him. Hugh liked patrol work and scoffed at desk jockeys playing banker in their suits and ties.

Tonight, Connor had been particularly quiet during dinner, his gaze often resting on Maddie. John knew he was working a vicious rape-beating case of a little girl. She'd been left in a coma.

With the kids upstairs and out of earshot, John asked him about the investigation.

Silent for a moment, Connor shook his head at last, bafflement written on his blunt face. "What the hell. There's no doubt Mama's boyfriend did it. She's the only one who won't believe it. Says some stranger broke in." He grunted. "Of course, he had to have locked the door on his way out—oh, yeah, and put the chain on. The place was locked up tight."

"Idiot," was John's comment.

Expression hard, Hugh said, "I hope you broke all his fingers."

His big hand squeezing the beer can until it began to crumple, Connor growled, "I'd like to do worse than that to him, but I was civil." He paused. "I don't envy him once he's in the pen. Boys there don't like child rapists."

Nobody commented; they didn't have to. At the Washington State Penitentiaries in Walla Walla and Monroe, child abusers were often kept in solitary for their own protection. The toughest drug lord had kids. You might sell heroin to a thirteen-year-old, but you didn't rape a six-year-old girl.

"Another beer?" Connor asked and, after a round of nods, went to the kitchen. The biggest and beefiest of the three brothers, he was dressed down tonight in faded jeans with holes worn at the knees and a T-shirt that might once have been green. On his return, he tossed them each a cold one. "We should have cleaned up earlier," he announced. "Now I don't want to."

"I cooked," Hugh said peaceably.

John shrugged. "I'll do it later."

His youngest brother peeled the tab and took a swallow. Nodding at John, Hugh asked, "You getting anywhere on Natalie Reed's body?"

"That could be taken two ways," Connor observed, an undertone of humor in his voice.

"No," John snapped, giving his brother a sizzling stare. "It couldn't."

Both paused with beer cans suspended halfway to their mouths and studied him with raised brows. "Touchy," Connor said at last.

"She's a widow," John said between gritted teeth.

"Widows remarry."

"Or screw traveling salesmen," Hugh suggested.

John uttered an obscenity. "Stuart Reed was my partner. I'm taking care of his widow. End of story."

"Uh-huh." Doubt from middle brother.

"Yeah. Sure." Mockery from baby brother.

John swore again. They laughed.

Connor had the grace to sober first. "We're just giving you a hard time. She's a looker and a nice lady. It's time you noticed."

"We're friends."

"I hear tell that you can be friends and lovers both."

Hugh was shaking his head before Connor got half-way through the sentence. "Men and women can't be friends. Sex gets in the way."

They had an amiable argument on the subject that got them past the rocky moment. Connor finally directed them back to the beginning.

"This Floyd. You find out anything?"

"Damned little." John told them what he'd done so far and what he'd learned. "With everything I know about this guy, I'd have bet he'd go straight back to dealing." He gestured with the hand that held the beer can. "So he got arrested. Them's the breaks. He knows that. He also knows that if he can avoid making an enemy who'll tip us off, chances are good he'll never see the booking room again. Moving drugs through Port Dare isn't all that hard."

Hugh crushed his empty can with his hands. "Your point?"

Connor's thoughtful gaze didn't leave John. "Come on, boy. His point is, what the hell is a drug dealer doing in Natalie Reed's house?"

Hugh of the dark hair and icy eyes said offhandedly, "Looking for drugs. What else?"

In unison, his older brothers turned their heads to stare at him.

He shrugged. "You know the rumors that a P.D. cop waltzed off with a huge shipment of heroin. What was it, a year and a half, two years ago they started? Okay, so nobody has turned in his badge to move to Minnesota or suddenly inherited a million bucks from a great-aunt once removed. Doesn't stop the rumors. Must've happened, right? What if Floyd thinks he knows something? Why couldn't Stuart Reed have been the man?"

"Because he was my partner. Because I knew him." John was uncomfortably aware that his voice didn't hold the force he'd meant to inject into it. Once in a while, he'd wondered about Reed's ethics. But their arguments had been over a pocketed "tip," not stealing a shipment of heroin.

Connor made a dismissive sound in the back of his throat. "There's always worthless gossip like that. You don't take it seriously, do you?"

Hugh laid his head back on the couch, set his feet on the coffee table and tossed the crushed beer can into the air, caught it and tossed it again. "Nah. Which isn't to say that somebody else doesn't."

John surprised himself by saying, "Any way you two can try to track down this rumor? If I start asking, people will know why."

Connor nodded his understanding. "And you don't want Natalie to hear you're even considering the possibility her husband went rotten."

John sidestepped that one. "Hugh especially might get further asking questions on the street."

"Don't mind trying."

Connor shrugged. "I'll do my best."

Silence settled, all of them slouched comfortably, Hugh still throwing pop-ups and catching them.

"I should get home," he said finally. "What time is it?"

John turned his head. "Midnight."

"Thought you had Saturdays off," Connor remarked.

"Big plans tomorrow." Hugh sounded satisfied. "I'm going sailing with a pretty lady. John's rumors will have to wait."

"Hell, it's not like I'm racing toward an arrest."

Conversation continued in a desultory manner, nobody eager to hit a lonely bed. John was starting to suspect he was going to be sorry tomorrow morning about seven o'clock—if he was lucky—when Evan unfailingly started his day. Maddie was old enough to sit her brother down in front of Saturday cartoons and even pour them both bowls of cereal. He'd hope they had a rare hour or two of harmony, with no noisy squabbles only he could settle. Having children killed any desire for a nightlife, and not just because you had to pay baby-sitters damn near minimum wage these days.

Hugh decided first that he had to go, with Connor groaning and levering himself off the couch to follow at his heels. John was seeing them to the door when the phone rang. His brothers stopped and turned with him. No good news came at—he shot a glance at the grandfather clock in the front hall—12:54 a.m.

One of the four phones in the house—lazy Americans—hung in an alcove under the stairs. He snatched it up. "McLean here."

"Detective, this is Isabelle Simon in Dispatch. You asked us to let you know if there was a call from 2308 Meadow Drive."

Adrenaline shot through him. The phone creaked when his grip tightened. "What is it?"

"Possible intruder in the house. A unit is en route."

"So am I," he snapped, and tossed the phone onto the table. He went straight to the small safe he'd had installed. Grimly he said, "That was dispatch. Natalie thinks there's someone in her house."

His brothers swore and turned toward the door.

John, who'd paused only long enough to grab his

piece and a backup, brushed past. "Somebody stay with the kids."

"I will," Connor said quietly. "You go with him."

Hugh leaped in on the passenger side an instant before John rocketed his car out of the driveway. Steering with one hand, he slapped the light on the roof. The streets in Old Town were empty and dark; the few cars he encountered on the highway made way for the flashing red and blue.

In a remote, cold part of his brain, he knew he was driving faster than was safe or justified. He didn't give a flying you-know-what. Hugh was smart enough not to say a word, only picking up the pistol John had tossed onto the seat. Discarding the holster, he shoved the gun inside the waistband of his jeans.

The radio crackled; a patrol unit reported having arrived. A moment later an officer murmured that a window was broken and asked for backup.

Hugh got on the horn and gave their position and ETA. Patrol and dispatch both acknowledged. John slowed briefly when a light turned red, then sped across the intersection once oncoming traffic stopped. His gut was clenched with naked terror.

His vision was double right now: the street ahead, a peripheral awareness of other vehicles; and Natalie alone in her bedroom, dialing 911, cringing with each beep as she depressed a button, whispering her address as she waited for someone to burst into her bedroom with a length of pipe swinging at her head.

He swore aloud, harshly. That lock on her bedroom door was useless. Worse than useless, because it gave a false sense of security. He could have installed a sliding bolt—but a determined killer could slam through one of those flimsy, hollow-core bedroom doors whatever the lock on it.

He took the last corner on two wheels and careened to the curb. While Hugh got flashlights from the trunk, John consulted in low voices with one of the two patrolmen. Normally the first officer on the scene would have been lead, but knowing John and whose house this was and seeing the look on John's face, Wently backed off fast. He and his partner would ride shotgun tonight.

John and Hugh followed him around the house, moving quickly past windows, keeping close to the walls.

A back window was wide-open. Somebody had smashed a jagged hole in the glass just large enough to reach a hand in to the latch. Crouched to one side of the window, John used the faint light from street lamps a block over to scan the family room in the daylight basement. The couch was against the wall, and none of the other pieces of furniture were substantial enough to offer any real cover. Nodding to Hugh, John went in, dropping five feet to the carpeted floor. While his knees were still absorbing the shock, he had his gun extended in both hands and was turning in a quick semicircle.

With a soft thud, Hugh landed beside him. Silently they crossed to the door, took simultaneous peeks into the hall and, with John's nod, went through it, each covering one direction. As smoothly as if they'd worked together for years, they swept the house room by room. Thank God, the crime scene tape and seal were intact across the door to the garage. It would have been a nightmare to search. As it was, John was fighting a raging need to race up the stairs and find Natalie, to hell with procedure.

The brothers took the stairs in a rush, John checking out the study while Hugh handled the sewing room. The bathroom door stood open; his flashlight picked out the tub enclosure behind sliding glass.

He and Hugh communicated with a glance. Both took up position in the hall, away from the bedroom door.

John raised his voice but kept it calm. "Natalie, it's John. You okay?"

A dense silence answered him. He waited rigidly, counting the beat of seconds, feeling a muscle jerk in his cheek.

What if they were too late?

No! he answered himself fiercely. God damn it, they weren't too late! She was being cautious. Smart.

"Natalie," he said again, pitching his voice a little louder. "You there?"

He caught a faint gasp and then, "John? It *is* you?"

Relief rocked him. He braced a fist against the wall to keep himself from staggering. Somehow he still sounded collected. "Hugh and I are both here. Are you alone?"

The next sound might have been a muffled sob, followed by a scramble of feet, a strange scraping and then the click of the flimsy lock.

When she flung open the door, he met her in the opening. Her bedside lamp was on, and he had a brief glimpse of her, all legs in another oversize T-shirt, brunette hair tumbling over her shoulders, eyes huge and dark. The flashlight thudded to the floor. With his free arm, he crushed her against him. She hugged

him, fingers gripping his shirt and biting into his back,
her face burrowing at his chest.

"It's okay. It's okay," he heard himself murmuring
hoarsely, his mouth against her hair. The slam of his
heartbeats damn near deafened him.

After a moment he had the presence of mind to
shove the gun inside his waistband at the small of his
back so that he could use both arms to hold her. He
moved his hands over as much of her as he could
reach, kneading, soothing, satisfying himself that she
was well and whole.

At long last, but too soon, Natalie gave a hiccuping
sob, then a sniff and lifted her head.

She peeked past John's shoulder. "Hugh?"

His brother's voice came from just behind him.
"I'm here, Natalie."

"Were you...were you the one sent when I
called?"

"No, ma'am. I happened to be at John's. Two other
officers are outside. I'd best go relieve their minds."

John felt her shaky breath. "Thank you, Hugh."

"Anytime," his brother said easily. He gave John
a light tap on the back and moved down the hall.

Belatedly John realized how Hugh would read this
embrace. Natalie was still plastered against him, still
holding on tight, and he sure as hell hadn't made a
move to ease back. Little brother wasn't going to believe he was just offering comfort.

John wasn't so sure he believed it himself, not on
the heels of the fear and relief that still had his heart
thundering and his knees weak.

How could he believe it, when he was suddenly
becoming aware of the pillowy feel of her breasts
flattened against his chest, the curve of hip just below

one of his hands, those glorious, bare thighs against his? He took a ragged breath, then went completely still in shock and—God help him—arousal. Was she wearing anything at all beneath the T-shirt that barely covered her butt? Or, if he moved his hand lower still and gathered the fabric in his hands, would he find smooth skin and plump flesh?

He swore silently. Damned if he wasn't getting hard. He couldn't let her notice. She was taking another hiccuping breath and letting her forehead rest against his chest.

"You came," she whispered. "I wanted you to come so badly."

If he'd been hoarse before, now his voice was a rasp, painful to hear. "I asked to be notified night or day if there was a call to this address."

"Oh."

John felt the instant when some kind of awareness rippled through her, tightening muscles. As she pulled back, he let her go too hastily, hoping against hope that she was too preoccupied with fear and gratitude to have noticed his arousal.

Natalie swallowed and brushed her hair back from her face with one hand, the movement lifting the hem of that damned tee a couple of perilous inches higher. He forced his gaze to her face, seeing that her downcast eyes looked puffy and damp.

"Why don't you sit down?" he suggested.

She looked vaguely around. "I should put something on."

"You're fine. I'd see you in less at the beach."

Right now, to see her in less he would have given any body part demanded except... He slammed a door on that one, shocking even himself at this raw lust for a woman he'd never regarded sexually before.

Her tongue touched her lips, and he saw her swallow. "Oh," she said again, and backed a few steps into the bedroom.

Relief, he told himself intensely. Damn it, this was just relief. Or adrenaline. Somehow it had gotten out of hand. His brothers ribbing him this evening had put the idea in his head. They'd primed him to notice, big time, that Natalie was a sexy woman with incredible legs, voluptuous hips, a pretty mouth, and a mass of hair any man would want to tangle his fingers in.

He almost groaned.

Find her bathrobe, he thought desperately. But how could he, now that he'd assured her she was fine in that oversize shirt and nothing else? She'd be humiliated if he suddenly tried to cover her up.

The lamplight touching her face, he could see that she was blushing although her chin was high. Her voice was small when she said, "There wasn't anybody in the house, was there? And I scared you, and brought half the Port Dare Police Department rushing over here just because I heard a bump in the night." She was talking fast now, not giving him a chance to break in. "Or maybe I didn't hear anything. I could have been having a nightmare and thought it was real. John, I'm so sorry! It was partly Geoff, seeming so sure I wasn't safe here. But I can't blame him. It was me. I…"

He laid a hand over her mouth. Natalie gazed mutely up at him over it.

"There was somebody in here."

Her mouth moved against his palm, but otherwise she was completely still.

"The family room window is broken. Looks like he used a rock from the edging around the flower bed. One of them is lying right there. He tapped the glass, made a hole just big enough to get his hand in and unlock the window. It's wide-open."

A small shudder rippled through her.

He let his hand drop. "Tell me what you heard."

"I…" She backed up blindly until she came to the bed, where she sat so suddenly it was as though her legs had given out. "A thump. No, two thumps. That's all."

He followed her, noticing with a brief, raised brow the chair that sat beside the door—smart, he thought approvingly. Sitting beside her on the edge of the bed, John tried not to notice her thighs. "Where?" he asked patiently.

"Where…" She sucked in another, shuddering breath. "I think, in the study."

John swore.

She seemed not to notice, and her brow creased as she concentrated. "As if he'd bumped against the wall. Staggered. Or…or was carrying something cumbersome and misjudged distances."

"Like a cardboard box," John said thoughtfully.

"Or…" She swung a pleading look his way. "Did you go into the study? Tell me there's not another body."

"No body," he said positively. "I can't swear one of the boxes in the closet hasn't been taken, but I'd have seen a body."

"Oh." She slumped with relief, then stiffened again. "Could…could there be one somewhere else in the house?"

"No body," he repeated patiently. "We checked

out the whole house. What do you think, your place has become a dumping ground for the mafiosa?''

Natalie let out a choked laugh. ''Well, you have to admit finding the corpse of a total stranger in your house is a little odd. Followed by somebody breaking in during the night a week later.''

Oh, yeah, he thought sardonically. ''Odd'' about covered it. Tonight's episode left him considerably less satisfied with the ''burglar turning on burglar'' theory about the murder.

He nodded toward the door. ''Did you have the chair under the knob?''

Her hair fell over her shoulder when she nodded. ''I felt really silly when I braced it under there, but it just made me feel more secure.''

''Smart,'' he said.

''As it turned out—'' she gazed doubtfully toward her maple dining chair ''—I don't know how well it would have held under a determined assault.''

''I don't, either, but at worst it would have slowed our guy down.''

She nodded again, saying nothing this time. The silence felt less comfortable than it once might have, maybe because John was trying so hard not to stare at her thighs.

Hearing voices from just downstairs, he said hastily, ''Maybe you should find that bathrobe before half the Port Dare P.D. strolls into your bedroom.''

She gave another tiny laugh and slipped off the bed, heading for the closet. John took one hungry look at her incredible legs and then squeezed his eyes shut.

''Is something wrong?''

''What?'' His eyes snapped open.

She was shrugging into a terry-cloth robe and looking inquiringly over her shoulder at him.

"Oh." He pulled himself together. "No. Just thinking."

"About?"

"You. We can go two ways here. If you want to grab some stuff, we can head for my place. Or you can go back to bed, and I'll get some shut-eye on your couch."

"But…" Her eyes widened and she said in alarm, "Maddie and Evan aren't home alone, are they?"

"Connor's with them. I expect he'd bunk down there if I call."

"What would you prefer?" she asked simply. "Whatever is easier for you."

He rubbed the back of his neck, thinking. "If you're okay with it, why don't you just go back to bed. We can get your statement in the morning. Tell me where to find a pillow and blanket, and I'll stretch out downstairs on the couch."

"He won't come back, will he?"

John knew who "he" was without asking. With regret and a certain ferocity, he said, "I wish he would. But, no. The etiquette book for crooks suggests no more than one visit in a night."

He loved her chuckle, especially under the circumstances.

Her eyes were shadowed but her mouth still soft from the smile when she came toward him. "Okay. I feel safe with you here. Tomorrow I'm going to order a security alarm."

"And you're coming home with me again until it's in," John said, tone inflexible. "No. Don't argue. Or at least, not until we've had breakfast."

"Okay," she said again. When he stood, she made an abortive move toward him, but was suddenly fiddling with the belt on her robe, her gaze downcast. Had she nearly kissed him on the cheek again?

He had a vivid flash of the night she'd surprised him with a kiss. Darkness beyond the kitchen, quiet, her bare toes curled around the stool, the rush of air as she neared and the scent of her hair and the texture of her skin up so close and the soft brush of her lips.

If she'd done it tonight, he would have had a hell of a time keeping from turning his mouth to meet hers.

Until he cooled down and figured out what to do about this unexpected lust for a woman he considered a good friend, it was probably just as well if she didn't kiss him.

"It sounds like Hugh's coming," Natalie said. Footsteps neared in the hall. "Um, I'll just go back to bed."

He was between her and it. No wonder she sounded tentative. She couldn't quite say, *For crying out loud, will you get out of here?*

"Yeah. Sure." Somehow his feet weren't moving. The bed was two steps away. She was right here in that short T-shirt and maybe nothing on under it. He had to curl his fingers at his side to keep from reaching out to plunge them in her hair. If she lifted her mouth he'd ravage it with his. He could get rid of Hugh in short order and...

From the doorway, his little brother said, "What's the plan?"

He gazed contemplatively from Natalie to John, blue eyes missing nothing, thoughts unreadable.

John cursed himself for the hoarseness still in his

voice. "I'm going to see if Connor can spend the night, and I'll bed down on Natalie's couch. Tomorrow, she's getting out of this place again."

Hugh's brows twitched, but he nodded. "Then I'll hitch a ride home with Wently and Jacobson." He gave Natalie a surprisingly gentle smile. "Sleep tight."

"Thank you," she said again.

He lifted a hand and disappeared from the doorway.

John picked up the telephone beside her bed and dialed home.

When his brother answered, he told him the situation. "Can you stay with the kids?"

"And make 'em the best dang pancakes they've ever had in their life," Connor promised. "Rest easy, and no rush tomorrow. Give Natalie my best."

When John passed on the message, tears sprang to her eyes. "All of you have been so nice." She dashed away the dampness on her lashes.

"Hugh's right." John went to her, rested the back of his hand against her cheek, and felt her nuzzle it. "Go to bed. Sleep tight."

She blew her nose and insisted on getting him the pillow and blankets. A moment later, the bedroom door was shut firmly in his face.

He checked to see that the broken window had been blockaded—it had, crudely, with an ill-fitting piece of plywood the men had found who knows where—and that the house was otherwise locked up, turning off lights as he went. Stretched out on her living room couch, which wasn't quite long enough for his six foot two frame, John was left to stare at the dark ceiling, ignore the sexual ache that he couldn't conveniently turn off, and brood.

Were these feelings artificial, an outgrowth of his brothers' razzing and the scare he'd gotten tonight? Or was he in real danger of falling for Stuart Reed's widow?

And even if he was, what, if anything, did he want to do about it? He liked Natalie. He could talk to her. He'd miss her more than he liked to admit if any advance he made blew their friendship.

Whether she gently rejected him, or kissed him torridly back, nothing would ever be the same again. Change could be good, but it was more likely to be bad. He didn't want to risk losing her friendship just so he could scratch an itch.

Adjusting the pillow, he tried to get comfortable. He clunked his heel against the end table and swore. His exasperation with the too-short couch was tempered by the knowledge that tonight, hyperalert for any sound, sexually aroused, in turmoil about what he felt, he wouldn't have been comfortable in a king-size feather bed.

An itch.

The convenient if vulgar explanation for his hard-on played in his mind.

Even the ferocious itches from chicken pox passed, John thought grimly. This one would, too, unless it was more complicated than that. If so... He swore again, quietly, the word lingering in his ears.

If so, he might lose the only woman friend he'd ever had.

CHAPTER SEVEN

JOHN MET HIS PARTNER at the curb in front of Natalie's house the next morning and told him the tale of the night.

Baxter, still standing on the driver's side with his car door open, rapped his fist on the roof. "Son of a bitch! I knew it!"

"It's not nice to say 'I told you so.'"

His partner gave him a feral grin. "If you'd just accepted my superior wisdom in the first place, I wouldn't have to be saying 'I told you so.'"

John made an obscene suggestion regarding the superior wisdom, to which Baxter only laughed.

"What say we go do what we should have done in the first place and take this house apart?"

"Maybe our friendly visitor last night left with what he was after," John suggested, playing devil's advocate.

Baxter slammed his car door. "If it had been that easy, he would have taken it the first time."

John waited until his partner joined him on the sidewalk. "The fact that he was back in the study last night doesn't sit right with me. He had time after he conked Floyd over the head. The garage...well, now, that might take you a month to search. But unless the guy is looking for something so small it could be anywhere…hell, say, a microchip, he had plenty of time to check out the study.''

''Unless he panicked.'' Baxter gazed at the house with the avid look of a hunter sizing up a set of antlers from a blind.

John grimaced. ''Possible.''

''Natalie home?''

''She went to work.'' He'd wondered about that, since it was Saturday, but she'd claimed she had to. And maybe it was just as well that she'd be busy today.

''What's she going to do tonight?''

''Sleep in my guest room. She intends to have a security alarm system installed, but that'll take a few days. In the meantime, I don't want her here.''

The balding detective jerked his attention from the house. ''Did he know she was home last night?''

''Car was in the driveway.'' That really bothered John. It took serious balls to break into a house knowing the home owner was sacked out in the master bedroom. Had the intruder been willing to kill again? Hell, he'd done it at least once before. Was the idea now so casual to him, he didn't mind taking that kind of risk? Or, worse yet, had he half hoped he'd have an excuse to do her? Even more sickening, had he *intended* to kill her when he was done in the house? Maybe rape her first?

Those were the fears that made John sweat.

Baxter grunted. ''I didn't like her moving back in here.''

''We noticed,'' he said dryly. ''And, yeah, you were right. Consider it acknowledged.''

Geoff Baxter's grin didn't last long. ''This is one time I wish I'd been wrong. I don't like to think of

Natalie in there with the bejesus being scared out of her.''

''I think she's tougher than that.'' Like many cops, John didn't much like the idea of every home owner keeping a gun under the pillow, but he was going to suggest that Natalie buy one and take a few lessons at the range on how to use it. If that bastard had come through her bedroom door last night, he would have been asking to get blasted.

Once in the house, he and Baxter each took a room and began a meticulous search of the residence. Bookcases: every book came down, got flipped through, the space behind examined. Using a small screwdriver, one or the other took the back off all the electronics components to see if something had been tucked away. Baxter pulled up loose carpet in a corner of the study; John yanked a few more inches of peeling vinyl in a corner of the utility room. Light fixtures that weren't encased in years' worth of dried paint came off so that one of the two detectives could reach a hand into the cavity behind.

When they started on the kitchen, neither man commented on the implications if they found something here or in Natalie's bedroom. They searched the cupboards—behind the pans and the soup cans and the bucket in the broom closet. They looked for false cans designed to hide valuables, opened the tops of spice containers, checked to be sure cereal boxes held cereal. John's partner pulled the panel off the front of the dishwasher, groped the pipes under the sink, felt to be sure nothing was taped to the top of a cupboard. They didn't look at each other when they were done, but John at least breathed a sigh of relief.

Feeling even more squeamish, he took Natalie's

bedroom while Baxter went down to the utility room. One of the two closets he found nearly empty. She'd evidently either packed away most of Stuart's things or given them to the Salvation Army. Nonetheless, he inspected the closet carefully. The master bath didn't take long. Natalie was neat, her makeup relatively simple and all in one drawer. Nothing was concealed in the toilet tank or on the rim along the top of the shower stall.

Trying hard to divorce himself from images of Natalie splayed on the bed, John lifted mattress and springs and found more of nothing. The woman had even vacuumed under it, clearly. He couldn't remember the last time he'd moved his own. Lining up the pillows, tucking in sheets and respreading the comforter tested his discipline. Her scent, flowery in a way that never cloyed, clung to the bedding. For just an instant, he *saw* her, hair spread on the pillow, arms flung above her head, nightgown pulled tight across her breasts and high on her thighs, which were splayed invitingly. Her dark eyes laughed at him.

Swearing, John turned to her closet.

It was as neat as the bathroom, shoes set in pairs on the floor, the suits, dresses and blouses that hung all categorized. Feeling like a bastard, he checked pockets, the boxes on the shelf, the depths of ski boots and riding boots.

He was probably too hasty by the time he got to the dresser. One drawer held nightgowns, a couple of T-shirt ones on top of an old-fashioned lacy white gown—the kind parents bought their daughter and hoped she'd wear on her wedding night—and at the bottom a spaghetti-strap, teal silk number that would cling to her body like a teenage boy's wet dream.

John tried to refold so that she wouldn't know he'd looked.

Jeans in another drawer, T-shirts in a third, and underwear and bras in the top. He shoved it closed without hunting. The low-cut, lace-edged satin bra on top would haunt him as it was. If Natalie had a secret, he reasoned, she wouldn't have left it to be found by the cops she knew were searching her house today.

The relief John had felt at finishing in the kitchen was nothing to the sense of deliverance and shame he had as he walked out of Natalie's bedroom.

He and Baxter met in the family room, where there was plenty of the crap Stuart Reed had carefully packed away in cardboard boxes, the tops sealed with tape. Fishing lures, tangled line and old reels, saved by a man who hadn't hooked a fish in ten years. Paperback westerns and thrillers that could have been traded or given to the library before the pages yellowed. Bowling ball and shoes.

"Oh, hell, maybe he used those," John muttered.

One box was packed with childhood memorabilia, the kind of stuff a mother saved. It was with both melancholy and unease that John sifted through drawings a dead man had done when he was five and his second-grade report cards. The photo albums couldn't be ignored. John found himself getting caught up in those, in the story he hadn't known of a skinny boy who was sulky in nearly every one and who seemed to shrink away from his father in the family snapshots. A newer album held newspaper clippings about every arrest of note Reed had ever made, all with his name highlighted.

Baxter wasn't interested. "Just make sure nothing's stuck between the pages," he said impatiently. "He'd have shown these to Natalie. If he hid something, it's in the garage.''

Baxter's mood was deteriorating. John watched him dump thick etched glass and china beer steins back into a box without rewrapping them in newspaper. A clank as he kicked the box into the corner of the family room made John wince.

"Natalie could sell those if you don't break them," he said mildly.

"They're too damned ugly for anyone to want." There was something almost feverish about the way he ripped the tape off the next box, then moments later lost interest in what appeared to be really old family photos—even tintypes—and petulantly jammed them back into the carton before grabbing for the next.

"Looks like the last of these," John said at last.

Crouched on his heels and shoveling through some kind of financial records, Baxter didn't seem to hear him.

John laid a hand on his shoulder.

His partner jerked and wheeled, abruptly relaxing. "Damn, don't sneak up on me!''

"Interesting?" John nodded at the stock report in Baxter's hand.

The other man gave him a blank look. "Why do I care what stocks Stuart Reed inherited from his mother? He probably spent the proceeds on beer mugs.''

"Let's lay off for the day," John said mildly. "We can start in the garage Monday.''

Baxter's face darkened. "Should be tomorrow. He might come back.''

"I take the kids to see Debbie. Anyway, he's not going to come back in broad daylight."

"Tomorrow's Sunday?" It could have been a revelation.

"Pretty sure."

As if the concession were grudging, Baxter gave an abrupt nod. "Yeah, okay. Monday."

"Natalie will be home any minute."

"Right." He scowled impartially around the family room, then dropped the year-end report he held back in the box and closed the top. "I need to head home anyway."

Edging into the personal more than usual, John asked, "Is something wrong?"

Baxter made a disgusted sound. "What would be wrong?"

The list of possibilities was long: his wife had thrown him out of the house or found a lump in her breast; he'd discovered a thousand-dollar mistake in his checking account or rot in the subfloor of his upstairs bathroom.

John settled for a mild, "You're in a bad mood."

"This is just such a G.D. waste of time," his partner snarled. "And we've got another couple of days of it."

John didn't say that he'd always figured that searching Natalie's house was a waste of time. Instead, he said, "My bet is, we don't find a damn thing."

Baxter savagely kicked one of the boxes, then swore. "Something has to be here. It's the only explanation."

Was it? John didn't say anything. Cops all had

cases that hit where it hurt for some reason. Stuart Reed and Baxter had been friends.

Hell, maybe Geoff Baxter was better friends with Natalie, too, than John had realized. The idea irked him, but he couldn't put his finger on why. It shouldn't be a surprise: Baxter had mentioned being over here for dinner just the week before the murder, and John knew he'd done work around the house for Natalie, too. Evidently it had been with his wife's blessing, as Linda and Natalie seemed to be friends as well.

Well, Baxter wasn't the only one who was hot and bothered about this murder. Security system or no, John was grimly determined that Natalie wouldn't be moving home again until they'd made an arrest. He hadn't mentioned that to her yet. He figured he'd save the fight for later.

His partner left and Natalie rolled into the driveway not five minutes later. John had been waiting at the front window like a nosy old lady. He met her at the door.

Strain showed on her face as she set down her purse on the hall table. "Did you find anything?"

She didn't say, *Any luck?* She was between a rock and hard place here. Without clues, they wouldn't find the murderer, but anything cached in this house that was worth killing over would point a nasty, accusing finger at Stuart. For her sake, John hoped he and his partner wouldn't uncover that reputedly stolen shipment of heroin.

"Nothing," he said now. "Didn't expect there would be."

She gave a jerky nod, lips pressed together. "I'll

just pack. You don't have to wait. I know the way to your door.''

"I'd rather you're not here alone.''

"The Porters probably have their binoculars trained on us right this minute.''

He crossed his arms and leaned against the wall. "Unless it's nap time.''

He was glad to see amusement mingle with her exasperation. "Anybody ever tell you, you're a stubborn man?''

"My mother,'' he said laconically.

Sounding thoughtful, Natalie said, "She tells me Maddie is stubborn, too.''

"As a mule. Maybe it's hereditary.''

"Or learned,'' she suggested with a wry look over her shoulder from halfway up the stairs.

While he waited, John thought reminiscently of the fights he'd had with his firstborn when she was a pre-schooler because she was determined to wear some eye-popping combination. She always wanted to express her feminine side—that was how he humorously saw it, anyway—with something like pink flowered leggings, and the fact that she was a modern woman in the making with a neon orange or black-and-white zebra-striped top. Whatever shoes he or Debbie would get out for her were never right. She'd scream her head off if she couldn't wear sandals in the snow or galoshes in August. The parents of the other pre-schoolers must have whispered about Maddie's mom and dad. Hell, maybe they were right to. What normal adult consistently lost every skirmish with a four-year-old?

He was still waiting patiently in the entry, leaning against the wall, when Natalie came downstairs with

a suitcase and a cat carrier. She looked tired and subdued. His guilt made him wonder whether she'd noticed that her clothes had been disarranged or the contents of her medicine cabinet inspected. Had she
known he would have to search her drawers, too? Or
had it never entered her head that he might be obligated to suspect her?

He hoped the latter. He didn't want her wondering
uncomfortably what he'd thought of her choice in lingerie.

Hell, he didn't like the fact that *he* was wondering
whether the bra she wore was anything like that lacy
peach-colored one.

John waited while Natalie locked up. He loaded her
suitcase and cat paraphernalia in the trunk of her car
and then followed her home, where he carried the bag
and Sasha's belongings into the guest bedroom, untouched since Natalie had left it only a few days ago.

"I should have changed the sheets," he apolo-
gized.

"Don't be silly." Natalie sank down on the bed as
if she didn't know what else to do. She was clutching
the plastic cat carrier as if it were a lifeline.

He guessed she hadn't done much sleeping last
night, even with him downstairs on the couch. What
would she do if he sat next to her and gathered her
into his arms?

The very thought had him backing toward the door.
"I'll get dinner on."

Her eyes focused some. "I should help."

Oh, yeah. Having her brushing him as they passed
in the close confines of the kitchen, smiling, teasing
him with words and scent, that was just what he
needed.

"I'm good. Take a nap if you want. I'll call when it's ready."

"I'm a mooch." She looked ready to cry.

"You're a friend in need."

"No, I'm..."

On a burst of irritation, John said, "Fine. Knit me a new sweater tomorrow. In the meantime, for God's sake, take a nap."

She was still staring at him when he stalked out.

In the kitchen he took his irrational frustration out on the carrots, celery and green beans he chopped for a stir-fry meal. What was it with her, anyway? Had she spent the past year figuring he was going to want payback for every single damned thing he'd done for her? What did she think, that he'd demand a romp in bed in return for painting her house and putting her up in his guest room?

Wasn't a romp in bed exactly what was on his mind? his conscience asked.

Not that way, he answered silently. Sex had to be given freely or it was no good.

And he hated like hell the thought that she might offer herself instead of a sweater, because she thought she owed him. Was that what the kiss on his cheek had been, a first tentative offering?

He swore, his voice loud in the kitchen.

To save him from his bad mood, he heard his children coming in the back way via the brick patio. Maddie's chatter was underscored by Evan's squelched attempts to contribute and by Connor's slow, deep-voiced comments. The door opened, the screen slammed, and the kids raced to him.

John set the wok on the countertop and turned to

hug Maddie and then swing Evan up in the air. "You guys have a good day?"

"Uncle Connor took us hiking. My feet hurt," Maddie announced.

Evan slid down his dad's body. "Mine, too."

She rolled her eyes. "*He* kept wanting Uncle C to carry him."

"He's five," John said mildly. "Short legs."

"He's a baby."

His brother grinned at him over their heads. "They got along great all day long."

Great. Wonderful. They'd saved their pettishness for Daddy. He gripped his patience and said, "Natalie is here. Let's try not to squabble too much. She didn't sleep well last night."

Wide-eyed, his son said, "Uncle Connor says a bad man sneaked into her house. Was she really, really scared?"

"You can ask her." John plugged in the wok and reached for the vegetable oil. "Go wash up. Dinner will be ready in about fifteen minutes."

They thundered out, arguing about who got the bathroom first. If Natalie was napping, she wouldn't be for long.

"You're a lifesaver," he told his brother.

"We had fun." Connor pulled up a stool. "They're good kids."

John knew what he meant by that. Connor had confessed before that he found Maddie and Evan to be a nostrum for the cynicism that had begun to beset him. "They're never quiet and pinched," he'd said. "Their eyes are never filled with terrible anxiety."

"They worry about their mother," John had said

then, his own anxiety finding voice. "She's been stolen from them."

"But they see her, talk to her. Hey, you two are divorced. If she was healthy, they'd be experiencing the same thing, only you're the one they wouldn't see as often. The only difference is, you're the custodial parent instead of her."

"And Mom can't come to open house at school or watch Maddie's dance recital or Evan's T-ball game."

"But they understand why and she does what she can," his quiet, down-to-earth brother had said.

Now Connor studied him shrewdly. "Tomorrow's your day to take the kids to see Debbie, isn't it?"

John dumped the chicken into the wok with the hot oil. "Yeah. Why?"

His brother shrugged. "Just asking. You're in a foul mood."

"So?" His tone struck even him as belligerent.

"You always are the night before," Connor observed.

John gave a short, unhappy laugh. "If we were still married, she could be at home. I could pay for a nurse. She'd see her kids every day, be part of their lives. She wouldn't be in this on her own."

"She's not on her own. She has her parents. And, yeah, if you were still married, she could be at home. But you're not. You weren't when she got sick."

In the turmoil he'd never managed to calm, John swore when he stirred carelessly and oil splattered his hand. "She could still be here. Maddie and Evan would have their mother."

Connor had heard it all before, said it all before, but he was patient enough to repeat himself. "She's an adult. You cannot take responsibility for her forever because you were once married.''

"She's the mother of my children."

"What kind of life would you have if she lived here? And would it really be best for the kids to live with the reality of oxygen tanks and midnight crises and a nurse ruling their mother's life?"

The truth was, he didn't have a clue, never mind answers that satisfied him.

"Here come the kids," his brother warned quietly.

Natalie was right behind them. Dark circles under her eyes gave him a renewed pang of guilt. She might have gotten some sleep if he hadn't been a jackass.

Dinner table conversation was carried by Connor and the kids. Natalie tried but would lapse into silences from which she roused with an obvious effort. Grateful for his brother's even-tempered presence, John figured it was just as well if he kept his mouth shut. Guilt in its many-layered forms was best not laid on others like a too-heavy quilt on a hot summer night that made you sweat and itch.

Connor left right after dinner, saying a few low-voiced words to Natalie on his way out. Maddie and Evan raced off to watch a rerun of *Full House*. Natalie began automatically clearing the table.

"You don't have to…" John began.

She marched past him with dirty plates in her hands. "Don't be silly."

Leave me in peace, he wanted to say, without knowing why she disturbed his peace. Oh, hell, he thought irritably, he knew why she unsettled him. Wanting a woman you couldn't have was never comfortable. What he didn't get was why her, and why now.

And he didn't like the fact that the wanting wasn't as simple as imagining her in his bed upstairs. Earlier, when he'd been talking to Connor about all the reasons he should move Debbie out of that damned nursing home into the spare bedroom, he'd faced a new dimension of guilt: he was starting to picture Natalie here for good. No room for an invalid ex.

Out with the old, in with the new.

Irrational, of course, since he and Debbie had been divorced for three years now. She hadn't begun to develop symptoms until later. Connor was right. A man couldn't spend his life caring for his ex-wife, a woman he often didn't even like.

Which didn't mean he couldn't feel guilty as hell over the cards she'd been dealt. Here he was, lucky enough to have a job he loved, their kids and his health. Dreams. She had a future in which remission was the best she could hope for. Multiple sclerosis was not a kind disease.

"Connor accused me of being in a bad mood," he said, following Natalie to the kitchen with dirty silverware and glasses. "You've gotten the brunt of it. I'm sorry."

"No." She lowered the plates to the tiled countertop beside the sink and faced him. "You were right. What you said earlier, I mean. I do hate being in debt to anyone."

He set down his load. "I don't like thinking we aren't good enough friends for you to accept anything from me."

Her tongue touched her lips. "I've always known that you were...well, taking care of me because of Stuart."

"Not true."

She studied him in perplexity. "Not?"

John opted for honesty. "At first, sure—Stuart was my partner. If it had been me, he would have done what he could for my kids."

Her makeup was smudged, he saw, her tiredness giving her fine-boned face a look of vulnerability. But her tone was steady. "That makes you a good man."

He ignored that. "Within a few months, I did what I did because you'd become a friend. Stuart and I were buddies because we were partners. We never would have been otherwise. You, I can talk to. I thought you felt the same."

"I did," she said softly. "I do."

He found his teeth gritting. "Then why the hell…"

"…can't I gracefully accept a helping hand?" Natalie gave a twisted smile. "That's what I wanted to tell you. It doesn't have anything to do with you. It was my stepfather."

She'd mentioned a mother and a sister. "I didn't know you had one."

"He died a few years back. Lung cancer. He was a smoker."

John absorbed that. "Is this a long story? Do you want a cup of coffee?"

Her smile was a ghost of its usual, more vibrant self, but it was something. "I should protest that coffee would keep me awake, but the truth is, I don't think anything will keep my eyes open once I lay my head down."

He mightily resisted the need to touch her, instead pouring them both cups from the dregs in the pot. "You have circles under your eyes."

"Even knowing you were there last night, I

couldn't stop listening. I almost came downstairs, but I thought maybe you were asleep.''

On a thrill of regret as well as alarm, John wondered, What if she had? As close as he'd come to kissing her earlier, upstairs, what if he had opened his eyes to find her standing in front of him in the darkness, saying softly, ''I can't sleep?'' He'd have had to pull her down beside him on the couch, hold her and comfort her as he would have Maddie after a nightmare. Only, she wasn't Maddie and his body was still aroused. What snatches of sleep he'd gotten had involved confused, erotic dreams. If Natalie had suddenly been cuddled up to him, head on his shoulder, sweet scent in his nostrils, his hands finding yielding flesh, would he have been able to be nothing but a friend?

He was intensely grateful that he didn't have to find out.

''You could have come,'' he said anyway.

''I thought…'' She blushed. ''Never mind.''

''You'd be bothering me?'' Was this more of the same? She couldn't ask for anything from him, even simple comfort?

''No, it wasn't that. Really. I just…'' She was trying damn hard to sound offhanded, even humorous. ''I guess I felt odd, the way I threw myself at you earlier.''

''You were scared. I held you.'' His voice was gritty. ''Isn't that what friends do?''

She seemed to shake herself. ''Yes. Of course it is. We've just never…'' She heaved a sigh. ''Oh, forget it. I was self-conscious, which is ridiculous.''

''Yes, it is.'' He nodded at the mug she held. ''Drink your coffee and tell John all.''

They sat on the stools at the breakfast bar where they had that night when he'd come home late. Sitting side by side, shoulders nearly touching, thighs inches apart, made him painfully aware of her, yet the fact that they weren't facing each other made it easy to talk.

He didn't have to prod. After a meditative silence, she began, "My father died when I was two. I don't remember him. He had his own small plane. He came in too low for a landing and hit an electrical wire." Natalie cradled the mug in her hands and inhaled the scent. "Mom remarried two years later. He—my step-father—thought we should all be grateful to him. After all, he'd rescued us from poverty, which was true," she added in fairness. "But he never let us forget it. He wasn't abusive, exactly. He never hit us kids, and I'm pretty sure he didn't Mom, either, but he was lord of the castle and he couldn't stand even being taken for granted. We were supposed to adore him and be constantly grateful for the bread he put on the table and the fact that we had decent clothes and a roof over our heads." Bitterness laced her voice. "I went through a stage in my early teens where I was always on restriction. I'd hear him downstairs giving my mother hell because she'd raised an ungrateful brat."

John watched her gaze at her past as if it were playing right here in his kitchen in living color. She'd become nearly unconscious of his presence as she talked.

In the midst of remembering, she squared her jaw. "I finally figured out a way to best him. I did things for him. I brought him his newspaper. I cooked favorite meals. I mowed the lawn so he didn't have to on Saturday. If he took us out to dinner, I made sure I'd already done something to even the score, so he couldn't say, 'Look at what I do for you.'"

"You knit him sweaters," John said, understanding.

Suddenly Natalie bowed her head and pressed her hands to her cheeks. "Oh, Lord. I even did that. It was a game, a war. He knew it, but he couldn't prove it, which ate at him. I was so sweet, and I hated every minute. I hated him."

"How did your mother feel?"

Starkly Natalie said, "She was grateful."

John waited.

Finally she lifted her head and looked at him, eyes wide and dark. "I swore I'd never owe anyone again."

"I never expected payment." He wanted to make sure she knew that.

"I didn't really think you did. It's just automatic." She held her head high. "I want you to know that. I didn't consciously think, *He hopes I'll be grateful.* I tried to make sure I didn't have to be. That's all." Natalie frowned. "The trouble was, you did big things for me, and I couldn't think of anything but small ones to do in return. I'm in arrears."

Please, God, don't let her have thoughts of offering herself, he prayed.

His gaze holding hers, he said, "Your debt is hereby dissolved."

"That easy?" she marveled.

"Nothing to it." Something was bothering him. "You were married. Didn't Stuart tell you the same thing?"

"I didn't—" Realization crossed her face like a

shadow, stopped her mid-sentence. "Of course I did," she said softly. "I suppose I always do with all my friends, too. Little gifts, I pay for lunch, I recommend them for jobs."

"None of which is so bad."

"Except for my ignoble motive." Natalie heaved a sigh. "Stuart never noticed. *I* never noticed. I was supposed to love him, which made it natural for me to buy him things or make special dinners or—"

John didn't want to speculate on what brought her to an abrupt stop this time. What would she have said if she'd finished?

Or met him at the door in my teddy and garters? Indulged his fantasies in bed?

Until this moment, John hadn't been actively jealous of Stuart Reed, but now he was. Pretty damn ridiculous, considering the man was dead and buried.

Sounding curt, he said, "It was natural."

"Except for—"

"Yeah, yeah. Your ignoble motive." He felt impatient, almost angry, but knew damn well it had nothing to do with her confession. "Nobody's generosity is uncomplicated, Natalie. We all have selfish moments. And you weren't even being that. You were defending yourself."

"Defending myself." Her eyes went soft, unfocused. "Maybe."

John took an unwanted slug of thick, strong coffee. "You didn't let me say my piece earlier."

Her gaze sharpened. "I'm sorry. What...?"

"I was trying to apologize for being a jerk. Connor tells me I'm always in a bad mood the night before I take the kids to see Debbie."

"Oh." Natalie scrutinized his face. "I've noticed before."

His mouth twisted. "Everybody but me, apparently."

"I know it must be hard."

"Hard? For whom? Me?" He gave a harsh laugh. "I came out of this with everything, didn't I? Sure, it's a nuisance to have to drive to Bremerton to see my ex-wife every other Sunday, but 'hard'? I don't kid myself. For Maddie and Evan? Yeah. I don't know whether they want to go or not. They think they should, but then they get so damned quiet when we're almost there. On the way home they look beaten. I try to do something to make it up for them, ice cream or a stop at a playground or even a movie, which makes me feel like I'm in some kind of competition with Debbie. See? Daddy is more fun than Mommy." He rotated his shoulders and made himself return to the bitter point. "Hard for Debbie? Oh, yeah. She wants to see the kids desperately, but all I can give her is a tantalizing taste. Hi and bye. I hear her crying as we leave."

Understanding welled in her huge, dark eyes. "It's unfair, and you feel guilty."

He shoved the stool back and stood in one frustrated, angry motion. "Shouldn't I?"

"You are not responsible for her illness. You didn't leave her because of it."

"But it's still goddamned unfair and I dread Sundays when I have to rub her face in it."

Her brow knit and she slipped from the stool. "You don't honestly think Debbie feels that way, do you?"

John made a raw sound. "No. God. No. She's...grateful." His laugh wasn't a laugh. "There's your idea of torment. She has to be grateful, and she can't pay me back in any way."

"Don't you really go for Maddie and Evan?" Despite the aching compassion in her eyes, Natalie's tone was brisk.

He scowled. "Who analyzes why the hell you do something like this?"

"You, evidently. Isn't that what you're doing?"

His scowl deepened. "Can't I just feel guilty?"

"Why not? I was just making the point that Debbie knows you're doing your best for the kids you both love. Of course she's grateful she chose a father for her children who she could trust to do that."

"For better or worse." He had to say the words. "Where am I, now that the worst has come?"

"Taking care of your children, which is what she needs most from you." That same brisk, practical tone should have grated but, oddly, comforted instead.

His grin was wry but real. "Okay, okay. I give up self-pity. For tonight, anyway."

CHAPTER EIGHT

AFTER TOSSING THE SADDLE over the top rail of the fence, Natalie slapped Foxfire's sweaty neck. He whickered softly and turned to playfully close big, yellowing teeth on her arm.

"Bite me and I'll bite you," she warned.

The stallion rolled his eyes and paused just long enough to say, *Yeah, but I've got bigger teeth*. Then, releasing her, he nickered again and tossed his head, for all the world as if he were laughing.

She did laugh, feeling the carefree, belly-deep joy a good joke might bring. She wished Stuart could know what a perfect gift he'd given her. Foxfire might occasionally be exasperating—like the time he'd tossed her on an asphalt road a mile from the ranch and left her to hobble home in the rain. But he also gave her wonderful moments of freedom and companionship, letting her experience his power and speed. She found a simple pleasure in the crisp air, open fields and hard gallops. This past year would have been so much tougher without her three or four times weekly escapes to ride her Arabian.

Today she walked him until the dark patches on his coat dried, carefully avoiding the quarter horse mares pastured below the barn. The one time he'd frightened her was when he caught the scent of a mare in heat and began fighting her. It was then that she knew she should geld him if she wasn't going to put him up for stud.

This walk was peaceful, the sun warm on her back, the stallion's hooves clopping on hard-packed dirt as he ambled behind her. Twice he nuzzled her back and made her laugh again. They paused so he could snuffle curiously in a pile of fallen maple leaves, huge and lemon-yellow and crunchy when he nibbled one experimentally. Like a child, Natalie kicked the edges of the heap until she gave guilty thought to the ranch hand who had tediously raked these.

She groomed Foxfire and restored him to his stall and paddock, leaving him contentedly munching on hay. It was only two o'clock. How long, she wondered, did the trip to Bremerton take? Would John stop today to take Maddie and Evan to a movie or…what else? Visit a toy store? An arcade? Or would they come straight home?

And why should she care?

They were friends, she told herself defensively. Couldn't she worry about him? Want to see that he hadn't been made silent, withdrawn and frowning by the visit to his ex-wife?

Getting into her car, Natalie sat for a moment without putting the key in the ignition.

Yeah, okay, they were friends. Gripping the steering wheel, she closed her eyes for a moment. Friends. Only, she had a suspicion that *friends* didn't have quite such a tangle of feelings for each other. Compassion for his anguish was mixed with jealousy for the hold his ex-wife still had on him. Natalie's loneliness because she was excluded today turned all too easily into a desire to hold John when he did brood.

Please, God, never let him suspect, she prayed.

Natalie took a deep breath, opened her eyes and started the car. Proximity, she told herself desperately, that's all it was. She'd been fine until the day she found Ronald Floyd's body in her house and had to go home with John. It had to be the fact that she was staying in his guest room—sharing a bathroom with his children, passing the milk at the breakfast table, peaceably inquiring what time he'd be home for dinner, as if she had a right—that was doing this to her. Giving her ideas.

She would be fine again once she could go home.

Quelling her deep reluctance, even repugnance, at the idea, she thought tartly, *If people would quit breaking in and leaving dead bodies, the house might start seeming more like home again.*

And if not—she would sell it. Simple as that. What equity she got out of the sale, Stuart's modest investments and Foxfire would be the only legacies from her marriage. Which was okay with her.

Thinking about the house made her realize she'd automatically taken the turns that would bring her home rather than to Old Town and John's shingled cottage. This would be a good time to grab some more clothes, Natalie decided. She'd be safe in her own house for a few minutes in the middle of a Sunday afternoon. It wasn't quite the same as being alone there in the wee hours of the night.

The moment she turned onto Meadow Drive, she saw that she wouldn't be alone anyway. A dark sedan sat in the driveway. She knew an unmarked police car when she saw one.

Natalie parked beside it and let herself in the front door. The foyer was empty and quiet.

A little nervous for the first time, she made sure to

leave the front door open and only took a few steps inside before she called, "Geoff? Are you here?"

A door opened and closed and the middle-aged detective came from the direction of the kitchen. He'd been in the garage, she realized. Seeming annoyed, he said, "Natalie. What are you doing here?"

"It is my house." She sounded almost apologetic.

"Is John with you?" He looked past her.

"No, he's in Bremerton with the kids. Didn't you know this was his Sunday? I just thought I'd pick up some more clothes." Confidence returning, she added, "Why are *you* here?"

Something shifted on his face, making him for a disconcerting moment into a stranger. The next second, she realized she'd imagined it when he grumbled with familiar irritability, "We shouldn't have laid off today. Damn it, the place could be cleaned out in the middle of the night! Stuart had something here, and if we don't figure out what, you won't be safe."

She stepped forward and placed a hand on his arm, feeling muscles rock hard. "Geoff, relax. You can take a day off. Think about it. I'll be safe either way. If…if the killer finds what he wanted, he won't be back. I know that would be frustrating for you—all of you take such pride in solving every case, and this one must hit hard. But whether you or our bad guy finds whatever is here, he won't be interested in me."

He gripped her hand, gaze intense. "Unless neither of us can find whatever it is. Then he's going to think *you* might know something. That you might have hidden it somewhere else."

The chilling thought had occurred to her, along with a corollary. "What if Stuart didn't *have* anything? What if this guy is looking for something that doesn't exist?''

Geoff Baxter's face hardened. ''You'd better hope that's not the case.''

She searched his eyes. ''But you knew Stuart. You don't really think he…oh, turned crooked? Because that's the only way he'd have something so valuable hidden here, isn't it? Something he never told me about.''

For a moment that stranger looked at her and his hand tightened until her bones creaked. Then he muttered a profanity, released her abruptly and let out a sigh that left his shoulders slumped.

''I don't know.'' He sounded reluctantly honest. His face was haggard below the receding hairline. ''He was my friend, but there were times…'' Geoff swallowed. ''I don't know, Natalie. He took the easy way sometimes. Didn't you see that?''

She shook her head, then wasn't sure she was telling the truth. Stuart had seemed to love his job, but she had begun to suspect it was the adrenaline rushes and seeing his name in the newspaper that satisfied him, not the mundane work that made up a cop's day-to-day life. And it was true that he hadn't really liked working around the house, or working, for that matter, on his marriage. None of which meant he'd steal…*something*—a something so valuable men would kill to get their hands on it.

And if he'd had such a thing, why hadn't he cashed it in? Told her about it? Even lied to her about it? *Honey, this great-aunt I've never mentioned died up in Pittsburgh and left me a whole shit-load of money. Easy Street, here we come.*

Because he never had anything.

She stared unseeing at Geoff and made herself face a niggling fear.

Had Stuart not told her because he hadn't stolen anything? Or could it have been because he never intended to tell her about it?

It was true that he'd become increasingly distant with her. They'd had sex less often those last months, and too many of those times at her initiation. Was it her fault he was losing interest? she'd wondered, ashamed. But he did respond to her in bed, so she had convinced herself he was just going through a bad patch. Midlife crisis, with his fortieth birthday approaching. Or maybe the romance went out of every marriage unless the two people involved really worked at staying connected. If work was what it took, and she was the one who had to do it all, well, so be it, Natalie had believed.

Now she gave voice to a thought she hadn't wanted to acknowledge.

"Was he going to leave me?"

Geoff reared back his head, eyes rolling like a spooked horse's. "What the hell are you talking about?"

Her jaw and voice firmed. "You were friends. Tell me. Was he planning to leave me?" Better to know.

He swore. "Don't be ridiculous. Stuart never said any crap like that. You two hadn't been married three years! You're a beautiful woman, Natalie. Why in God's name would he leave you?"

Her mouth quirked in a smile whose sadness she could feel. "Thank you for the compliment, Det. Baxter. But you and I both know that my beauty—or lack," she added wryly, "has nothing to do with whether Stuart was happy married to me." When she saw that he was about to argue, she said, "Would you leave Linda if she put on weight or was scarred in an accident?"

He shook his head in exasperation. "Damn it, you know I wouldn't, but we've been married for twenty years. What I'm saying is, a man doesn't get tired of a woman like you in less than three."

Uncomfortable with his insistence on her beauty, something she knew darn well she didn't possess, Natalie gave up the argument, saying only, quietly, "Geoff, I'd rather know what he was thinking. Don't try to spare me." She shook her head when he started to speak too quickly. "Think about it. That's all. Moving on might almost be easier if I knew..." She stopped, pressed her lips together, then managed a rueful smile. "I'm going to go pack. You need to go home and take your wife out to dinner. Appreciate what you have."

"After twenty years, that isn't a hell of a lot," he growled, but she thought he was pretending disgruntlement. He and Linda didn't have children, and she guessed that he regretted it, but they had a nice house and traveled often. Cops didn't go into their line of work for riches.

He waited while she packed and then did leave, the dark sedan following her compact until she turned off the highway toward Old Town. Geoff and Linda owned a modern three-bedroom ranch house with half an acre and a view of the strait. He often gave John a hard time about his ninety-year-old restored cottage.

"What is it this week? The furnace?" His brow would crease in exaggerated thought. "No, you bought a new one last year. Let's see. Termites? Roof caving in? Does the wiring still have those little glass transformers, or whatever the hell they are?''

"Hey, come on," John would say. "The place wasn't wired until the Depression. Modern. Nothing to worry about."

Smiling, Natalie parked to one side of the packed-gravel driveway, noting that he wasn't home yet. The house was actually a charmer, with all the character her inherited split-level lacked. The deep front porch had the kind of swing where you sat on summer nights and visited with your neighbors, or necked with your boyfriend if you were young and the porch light was off. The exterior was painted a pale sea-foam green with the fancy trim typical of the era picked out in white and deep teal. Arbors framed a brick patio in back and a secret garden surrounded by boxwood hedges that John grumbled about but kept impeccably trimmed. Inside, the house was comfortable with oak floors and high ceilings and wonderful woodwork. Natalie envied John his house.

She remembered the first time she'd seen it, when John and his wife had her and Stuart over for dinner right after their honeymoon. She'd felt an acute, nearly painful pang. Both men were detectives; they'd both grown up in Port Dare. Why had Stuart settled for a characterless, 1980s split-level house decorated only with big-screen TV and stereo system when he could have created a home like this?

At the time, she'd suppressed the disloyal thought. John was married. Stuart's house was typical for a bachelor. They'd create a real home together.

Shaking off the memory and the regrets, Natalie unlocked the back door and carried her extra suitcase into the guest bedroom. Cautiously Sasha emerged from under the bed for a visit. As Natalie hung clothes in the closet, part of her was listening for the sound of a car in the driveway.

The rush of pleasure she felt when she heard it disconcerted her. He was a friend. No more. And today, of all days, he probably wished she wasn't here.

The back door rattled and Evan shouted, "Natalie's here!"

Sasha shot back under the bed.

"Evan!" his sister protested. "I can go say hello, too, if I want!"

"But I said I wanted to see her first!"

"Guys!" came their father's deeper, exasperated voice. "You're not dogs, and she's not a bone."

With a faint laugh, Natalie wondered if they'd even heard him. The kids were already jostling at her door for the right to enter first.

"Hey," she said mildly. "Don't hurt yourselves."

Evan gave his sister a look of dislike. "*I* just wanted to see you."

"*We* wanted to see you." His blond sister cast a quick glance at the suitcase. "Are you leaving?"

"Settling in a little more, I'm afraid," Natalie admitted. "I needed more clothes than I had."

"Oh." She sounded unaccountably relieved.

"Did you have a good visit with your mother?"

Maddie shrugged. "It was okay."

"I beat her at rummy. I'm a good rummy player," Evan declared.

"Well, *I* beat you. *And* Mom," his sister said with a sniff.

"You're bigger," he said simply.

Behind them, John filled the bedroom doorway. His

searching gaze took in the suitcase, too. "You stopped by your house?"

"Geoff was there," she told him, feeling absurdly self-conscious to be folding a nightgown and laying it in a drawer. As though she hadn't paraded around his house already in her gown and bathrobe. And then there was the night she'd launched herself into his arms wearing one. She'd seen the way he carefully kept his eyes trained on her face as he gently suggested she don a robe before the rest of the Port Dare P.D. came into her bedroom.

John frowned. "At your house? Did you ask him to go with you?"

"No, he was there. He admitted that he hadn't wanted to take today off." Aware of Maddie and Evan, she said lightly, "He's sure the two of you are having a race with time and the bad guy to find the holy grail."

John's jaw muscles tightened. "He had no business there by himself."

Remembering that momentary, queasy impression that she didn't really know Geoff Baxter, Natalie couldn't help asking, "Don't you trust him?"

His look was frankly astounded. "Don't be ridiculous. He's my partner. What are you suggesting?"

"*I'm* not suggesting anything," she pointed out. "You're the one who doesn't want him in my house without an escort."

The lines from mouth to nose deepened. "We don't run off half-cocked on our own. He knows that."

"Talk to him." She smiled at the kids. "Have you guys had dinner? Did your dad buy you fast food all day?"

Evan climbed onto the bed and wrinkled his nose.

"He packed a lunch and made us eat at the park. I wanted McDonald's."

"Egg-salad sandwiches," his sister agreed gloomily. "And *carrot sticks.*"

"Don't forget the apples," their father reminded them with a quirk of his mouth.

"We didn't even get cookies," Evan concluded.

John's smile was gone. "The point of these Sundays is visiting your mother, not stuffing yourself with junk food."

Evan made the mistake of whining, "But usually…"

"Yeah, well, no more." John sounded hard, almost angry.

Their eyes widened. After a moment, he sighed and rubbed the back of his neck. "Maybe sometimes."

"We ate our carrots," Maddie said, almost timidly for her. "So we've had a vegetable and a fruit already. Can we order pizza for dinner?" She added innocently, "Then you wouldn't have to cook."

Natalie saw him on the edge of refusing before his mouth twisted. "Maybe." He held up a hand. "You guys scoot. Let me think about it."

They were smart enough to obey without another word.

"I'm weak," he said, once they had clattered downstairs.

Tempted to laugh, Natalie stopped herself. "Because you want them to be happy?"

"Instant gratification doesn't make for a healthy, well-adjusted child."

"Nor does an occasional pizza corrupt your children." The moment the words were out, she shook her head. "Wait a minute. What do I know? I don't even *have* kids."

"You were one."

"So was Scrooge."

"My two love you."

"I'm a novelty," she argued.

He shrugged, but a faint smile played at his mouth. "They didn't like the novelty of Daddy packing carrot sticks for lunch instead of driving through Hamburger Heaven."

She rolled her eyes. "That's because I'm not issuing orders or frowning disapproval. I'm like…like candy."

The smile lingered in his eyes. "Versus carrot sticks."

Knowing she was being laughed at, still she said stubbornly, "Right."

The grin showed. "Suit yourself." He watched her hang up a blouse. "So, what do you like on your pizza?"

She smiled over her shoulder. "Anything not fishy."

He nodded and disappeared.

Natalie finished unpacking and then loitered in her room, having a cuddle with her cat and listening for the pizza delivery. Cowardly, maybe, but she was most comfortable with him when Maddie and Evan were around, too.

She emerged when she heard the doorbell half an hour later. The kids, crowing in triumph, barreled down the hall. For safety's sake, Natalie let them pass before following.

The evening was fun. They ate at the dining room table, but with paper plates. John brought pop cans and no glasses. "This is Maddie and Evan's night to clean up," he said.

"Okay," Evan said agreeably.

His sister surveyed the table first with quick suspicion to make sure she wasn't being tricked before nodding as well.

Natalie noticed they didn't talk about their mother. Instead it was school, soccer practices, dance lessons and Uncle Hugh, who apparently could make a really great farting sound with his armpit.

"He always was good," John admitted with a reminiscent gleam in his eyes.

After dinner they played board games, including a cooperative one where deep-sea divers shared oxygen and tools to bring up treasure from the bottom of the ocean. Natalie laughed and bickered and felt positively childlike.

Except, of course, when she met John's quizzical, amused eyes. Darn it, this evening was not aiding her determination to regain her feelings of pure friendship toward him.

When he told the kids to get ready for bed, Natalie stood and stretched, too. "Good idea. Where do you keep the games? I can put them away."

"Why don't you have a cup of coffee with me?" The tone was one he might have used when telling a suspect he couldn't leave the area.

Half amused, half annoyed, she asked, "Am I in trouble?"

Passing her, Maddie wrinkled her nose. "Dad always talks like that."

He raised a brow. "What?"

"Nothing," his daughter said hastily, scooting out the door.

"You sounded dictatorial," Natalie told him. "Maddie says you always do."

"Sorry." This tone wasn't particularly repentant. "Stock in trade."

She hesitated, her hand on the back of the chair. "Was there something you especially wanted to talk about?"

"No, I...just hoped for your company." His expression became shuttered. "But if you're tired, we can skip the coffee."

His awkwardness and quickly hidden disappointment got to her where a demand didn't.

"No, I'd like to keep you company." Still on her feet, she said, "I'll pour the coffee."

When she came back from the kitchen, he still sat at the table, but he was massaging his temples. When he heard her, his head came up and he dropped his hands to his sides.

"Headache?" she asked.

"It would seem so." He grimaced. "Another of those every-other-Sunday symptoms."

"Hard day, huh?" She remembered his previous reaction to that choice of words. "Harder for her, I know," she amended as she set his cup in front of him and took her own to a safe distance on the other side of the table. "Which doesn't mean it can't be stressful for you."

"You know what hits me every time?" He cocked his head, and she realized he was listening to be sure Maddie and Evan were really upstairs and unable to hear him. "It's discovering all over again that she and I can't just talk. I can't say, 'Please don't make Maddie and Evan feel guilty because they can't come more often.' Hell, no, if I say that she accuses me of trying to get between her and the kids. I pull my punches because she's in a wheelchair, but on the way home I remember that all of our conversations were like that, even when we were married. Every word I said was loaded, every word she said was. Nothing could be simple. No, 'Hey, I had fun tonight.' Because if I had fun at a party it must mean I'd rather spend every evening with the guys instead of her. If she said she had fun, it was a challenge. 'Didn't you see me flirting with so-and-so? Aren't you jealous?'"

He fell silent abruptly, then swore. "What am I telling you this for? I sound so damn petty. Debbie's entitled to a few temper tantrums. Who can blame her? Don't listen to me."

"But I am listening. Just because she's ill doesn't mean she can do no wrong."

His lean, handsome face looked gaunt and older, lines deeper. "My trouble is, somewhere near the end of our marriage I realized I don't even like her. Fine thing, isn't it, marrying a woman you don't like. Apparently, it took me a few years to notice." He took a deep breath. "And now I feel guilty, because the woman I don't like is condemned to life in a wheelchair at an extended care home. If she's lucky."

And he had it all.

Natalie touched his hand, lying slack on the table. "There's no way for you ever to feel better about this, is there?"

His hand closed on hers. "Looks that way, doesn't it?"

"Tell me about her, when you first got married." In a way, Natalie didn't want to hear. She didn't want renewed jealousy to replace her deep pity for the pretty, lighthearted blond woman she had briefly known.

He said nothing for a moment, seeming to study her hand. Finally he released it and exhaled.

"You knew Debbie. She was my high school girl-friend. Always cute, popular, a cheerleader. I felt lucky to have her. I went away to the University of Washington, she took classes at the community college. I didn't see enough of her during breaks to get disillusioned. I graduated, went to the academy, was offered a badge, and proposed."

When he fell silent again, Natalie prompted him. "Were you happy at first?"

He squeezed the back of his neck. "Sure. Why not? Until you have kids, life doesn't get complicated. Yeah, I started wishing she had more interests, wishing she had the stomach to listen to me talk about my job, but, hey, she was pretty and feminine and she'd smile and tease me out of any mood. And I had Connor and Hugh and my friends if I needed to talk." John shrugged. "She wasn't cut out to be a cop's wife. She loved to entertain, would have been great as the hostess for a businessman." He gave a crooked smile. "She actually dated our esteemed mayor when we were all in high school. Think what a mayor's wife she'd have been."

Natalie didn't speak the obvious: Debbie would still be in a wheelchair.

John's face closed, and she knew his thoughts paralleled hers. "She could have been happier with someone else," he said.

"And so could you have been."

His flash of anger startled her. "Meaning?"

She lifted her hands. "Life's a bitch."

Anger extinguished, he gave a humorless laugh. "Yeah, yeah. And then you die. In other words, what's done is done."

"Something like that."

"And she would have come down with MS no matter what." The admission, however obvious, seemed dragged out of him.

"Well, she would have."

He rotated his neck to ease the headache she could see shadowing his eyes. "I did love her."

When Natalie said nothing—didn't know what to say—he grimaced. "I'm good company. Sorry."

"I didn't mind listening." However inadequate that was.

John gave her an odd look. "Do you know, I've never had a woman friend before."

"I'm not sure I've ever had a man as a friend, either," Natalie admitted. "I mean, I have lunch with men from work, but I don't tell them my deep, dark secrets, either."

He cocked his head. "Have you ever told me your deep, dark secrets?"

"I guess I don't have any juicy ones." She made a face. "I'm not a very exciting person."

Cradling the coffee mug in his big hands, John contemplated her. "You're very guarded. I sometimes wonder how well I really know you."

"Would you believe I'm shy?"

His reflective gaze stayed on her face. "From what I hear, you're a bulldog at work."

"That's different." Natalie looked down at her own, nearly untouched, mug of coffee. "It's like acting a part. There's a certain excitement." She gave a small laugh. "Like hunting for antiques in out-of-the-way junk stores. When I bag a big account, I get a rush of adrenaline.''

''You want to stuff 'em and hang 'em on the wall?''

Her chin came up. ''You're laughing at me.''

''No.'' His smile faded. ''I feel the same when I make an arrest that really counts. Triumph, pure and simple.''

Natalie nodded, pleased that he understood. ''But I can do my job without it being personal.''

''You don't have to give anything of yourself away.''

She dipped her head.

''Which you don't much like doing.''

Natalie stiffened. ''Why the psychoanalysis?''

Frustration flared in his eyes. ''Because I've just been baring my soul, but you're not about to do the same, are you?''

Strangely, it was fear that rose in her. Fear of him? Fear that he could somehow compel her to reveal parts of herself she wanted hidden? Or fear that if she didn't, she would lose his friendship?

With dignity, she said, ''I didn't realize this was a game. What is it, truth or dare?''

Eyes glittering with intensity, he searched her face for a disquieting moment before he shook his head, slammed down the coffee mug and shoved back his stool. ''Forget it. I'm in a bad mood. You already knew that.''

She tried to make her tone light, as though nothing had happened, but her voice shook slightly. ''Yeah, I kinda guessed.''

''I've got to get the kids in bed.'' He turned away.

"John?" Her heart pumped fast and hard; she already knew she was going to be rash.

He stopped but didn't turn. "Yeah?"

"I think it's because you're a man," she said hurriedly. "I can't seem to get past that."

Now he did turn slowly, expression arrested. "Why?"

She was chickening out. "I don't know. Because you are. Because I never had brothers or male friends in high school or…"

"We've known each other a long time."

Natalie couldn't tell what he was thinking, and that made her more nervous. "Yes."

"Don't you usually quit noticing what friends look like, when you've known them long enough?"

She nodded almost reluctantly. It was true. Her roommate in college had been a girl with burn scars, but she'd no longer seen them after a while.

"So why," he said very softly, "can't you quit noticing I'm a man?"

Because she was attracted to him.

A tiny shock almost stilled her heart. She'd known the answer all along. Maybe, on some level, she had always been drawn to him.

Wordless, she met his eyes.

He took a step closer. She found herself sliding off the stool to face him. He was a large man; she did sometimes forget that. But right now she was exquisitely conscious of his broad chest and shoulders, his looming height, of the way he dwarfed her.

"Could it be," he said, in that same silky voice, "for the same reason I can't forget you're a woman?"

She sounded very strange, as if she heard herself through a long tunnel. "And why is that?"

His intensity arced to her, as powerful as a touch. "Because, God help me, I keep thinking about kissing you."

Natalie drew a shaky breath and chose truth. Her heartbeat deafened her. "I've...thought the same thing. Sometimes."

He said something she didn't understand, something rough, profanity maybe. The next thing she knew, one of his big hands wrapped around her nape and his mouth descended to hers.

CHAPTER NINE

UP UNTIL THE MOMENT his mouth closed over Natalie's, John could still hear the voice of his common sense.

Don't do this. Think about everything you have to lose.

One taste of her evoked stunning hunger that drowned that common sense. She was sweet, soft, responsive. The memory of how her body felt pressed to his had been imprinted since Friday night, as if the fear of losing her had sharpened sensation. Now she fit against him as if she belonged.

If he'd thought at all, he would have kept the kiss light, something they could both dismiss afterward if it wasn't a success. Friends pecked each other on the lips, didn't they?

Friends didn't kiss each other like this, with desperation and mindless passion.

One of his hands cupped the back of her head; the other gripped her buttock as he lifted and pressed her against him. He came up for air only when he had to. She let out small whimpers and tugged at his hair until he bent his head again. John backed her against the table and lifted her so that he could cradle himself between her thighs. He was so damned hard, aching for her, ready to have her here, now. With a free hand he lifted her T-shirt and cupped her breast, glorying in the weight and fullness and the hard peak of her nipple against his palm.

She wanted him. She had to want him. This wasn't one-sided.

The knowledge had been there all along, feeding his secret fantasies about her. Now it roared through him like a Gulf hurricane, the quiet eye of certainty surrounded by whipping turmoil.

She sighed, nipped his neck, her mouth damp. He knotted his fingers in her hair and lifted her face to claim her lips again. The drive of his tongue mimicked the primitive urge that had his hips shoving against her.

"Daddy!" came a distant, indignant cry.

John jerked and dragged his mouth from Natalie's. He was disoriented, taking a couple of seconds to realize his kids were just upstairs. Squabbling, of course. Wanting his intervention.

He sucked in ragged breaths as he fought for control. He'd forgotten his own children. How could he?

Natalie had stiffened under his hands. Her breasts were rising and falling as she, too, gasped for air. Her lips glistened and looked swollen. He wanted to nip her lower lip, demand entrance. He wanted to carry her into his bedroom and lock the door, to hell with his children.

"Daddy!" came Evan's whine. "Maddie's being mean!"

The telephone rang.

John groaned.

"It's…it's just as well." Natalie was inching back and trying to straighten her clothes.

"No, damn it, it's not!" he snapped, his fingers biting into her arms.

She lifted startled eyes to his. Her pupils were dilated, her cheeks pink.

He made himself flex his fingers and release her. "I've been wanting to do that for a long time."

He hoped for a glorious, shy smile and a whispered admission that she felt the same. Instead, her gaze slipped from his and she said, "Shouldn't you answer the phone?"

Tautly John said, "That's what the answering machine is for."

"Da-ad." His daughter's voice neared. "Evan's being a brat."

His own voice could be heard as the answering machine kicked in. "You've reached the McLean residence. We can't take your call right now. Leave a message."

The kids tore into the kitchen at the exact same moment that Hugh started speaking. "Call me, John. You asked me to check out those rumors. You're not going to like this, but it seems they're dead-on." Click.

Natalie had slid from the table and he'd backed up a couple of feet. Anyone older than eight would have caught some vibes. His children didn't.

His son launched the first salvo in a whine. "*She* says we have to watch…"

"No TV." John's voice had a snap they seldom heard. "You can't agree, you lose. Straight to bed."

Their mouths dropped open.

"But, Dad…!" Maddie began.

"*Now.*"

They went without another word, expressions chastened. Hell, maybe he should crack down more often.

Why should he play ump? Let them work out the rules.

He turned to see that Natalie was edging toward the door to follow them.

"Natalie…"

She shoved a hand into her tangled hair. "Let's not talk tonight, okay? Tomorrow?"

He wouldn't have known what to say anyway. *Don't read too much into one kiss.* Or, *Read as much into it as you want.*

Talking had never been hard for them, although they'd had their best conversations on the telephone. Maybe he should call her tomorrow at work. Say things that were difficult in person.

But he knew he wouldn't. Seeing the nuances of expression on her face had become too important. Words weren't enough anymore.

"Yeah. Okay," he said. His voice roughened. "Just don't…"

She paused in the doorway. "Don't what?"

"Don't be sorry."

From the way her gaze flitted from his, she already was, he saw with dread.

She only nodded and left. Fled, because he hadn't listened to the sane voice of his common sense.

Don't blow a friendship you need so badly, it had tried to tell him.

She was a guest in his house. What a time to come on to her. John faced how he'd feel if tomorrow she made an excuse to go stay with a woman friend. He'd been damned lucky she trusted him so implicitly.

But he was still hard, his body still thrumming with raw sexual need. He couldn't remember wanting a woman like this. How did you divert a hurricane from its path?

John swore aloud, his voice harsh in the empty room.

He was almost grateful to remember Hugh's message.

Until he pushed Play and listened to it again.

The rumors he'd asked him to check out had to do with a missing shipment of heroin and the dubious stories of cops who'd made it disappear. They were dead-on?

John went into his study to call his brother, who answered on the third ring.

"Thought that message would get you," he said, when John had identified himself.

John had no patience tonight. "What do you mean, dead-on?"

"I found somebody who says he'd testify in court that he tipped off Stuart Reed about a good half million dollars worth of white stuff coming into the country. Next morning, the boat was found adrift and the two men who were supposed to be on it weren't. I vaguely remember the incident. Coast Guard handled it, but they contacted Port Dare P.D. because they suspected drugs had something to do with it."

"We get tips all the time," John said impatiently. "You know most of them are worth crap."

"According to my source, there were actually three people on that boat. One of them got away. He might talk if we're persuasive enough, my informant says. And what he'll tell us is, cops had something to do with it."

John wanted to be shocked. Or disbelieving. Not coldly angry and convinced despite himself.

"You get a name?"

"I got a name," Hugh said in a hard voice.

"I think I can be persuasive."

"I figured."

John rubbed the back of his neck. "Your source thinks the cop was Stuart Reed."

"Yeah." Hugh was silent for a moment. "I'm sorry, John. I know he was your friend."

"Not that good a one, apparently."

Head pounding anew, John wondered how he would tell Natalie. She'd loved her husband. How would she deal with the knowledge he was crooked?

Or had she known?

"No." Not Natalie. She was too honest. Had been too shocked at finding the body in Stuart's den. Stuart couldn't have told her.

If anyone else was investigating this case, that wouldn't be enough.

"No what?" his brother asked.

"I was thinking aloud." John swore. "This opens a can of worms."

"Oh, yeah." Something rustled in the background, and John easily pictured Hugh unwrapping one of those peppermints he sucked incessantly since he'd quit smoking two years ago. "We should bring Internal Affairs into it."

"Not yet," John said, too quickly. He let his head fall back and lightly bump the wall. "Let's be sure first. For Natalie's sake, if not Stuart's."

His brother had the goodness—or the sense—not to question Natalie's honesty.

"You going to take Baxter to talk to this guy?"

John went with instinct. "I want you."

Silence. "You don't want Baxter to know?"

John closed his eyes. "Not yet. Let's keep it to ourselves until we hear this guy's story."

Funny, brothers could and did argue about anything. But they also knew when to say agreeably, "I'm all yours tomorrow."

HUGH'S SOURCE had even known where to find Jens Lindmark. He lived in a decent condo—owned, not rented, John had checked—with a waterfront view from the second-story balcony. He carried no mortgage and wouldn't have been given one, considering his lack of employment history.

At eight-thirty sharp, Hugh rang the doorbell. John contemplated the nice planter box with pansies peeping from beneath a purplish grass.

No answer. Hugh glanced at his watch and gave Lindmark one minute, than rang again. And again. Third time was the charm.

Muffled swearing and finally footsteps preceded the unbolting of a dead bolt. A thin, narrow-faced man in his thirties wearing nothing but low-slung pajama bottoms yanked open the door.

"What the hell do you want?" His eyes narrowed as he took in Hugh's uniform and then John, a step behind. He growled an obscenity. "Cops. You couldn't wait until nine o'clock? Ten o'clock?"

"The early bird…"

This obscenity was blistering.

Both men presented shields. "We want to talk to you," Hugh said.

"So does my ex-wife. I don't talk to her, either."

Hugh planted a hand on the door and effortlessly prevented it from shutting. "We hear you might know something about half a million bucks worth of heroin that went missing.''

Jens Lindmark gave an incredulous laugh. "If I did, you think I'd tell you?"

John said musingly, "Word on the street is that nobody knows where that shipment went. If it were to somehow get around that Jens Lindmark does know…" He paused, shook his head. "Why, we're probably just the first of many visitors."

"So you're dirty cops." Mouth curling, he appraised them. "Why didn't you just say so?"

"Because we're not." Hugh's voice was hard. "We're the honest kind."

"Then why the hell do you care what happened?" He rubbed his chest idly, scratching in the thin blond hair. "Junkies in Seattle have shot up the damn stuff long ago."

"Maybe. Maybe not."

His brows rose. John sensed genuine startlement.

"Can we come in?"

"Oh, hell." He backed up, giving another bark of laughter. "Why not?"

The condo was decently furnished, department-store style. He was a flunky, not a head honcho, or he'd be living in more luxury, but clearly he wasn't an addict himself and must be steadily employed in his chosen profession.

He waved them to seats on a nubby brown sofa and flung himself into a leather chair, planting bare feet on the glass-topped coffee table. "Tell me why you want to know."

Hugh and John exchanged a glance. John said, "We have reason to think someone is looking for that heroin."

"Someone?" Lindmark smiled unpleasantly. "A cop."

"We don't know that."

He put his feet on the floor and sat up. "Okay, then let me tip you off. You want a cop."

"What makes you so sure a cop was involved?"

"I was there." His shoulders twitched and he shot to his feet. "I know cops when I see them."

The brothers' eyes met again. Not *a* cop—cops.

"Did you recognize any of them?"

"Oh, yeah." He walked jerkily to the sliding doors, looked out, then turned, his eyes filled with sudden fear. "Damn! That's why you're here, isn't it? You didn't know anybody survived!"

John stood. "That's not…"

Lindmark flattened himself against the glass. "I've never talked." His Adam's apple bobbed. "I swear! I never will. You don't have to worry about me! I'm not asking for money, I'm not asking for anything. You've got to believe me."

Feeling a cold fury at his fellow officers sworn to uphold the law, John said, "We weren't there. But if cops were involved, we want to know who."

Lindmark was panting, his eyes flicking from one brother to another. After a moment he swore. "I'm stupid! Stupid to let you in my door."

"No. You're stupid if you don't take this chance to tell us what you know. We arrest the dirty cops, you can quit looking over your shoulder."

"I'm not looking. They didn't know I was there."

"Somebody did, or else why did we come knocking at your door?"

He paced and sweated and cursed but finally saw the sense in what John said.

"You're his partner, aren't you?" Lindmark was still twitchy. "I remember you."

Ice formed in John's chest. "His?"

"Reed's. He was there. I knew him."

John had seen Lindmark's rap sheet. Stuart Reed had once arrested him.

"You're sure."

"Oh, yeah!" The hand that pushed back his hair shook. "It was night, we had just slipped into the berth with the engine off. I noticed a rat swimming in the water. I looked up when Sanchez jumped onto the pier with the line and these guys in black swarmed from… God. I don't know where they came from. Just pop, pop, pop. Sanchez toppled back into the boat." He swallowed, and a nerve ticked in one cheek. "Willis, too. I heard they found the boat drifting later."

"Where were you?"

"In the dark on the other side of the cabin. I saw Sanchez go down, I rolled over the gunwale and let myself down into the water. Just as I let go, Willis's blood splattered the windshield. Some of it got in my eye and stung." Now he did look like an addict, muscles jerking all over. "It was a nightmare, man. A nightmare."

"How many men?" Hugh asked.

"I don't know." He sat down, then shot up immediately, beginning a restless circle of the living room. "Three, I think. I don't know. It happened so fast."

John injected doubt into his voice. "And yet you're sure you can identify Detective Stuart Reed."

"I know him. It was him that shot Sanchez. The

others, I didn't get as good a look at, but they were cops. They were wearing SWAT team uniforms.''

Cops in uniform. John's roiling anger hardened into black ice.

"It wasn't a bust that went bad?" Hugh asked.

"Hell, no! They didn't say a word. They just started shooting.'' He rubbed his thighs, the tic in his cheek going like a metronome. "If I'd been up in the bow, I'd be dead, too.''

"You didn't report any of this to your bosses.''

"I didn't have any bosses. This was Sanchez's baby. He hired me. I don't know who he was working for. Shit, man, what am I going to say? Yeah, I'm here alive and well, but your heroin is gone? You think they'd buy that?''

John watched Lindmark closely. "You know Stuart Reed is dead?''

"Know?'' His laugh held an edge of hysteria. "I held a party! I served champagne! Know? Oh, yeah. You can say that.''

He insisted he couldn't identify the other men in dark SWAT team uniforms. He couldn't swear there were three. Two, he knew for sure.

"You said 'swarmed,'" Hugh reminded him. "That sounds like more than two.''

He began twitching again. "I don't know. Man, I saw those guns and silencers and I wasn't carrying. They just came out of the night like they were part of it. Okay. I take back 'swarmed.' They *materialized.*'' He enunciated the word sarcastically. "Is that better?''

John let it go. "You swam away.''

"Underwater as far as I could hold my breath. I

came up on the other side of a sailboat. Man, I never saw anything else."

"Bullshit!" John said sharply. "You can't tell me you didn't look back, see what they were doing."

Lindmark yanked on his hair in a seemingly unconscious, convulsive way as he exploded, "Hell, yeah, I looked! All I saw was the boat drifting away. The engine started after a few minutes, so I guess they were on board. I didn't swim after them, if that's what you mean."

They ran him through the story repeatedly. He wasn't sure how many men had attacked the mooring boat. Two for sure, maybe three or even four. Definitely SWAT team uniforms. He couldn't be shaken from his identification of Stuart Reed, but only shook his head at the idea of recognizing the second man from photographs.

"I saw Reed, and I'm going, 'Shit, these are cops!' I hear this pop, pop, and Sanchez goes down. The docks aren't that well lit. I was scared. I don't mind admitting that. But I wasn't going to hang around asking, What color are that dude's eyes?"

Any mention of Lindmark testifying in court evoked naked fear. He held up both hands and shook his head so violently he was in danger of giving himself whiplash. "I'll lie, man. Somebody'd do me if I opened my mouth like that. Maybe you arrest two guys and there were three. No. Forget it."

His eyes wild, he was deeply regretting having let them in by the time they left, swearing he'd lie if they sent anyone else to ask questions.

"I wasn't there. I don't know anything."

John was behind the wheel as they pulled away from the curb.

"Scum," Hugh remarked.

John grunted.

His brother let him brood for a minute before asking, "Now what?"

"Now I don't know," John admitted. He muttered an obscenity. "Cops. Can you believe it?"

"Happens everywhere."

"Not here." He made a disbelieving sound. "We know everyone on the force."

"Could be Reed was the only one. He could have borrowed the uniforms."

John wanted to believe it and didn't. The operation sounded too smooth, almost military. Cops who'd worked together could operate that way. No wrinkles, just *materializing*.

"Whoever the partner was, he didn't get his cut."

"You think there was only one?" Hugh asked.

"Yeah. I think Lindmark wanted to believe there were more. Two would have been enough, if they were cops. With surprise on their side, why cut anyone else in?" He grimaced. "Why take a chance trying to find another dirty cop?"

It was his brother's turn to grunt. Hugh was staring straight ahead, his lean face grim. "If this partner is searching Natalie's place, he's not looking for money. He thinks the heroin was never sold." He glanced at John. "How long between the heist and Reed's heart attack?"

"Uh…" John had to think. "About three months."

"Heroin isn't the kind of thing you keep lying around the house."

"But finding a buyer might take you a while if you have to be extra careful. It isn't something a cop would want to be hasty about."

"True," Hugh agreed thoughtfully. "I know the right kind of people, but they'd laugh in my face if I suddenly announced I had some stuff to unload. They'd figure it for a setup."

"Here's a thought. What if Stuart was stringing his partner along, but he *had* unloaded the heroin."

"Then where in hell's the money?" his brother asked logically.

"Safe-deposit box. Swiss bank account. Anything's possible."

Hugh shot another, inscrutable glance at John. "You're sure about Natalie."

John's hands tightened on the steering wheel. "I can't believe she'd want dirty money."

"It's in her favor that Reed's been dead a year and she hasn't changed her lifestyle," Hugh admitted. "For all we knew, he might have had a great life insurance policy that left her a rich widow. Nobody would have wondered."

One of the many parts of this that bothered John was the implication for Natalie. If Stuart hadn't told her he was suddenly one hell of a lot richer, when *had* he intended to spring it on her? What kind of lies would he have used? Or was it possible she wasn't part of the new life he was planning?

She'd mourned him sincerely. How would she deal with the knowledge that he was not only crooked, he'd lied to her?

"On the other hand," Hugh continued, tone musing, "a smart widow left in her spot might just decide to let some time go by. In case anyone was watching. She's young. She's got time."

John swore viciously. "Can that kind of talk! I'd bet my life on her honesty."

"Would you." Hugh's gaze was unexpectedly penetrating. "Seems to me my big bro has a crush on the lady."

"We're friends. Can't you trust a friend?" Even John knew he didn't sound completely convincing.

"Sure. Why not? But, hey, I saw the way she flew into your arms."

"She was scared."

"I was there. Wasn't me she was looking for."

John didn't lie to his brothers. This wasn't a good time to start, given that he and Hugh were both obligated to take what they'd learned to their superiors and to Internal Affairs, and he was about to ask Hugh to ignore that duty. Not just because he thought he and Hugh would have a better chance of flushing out the bad guy themselves, but because he knew how this would look for Natalie.

If Stuart had stolen a half a million bucks worth of heroin, where was it? Where was the money? The department would figure she must know the answer.

John had pulled the car into his slot in the garage beneath the station, but he didn't turn off the engine. Beside him, Hugh waited, slouched bonelessly in the seat, the epitome of patience.

"I kissed her last night." John sounded hoarse.

Hugh waited some more.

"She kissed me back, but afterward she didn't want to talk about it. We were good friends. I'm guessing that's something she doesn't want to change."

"But you do," his brother said.

"I don't know." John let out a long breath. "I just can't quit thinking about her. I want…" He stopped.

"Her," Hugh finished succinctly.

"More, I was going to say." John squeezed his eyes shut. "But hell, yeah, I want her."

"Yeah, I kind of noticed." His brother's tone of faint amusement penetrated John's absorption.

His eyes shot open, then narrowed. "You think it's funny?"

"Connor and I both figure you've been half in love with her since you woke up one morning and realized she wasn't married anymore. It's just taken you a while to admit it."

John digested the fact that his brothers had been talking about him, then dismissed his irritation. "You know Natalie. Do *you* think she's lying about the money?"

"Nah." He hesitated, then shrugged. "The lady's got secrets. I never feel like I'm seeing all the way through her. But you know her better than I do. If you trust her, I trust her."

"I do."

His brother spread his hands and reached for the door handle. "Good enough for me."

Turning off the ignition, John nodded. He would have felt the same. He and Hugh had their differences, but in other ways they were tight.

"You know," he said into the silence, conversationally, "Internal Affairs would look hard at me, too. Stuart Reed and I were partners."

Hugh swung back, quick anger glinting in his eyes. "I'd better not hear that kind of crap from anyone."

"How could I not have known? Damn it, we *worked* together."

"We all knew him! He'd been in the department long enough." Hugh's brows drew together. "Maybe you overlooked his flaws. The way he encouraged people to whine, for example.''

''He did?''

''Hell, yeah. You probably didn't see it because you went home after your shift instead of stopping by the tavern. He didn't bitch about the department himself, but he'd egg everyone else on. I didn't like to sit with him at the Lantern when I stopped for a beer. Just seemed like everyone around him would be grumbling about pay or why our esteemed chief had his head up his you-know-what. Not my style. This one time, I overheard him drop a word in Bettelman's ear that Verbeek had been talking about how Bettelman had frozen at that shoot-out at First National. Remember?'' Hugh shook his head. ''Yeah, Verbeek said a few things, but he was willing to cut Bettelman some slack. The kid was young. Instead they both ended up with black eyes and they could have gotten the boot. Stuart Reed thought it was funny.''

Frowning, John said, ''I never noticed.''

His brother gave a grunt of laughter. ''That's because you're above such things.''

He scowled.

Dropping the comedy, Hugh got back to the point. ''The thing is, Reed listened to people. He liked to know when they were dissatisfied. He could have found somebody of like mind easy enough.''

''Why?'' John looked to his brother for answers he didn't have. ''That's what I don't get. Nobody goes into law enforcement for the bucks. You get caught, you lose your badge and end up flipping burgers.''

Hugh shrugged. ''Maybe he figured he was doing the world a favor knocking off a couple of dealers. If he got rich out of it, he deserved it, right? Slaving in the trenches all these years, why not get some payback? You could justify it.''

"He was a cop.''

"There speaks your honest soul. Maybe he soured. Maybe he was on the take all along, and this was just his big chance to score.''

"I thought I knew him.'' Damn it, he sounded plaintive.

"And now we have to doubt everyone.'' Hugh didn't look any happier than John felt.

"Let me think about our next step.''

Hugh only nodded. ''It's your call.''

Not an easy one to make. Not when it meant lying to friends and colleagues.

Starting with Geoff Baxter, his partner. John knew how deeply insulted he would be if the situation were reversed. Trouble was, he'd remembered something about Baxter.

John had taken some time off work last year, when Debbie had been diagnosed and they were trying to decide what to do and the kids were scared. In John's absence, Stuart Reed had had a temporary partner: Baxter. Six weeks, hand in glove. Funny coincidence that, during the same six weeks, Stuart Reed had apparently offed a couple of drug dealers and stolen a major shipment of heroin. *And* that Geoff Baxter was obsessively determined to search every cranny of Natalie's house.

Which had gotten John to thinking things he hadn't said even to his brother.

CHAPTER TEN

STUPID, STUPID, STUPID.

Natalie hid in her office, a cup of coffee growing cold as she stewed over the night before. She'd spent it tossing and turning, alternately chewing herself out, despairing and rejoicing.

She had never, ever, in all her life, felt such glorious, unrestrained passion. So much wondering, and now she knew. The ache low in her belly had helped keep her restless. Why hadn't he followed her? And why should she expect that he would? He'd made a reckless move. Would he wait for her to make the next one?

Half a dozen times during the night she'd wondered: What if she went down the hall and said, *I want you?*

Now, at her desk, Natalie buried a moan in her hands at the very idea. She knew she was a mass of contradictions: bold at work, pushy when she had to be, but shy with men and not *open,* even with her friends. She made friends easily enough, but most didn't seem to notice that she never mentioned her childhood or her doubts about her marriage or her growing anger at Stuart.

Or, God forbid, her crush on Det. John McLean.

All she knew was, she had never in her life done

something as brash and risky as walking into a man's bedroom and throwing herself at him.

Stupid, stupid, stupid.

She hardly knew whether she was bemoaning her cowardice, or the weakness that had led her to take that step toward him and to say, "I've thought the same thing." If their friendship was to be salvaged, *that* was the moment to have laughed and said something like, "It's probably inevitable, considering we *are* a man and a woman. Of course I've wondered, too! But let's not mess up a good thing."

She could have made it light enough to rescue their dignity. She could even have stayed and chatted a while longer.

But, no. She'd gasped, whispered, "I've thought the same thing," and walked into his arms.

For the most wonderful, sensual, sexy kiss of her life.

Only now was she remembering everything she had to lose. What if she did sleep with him, and it wasn't that great? Natalie let out something halfway between a sob and a laugh. Okay. She couldn't imagine that would happen. So, what if it was great, but sex was all they had? Sex plus friendship did not necessarily equal love. And only love and marriage and forever was worth risking all that could go wrong.

She'd expected some of the fall to begin this morning, when Natalie was certain they wouldn't be able to meet each other's eyes. What if he was already sorry about the kiss? What if sex was casual to him, and he didn't figure it would get in the way of their friendship?

But it would. It had to. Natalie was so afraid that if they became sexually involved, eventually one of them would lose interest, and then he wouldn't drop by anymore, or call her at night just to talk, or come running when she needed him.

Reason said she needed him as a friend more than she did as a lover.

Her heart whispered, yes, but what if he *could* fall in love with her? What if he had? Could *she?* Wasn't that possibility worth almost any risk?

She didn't know. Yes. No. Maybe.

With another moan, Natalie opened a drawer and stared inside blankly. She needed several files. But which ones?

Face it, Natalie thought, she had no idea how to *take* the risk, short of tucking her dignity in a drawer and presenting herself in his bedroom. No idea what to say to him tonight. No idea what to do if he didn't make another move and say anything to her.

She was a coward.

Coward enough to have been relieved to shower and dress and find John and the kids already gone that morning, only a note on the kitchen counter saying, *Had an early appointment today. Mom will take the kids to school. See you after work. John.*

Her day consisted of meetings. It had begun with their usual Monday morning quarterbacking session, when she and heads of other departments sat around a conference table and went page by page through competing newspapers to see how the *Sentinel* compared.

Generally well, she thought, at least on the advertising side. Editorials were sometimes mealymouthed, a sin common to newspapers from a community where everyone knew everyone. Local coverage was excellent, and wasn't that why the citizens of Port

Dare subscribed to the *Sentinel?* For the most part, she was able to tune out.

She'd calmed herself enough to recollect what information she needed to see one of several local businessmen who didn't like the expensive, glossy inserts run by chain stores. They couldn't afford to compete, of course, and her only answer was to suggest they host events that might make the news pages.

The owner of a hardware store, he glowered at her. "You mean, one of those damn things where I give away a car to whoever sits in it longest?"

"Why not?" she countered. "Think of *Survivor.* You know how the world watched." She'd paused just long enough. "On the other hand, if you don't want quite as much publicity, go for a simple donation to a needy family. I guarantee you'll get an article."

She left him thoughtfully eyeing the rows of ride-on mowers with balloons tied to their gear shifts. Dang, maybe she should change careers. She'd make a heck of a fund-raiser for a charity.

On the other hand, she didn't have the nerve to grab her cell phone and call John.

Contradictions.

Having brought her riding clothes, she went straight to the stable after work and rode in the large outdoor arena despite a slight autumn drizzle. The stallion was in an irritable, fidgety mood, fighting her every command. He wanted to gallop, not trot, and he refused to change leads as she reined him in a tight figure-eight. Some days Natalie would have thrown up her hands and opened the gate, taking him for a long, freewheeling ride in the foothills. Today she grimly worked him until sweat soaked his flanks and he did as she bid.

"Congratulations," Pam Reynolds said, as Natalie led him into the wide aisle of the barn, shook dampness from her hair and reached for the buckle to loosen the girth. "You usually let him ride roughshod over you."

"Oh, thanks." Natalie heaved the saddle off. "You know, I'm not trying to show him. He and I are supposed to be having fun."

The stable owner bent and lifted the foreleg of one of the horses she used for lessons. Loosing a pebble with the pick, she said musingly, "It's a shame. That horse is wasted here."

Natalie felt a blooming of a mother's pride. "You really think he has what it takes to succeed in the showring?"

"We have a couple of Arabians here. You've seen 'em. Nice horses." Pam set down the hoof and circled to the bay's other side. Her voice came over his back. "Your Foxfire makes 'em look like plugs."

"He cost a small fortune." Natalie felt a renewed pang of guilt at Stuart's extravagance and at her own in not having promptly sold the horse and invested the money for her future.

Pam's head appeared above the placid bay's back. "Twenty-five thousand isn't so much. Melissa Monroe paid ten for Baroness."

Baroness was a nice Arab mare, but not showring material. Even Natalie could tell that.

"Foxfire and I are buddies." To heck with prudence or anybody's opinion that her beautiful horse was wasted on her. "I don't want to sell him, and I don't have the skill or interest in showing him. Today was just to remind him that I *am* the boss. Even if I listen to, um, protests.''

"You let that horse get by with murder." Pam's leathery face was momentarily warmed by a smile. "But don't listen to me. I'm jealous, remember."

As always, Natalie offered the stable owner the chance to ride Foxfire. Also as always, Pam refused.

Grimacing at her wet hair and sweat-and-mud-streaked face in the rearview mirror, Natalie drove home. No, not home, she hastily reminded herself, to John's house. She was annoyed with herself when she saw his car in the driveway and wished she could sneak in and shower before she saw him. So what if she was grungy? He'd held her when she cried after Stuart died. He'd seen her with middle-of-the-night hair and a face scrubbed clean of makeup. Their friendship *was* doomed if she had to start worrying about what she looked like every time she saw him.

Especially since they were now, however awkwardly, living together.

"Hi." She breezed in the back door.

John was chopping onions in the kitchen, his back to her. He glanced over his shoulder, taking her in from head to foot. "Have a good ride?"

"Um." Natalie passed out of his line of sight as quickly as she could without being blatant. "I'll take a fast shower," she called.

His voice followed her. "No hurry."

That being the case, she took her sweet time, washing and drying her hair, discarding a couple of shirts before she chose one though she had only put on jeans, and even applying light makeup, something she rarely did in the evening. A woman had her pride, she excused herself.

Only when she reemerged from her bedroom did she notice how quiet the house was. Natalie paused in the hall and listened. No canned laughter from the TV, no bickering.

No children?

Her heart turned a somersault. Did she *want* to be alone in the house with John?

She momentarily pressed her hand to her chest, trying to quiet the wild beats. Deep breath. Seduction was not necessarily on the menu even if Maddie and Evan weren't home.

Finally she settled for faking poise. Strolling into the kitchen, where John had moved to the stove, she said casually, "I don't hear the kids."

"Mom has them." Lines carved his forehead and his expression was unexpectedly serious. "I wanted to talk to you."

The somersault her heart had taken became a belly flop. He sounded like a man who regretted a mistake and wanted to right it.

She knew herself the kiss shouldn't have happened, so why feel so crushed?

"If you mean last night," she began.

He looked blank. "Last night?" His face cleared. "Oh. I guess we should talk about that, too, but no. This is something else."

Now her heart raced. Why so grim if he'd learned something about the corpse in Stuart's den? Shouldn't he be *glad* if he'd gotten somewhere on the investigation?

She groped for a stool behind the breakfast bar and sank onto it. "What?"

He swore suddenly and turned back to the stove.

"Damn it, let me get dinner on the table. I just burned the sauce."

The acrid scent filled the kitchen.

"I'm sorry, if you're cooking just because I'm here."

"Don't be ridiculous," he said brusquely. "I have to eat."

Squelched, Natalie waited in silence while he discarded the blackened mess, cleaned the pan and got ingredients out of the refrigerator.

"Can I help?" she asked timidly at one point, but he waved her off.

"This just takes a minute. We're having chicken and broccoli crepes. Everything else is ready."

When he was done, they each put together their own, spooned Swiss cheese sauce over the filled crepes, and carried them to the dining room table, already set in a casual way.

Natalie picked up her fork, but she had no interest in eating. "What's wrong?" she asked quietly.

John balled up his napkin and squeezed it in a fist. "I don't know any way to say this, except straight out. It looks like Stuart gunned down a couple of drug dealers and stole a hefty shipment of heroin. I think it's either the heroin or the money he sold it for that has people breaking into your house."

Natalie suddenly felt numb. The fork dropped from her hand. "Stuart killed men for drugs?"

In a frustrated motion, John threw the napkin and reached across the table to grip her hand. "I talked to a guy today who saw him do it. Stuart had arrested him a couple of years ago. My gut says this guy was telling the truth."

Still, shock held her immobile. "Stuart?"

Her husband? The man who kept an album of newspaper clippings about the arrests he'd made and the medals he'd won and the groups to whom he'd spoken? The hero with whom she'd fallen in love? The man she'd married, the man who had made love to her, was not only capable of cold-bloodedly killing for drugs or money, he'd actually done it?

John's mouth twisted. "I don't want to believe it, either."

"Stuart? It couldn't have been Stuart. He was a hero!" she argued, as much with herself as him. "Do you remember that boy he pulled from the lake? No." She shook her head. "No, not Stuart. He couldn't have."

John's gaze held compassion. "I'm afraid he did."

She tried again to grapple with the unimaginable. "But why?" she asked in complete bafflement. "I don't understand."

His grip on her hand tightened. "I've had more time to think about this than you have. Stuart had gotten bitter about our pay. Do you remember how angry he was when the city council denied the chief's request for additional budget to add five officers and give an across-the-board five percent pay raise?"

She did remember. Stuart had come home that day with his face contorted with rage. His ranting had scared her. When she'd set dinner on the table, he'd picked up his plate and flung it against the wall, stomping out, only to stagger home late that night and fall into bed drunk.

"A lousy five percent raise," she said softly. "He kept saying that."

John let out a heavy sigh and released her hand. "His reaction was way out of proportion. I don't think it was the money. He saw it as a slap in the face. He wanted respect. He wanted it more badly than I realized.''

''Or than I did.'' Natalie stared unseeing at her untouched dinner. ''How was doing something horrible like that going to earn him more respect?''

''Maybe it wasn't supposed to. Maybe it was payback. Or maybe he was just fed up, and the money was a way out. Maybe, once the heat was off, he would have handed in his badge.''

She looked up swiftly. ''But he loved being a police officer! That's who he was!''

John's jaw tightened. ''Was it?''

An irrelevant realization diverted her, cracked the wall of numbness. ''That's how he could afford to buy Foxfire. I thought about it today, while I was riding.'' Pain seeped through. ''He bought me a present with stolen heroin. Drugs soaked in blood.''

John said nothing, and she saw in his eyes that it was true.

''How would he ever have explained...'' Throat closing, she stopped. He wouldn't have explained. She had known full well that Stuart had lost interest in her and their marriage. She had been an impulse. Or else she'd disappointed him in some way. She would never know now. But he had intended to leave her. No, to ask her to leave—the house was his, after all, as he'd made plain enough. She was the *outsider*. The one who didn't really belong.

''Foxfire was...a farewell gift.'' She laughed bitterly. ''Like rich men with mistresses. He knew I wouldn't want a ruby necklace.''

''You don't know.''

''What else?''

John swore. "How am I supposed to answer that? Maybe he just didn't understand how you'd see it. He loved you and wanted to share his newfound wealth."

"Oh, no." She was shaking her head hard. "He knew. Why else didn't he tell me?"

John said nothing. She looked down at his hand, fingering his fork. Slow understanding built into shock that made her chest hurt.

"You think he did tell me, don't you?"

He blinked. "Of course not!"

"Oh, my God." She shoved back from the table. "You think I've known all along."

Swearing, John blundered to his feet. "No, I don't. Damn it, Natalie."

The hurt was blinding. "Did I kill Ronald Floyd because he wanted the money?"

"Natalie…"

She backed away when he reached for her. "Don't touch me! I…" She pressed a hand to her mouth. "I need to leave."

He blocked her way. "You're not going anywhere until you listen to me."

"I don't have to!" she shouted. "Why should I? You've…you've been playing me all along, haven't you? Keeping an eye on me. What were you doing? Waiting until I slipped out to check my stolen millions in my secret safe-deposit box?"

She'd moved away as far as she could. He grabbed her shoulders and gave her a firm shake. "Goddamn it, Natalie, listen to me!"

Sobbing for breath, she stared at his furious face.

Voice low and intense, he said, "I know damn well that Stuart didn't tell you. You're a woman of integrity. Do you think I can't see that? I'd trust you with my life. It never crossed my mind that you have that money.''

Tears ran down her face, and still she stared.

"I promise," he said more gently.

"You...you believe me?" Her voice wobbled.

"Yeah. I believe you."

She swallowed. "Oh."

He growled something under his breath and yanked her up against him. Natalie went, burrowing into his shirt, instinctively seeking the powerful beat of his heart. When she found it and felt safe, she cried.

The sobs were deep and compulsive, beyond her ability to stop. It was as if she cried for every grief at once. Every pain swirled together in a kaleidoscope: her realization that her husband hadn't loved her; the loss of him, the thud of dark earth on the shiny casket; her loneliness, her bitterness, her denial; and, finally, this understanding that she had been so wrong about who the man she married really was.

She cried until her nose ran and her eyes swelled and the front of John's shirt was soaked. All the time, he squeezed her tight, his hands moving in a soothing rhythm on her back. He murmured something, probably nonsense. *It's okay. It'll be all right.* She felt his cheek against her hair, the small kisses he pressed to the top of her head.

Somehow, it was always John who held her. She didn't know why; she had no right. He wasn't a father or brother or husband. Stuart's friend, he had inherited her. She hated the sense that she was an obligation, like a pet he'd taken in because no one else wanted it.

She rested finally, forehead against the solid wall of John's chest. Her mind drifted. Was it true that he would trust her with his life? Was their friendship, then, not as one-sided as she had feared? Did he need those nightly calls as badly as she did?

He was still murmuring, his voice hoarse. Natalie took a shuddery breath and drew back. Only reluctantly, it seemed, did he let her go.

She kept her gaze downcast, not wanting to see his expression or him to see her swollen face. ''I need...''

John thrust a paper towel into her hand.

Natalie blew her nose firmly. ''I think I need to go wash my face,'' she said, and fled.

In the bathroom, she splashed cold water on her face over and over until the blotches paled and her eyes reappeared between puffy lids. Gripping the sink, the water still running, Natalie looked squarely at herself in the mirror and winced.

It was lucky she cried so seldom, since she obviously didn't have a gift for doing it prettily.

On one level, she knew she was examining herself carefully in the mirror to avoid thinking about John's revelation or John himself.

She didn't succeed for long. He would be waiting out there for her to reappear. They weren't done, she knew. Even if it was true that he trusted her integrity, the rest of his department had no reason to feel the same. Even the others who knew her would have to wonder. If her husband was a cold-blooded killer and a crook, what did that make her? They'd seen her mourn at his graveside, but didn't know that her marriage had essentially been over. How could John shield her?

Once they found the money, which she had no doubt they would, given their determination, how would she be able to prove she hadn't known about it? They might not be able to prove in a court of law that she had, but she was scared nonetheless.

Natalie washed her face one more time, brushed her hair and went back to the kitchen.

John stood almost where she'd left him, his head hanging, hands dangling at his sides. At the sound of her footstep, his head shot up.

"Did he sell the heroin?" she asked straight away.

"We don't know."

"Is it…is it the drug dealers he stole from who are looking for the drugs?"

His expression shifted, and for a moment she thought he intended to lie. Then he grimaced, rubbed a hand tiredly over his face, and said bleakly, "The informant insists there were two or maybe three cops. Stuart was the only one he got a good look at."

Now she gaped. "Two or three? Not just Stuart?"

"It would appear so." His expression had hardened. "Not necessarily Port Dare officers. He could have hooked up with a county deputy, maybe." He told her about the men dressed in black SWAT team uniforms who had raided the powerboat. "To salve his own self-respect, our guy wanted to believe there were at least three, but I'm guessing from his uncertainty that it was just Stuart and one other cop. Someone he worked well with."

"But you two were partners," she blurted, and then regretted immediately what sounded like an accusation.

A muscle jumped in John's cheek. "It has occurred to me that others will think the same. You're not alone, you know."

"So we'll both be investigated?"

"Eventually." He hesitated. "Unless we figure out first who he was working with."

"You mean, you and Geoff."

John said nothing for a moment, again seeming to battle with himself. At last he gave his head a shake and said, "Actually, Hugh's the one who uncovered the informant."

She absorbed that. Of course, his brothers knew everything. Taking a breath, Natalie asked, "Do they know you're telling me all this?"

"They assumed I would."

"They don't have any reason to trust me."

"You mean my brothers?" John shrugged, looking surprised. "One for all, and all that."

How easily he said that, she marveled. What must it be like, knowing so effortlessly that you weren't in any mess alone, that your word would always be accepted, your side of any story believed?

Natalie was friends with her sister, but their relationship was nothing like the one John had with Hugh and Connor.

Younger, Maryke had never resented their stepfather the way Natalie did. She was always good natured, malleable, less determined to fight than Natalie. "Why not just thank him?" she would say, not understanding her sister's truculence. Natalie had been left feeling alone, as she had felt ever since.

Until, she realized with slow astonishment, this very minute. John hadn't doubted her, and had implied that his brothers wouldn't, either. If John trusted her, they did.

Simple.

"I really didn't know." Natalie felt it needed to be said once.

He raised his brows. "Of course you didn't. You'd have left him."

Confession time. "I don't think we'd have been married much longer, no matter what. I should have told you that from the beginning. I'm sorry. You took care of me because I was Stuart's wife, and I didn't want to lose that. But the truth is…" Hesitating, she squeezed her fingers together and was grateful that she seemed to be cried out.

John was watching her with creases deepening between his brows. "The truth is…" he prompted, without giving away what he thought.

She moistened dry lips. "Stuart wanted me but had no real idea of what marriage involved. The house was always his, and I never felt like more than a guest." Humiliated at the admission, she said, "I…I tried so hard to pretend the marriage was more real than it was. But I think he was getting tired of me, and I was getting tired of pretending." She breathed at last, finishing starkly, "And then he died, and I didn't want to tell everybody that we weren't happy together." Natalie searched John's face for understanding. "It isn't that I didn't grieve, please don't think that. He was my husband! But the ending was just…just a different kind of ending than I expected. I felt sad for him more than for myself. I thought…" Oh, this got harder and harder to say. "I thought it was somehow my fault that our marriage didn't work better. That maybe I'm not very good at…at intimacy. You've said the same yourself."

He let out a gritty sound. "No, that's not what I said. I've been frustrated sometimes because I want to know you better than I do, and you don't make it easy."

"No," she said desolately. "I guess I don't."

A glow deep in his eyes, John gripped her shoulders again. "He couldn't possibly have been tired of you."

She tried to interpret his tone, hoping and praying he meant what she wanted him to. Lowering her gaze to the top button of his shirt, she said, "I'm not that exciting. I know that. I just wanted...I thought..." She made a face, finishing in a rush, "Marriage meant having one person who thought I was. Who *always* would think I was." She stole a shy look. "You know?"

His mouth had a tender twist. "Stuart was crazy."

Almost fiercely, Natalie said, "Now, I'm glad he *didn't* love me. I'm glad I already knew I'd made a mistake."

"The son of a bitch didn't deserve you."

The vehemence in John's voice widened her eyes and set her heart to drumming.

"Thank you." She tried to say it lightly. "What would I do without you to boost my ego?"

What would she do without him, period? If *he* tired of her?

He bent his head. His mouth a hairbreadth from hers, he said softly, with purpose, "Good thing you won't have to find out."

Natalie took that in, understood that he was promising...what? Eternal friendship? Or love?

Suddenly she couldn't bear to have one and not the other. Which was why she lifted her mouth to meet his, all her fears scattering.

This was a chance she had to take.

CHAPTER ELEVEN

HIS MOUTH DEVOURED HERS, his body was hard, demanding. Natalie's mind blurred and she was instantly filled with urgency as powerful as his. She wound her fingers in the thick, fiery silk of his hair and kissed John back, her tongue sliding against his. A low groan started in his chest, and while one of his hands cradled her nape, his other gripped her hip and pulled her tightly up against him.

It was all happening so fast. Instead of a timid awakening of sexual response, she felt a desperate readiness that must have been building for days. Weeks. When his hips shoved against hers, Natalie's thighs opened to allow his knee to press between. He lifted her, and shamelessly she rode his powerful, jean-clad thigh. But it wasn't enough. She wanted *him.*

Natalie murmured wordless demands. His groan deepened and his hand moved from her nape over her collarbone to her breast, where he gently squeezed and weighed and rubbed. She whimpered, hearing herself in shock. One kiss, and she was ready to lie down on his kitchen floor if only he would take her here and now.

Instead he swept her up in his arms so suddenly she shrieked and grabbed hold. Above her, his face was taut, a flush darkening his cheekbones and his eyes glittering. She had never seen John McLean be anything but gentle and patient. Seeing his expression of tense, hot sexual need gave her a jolt of gratification. This was the face of a man desperate for the woman in his arms. Her.

He carried her effortlessly up the stairs to his bedroom. Her feet brushed framed photographs on the walls of the hall, rocking and tilting them. John's long stride didn't check. She kissed his throat and loved the vibration she'd awakened.

Natalie had never been in his room. As he carried her the few steps to the bed, she had a kaleidoscopic impression of white walls and oak floor, Victorian oak dresser and dizzying circles in vivid colors on a wool hooked rug that hung on the wall.

At the bed, he paused. Natalie's mouth stilled on his jaw when she felt his muscles tighten, lock. After a moment, he let her slide exquisitely down his body, but instead of kissing her again or bearing her down onto the huge, comforter-covered bed, he looked searchingly at her with eyes that held a latent glow.

Alarm squeezed her chest. "What?" she whispered.

"Are you sure?" he asked hoarsely.

She didn't want to think. She would rather have been swept away. Of course she had her share of doubts! No, she wasn't sure. How could she be, when tomorrow and a month from now were so uncertain, so perilous?

But this very minute, Natalie couldn't bear it if he stopped, if he was gentlemanly and, while she straightened her clothes and retreated like the coward she so often was, said, *Fine. No, it's okay. I don't mind.*

Was she sure she wanted to do this, whatever her fears?

"Yes." She spoke more strongly than she'd known she could. "I'm sure."

The sound he made was raw, thankful. In one move he lifted her, put her on the bed and was on top of her, his mouth seizing hers. These kisses became less skilled, more frantic, his teeth nipping hard at her lower lip, hers at his neck, their every breath gasping. She struggled to tug off his shirt as he was pulling hers over her head. No, he hadn't lost his skill—the catch of her bra took one flick of his fingers, and he was murmuring a litany of pleasure as he kissed her breasts, suckled, rubbed.

Arching against his mouth, she cried out. She had never felt so beautiful, so powerful, so humble and needy.

So loved, and achingly aware of what she had missed all her life.

His patience snapped, and he rose above her to shed his khakis and slide her jeans and panties down her legs with that hot light in his eyes. He kissed his way back up her legs, shaven jaw rough against the soft skin of her inner thigh, breath molten as it ruffled her curls. He nuzzled only for a second, groaned and reached for the drawer in the bedside stand.

She watched dazedly as he rolled a condom onto himself. Insanely she would never have thought of it, hadn't known she could be so heedless.

"Thank you," she whispered.

Lids heavy, eyes a glittering, deep blue, he said, "Someday we'll make love without this." His hand splayed on her belly, he looked his fill at her body, sprawled atop his bed. "Someday," he murmured again.

The next instant, he rolled onto his back and lifted her above him. "Ready or not," he said in that same rough, urgent voice.

Oh, yes. She was ready.

Natalie sank slowly onto him, her body adjusting to the shock of the invasion, stretching, convulsively tightening even as she herself was the one to pull back. She withdrew until he was no more than a nudge at her core, then lowered herself again, back arched, head thrown back, a silent cry coming from her throat. He played with her breasts, let her set the speed, but she felt his gathering need in the way his hips lifted to bury himself more deeply in her.

Finally, when she faltered, he growled and gripped her buttocks, rolling her onto her back. She spread her legs wide and hung on as he thrust hard, faster and faster, sweat making his back slick beneath her fingers. Pleasure spiraled in her belly, tightening, tightening, until it convulsed like a spring pressed down and released. John groaned and jerked deep inside her, his last thrusts extending the wash of exquisite feeling that traveled as far as her fingertips and toes.

John being the man he was, he didn't sprawl atop her, but rolled again and tucked her into the crook of his arm. Feeling her breathing calm, listening to his steady heartbeat, Natalie realized she was smiling even as inexplicable tears stung her eyes.

This, too, she had missed. Stuart had become less and less tender in bed. When they had sex, he often turned away immediately as if she no longer existed. It had made her feel…used.

John smoothed hair back from her face, his hand lingering. He said unexpectedly, "Hugh says I've wanted you since the day I woke up and realized you weren't married anymore."

They'd been talking about her? Natalie wasn't sure how to feel about that. "*Hugh* says?" Did she sound the tiniest bit tart?

Apologetically he said, "Sometimes they know me better than I know myself."

She curled his chest hair around her finger, fascinated by the silky, springy texture. "You didn't know you were even attracted to me?"

"Not a clue." He gave a grunt of laughter. "That's probably not the most tactful thing to say to a woman you've just bedded. But, you know, I never would have admitted even to myself that I wanted my partner's wife. I guess I turned some sort of internal check on, and it took a shock to turn it off."

Natalie rubbed her cheek against his hand. "A shock?"

"A threat to you. Fear of losing you." His shoulder moved under her head. "Something out of the ordinary."

She nodded, knowing he'd feel the movement.

"What about you?" He reached down and pinched her bottom, making her jump. "When did you start lusting after my manly self?"

She giggled at his deepened voice. "Lusting?" she said innocently.

"You did lust?"

"I guess I must have, or I wouldn't be in your bed, naked, now would I?"

"And sure you wanted to be here," he reminded her.

"Did I say that?"

She earned herself another pinch. Her punch to his chest started a good-humored wrestling match that ended in a slow, sweet kiss.

With Natalie settled back comfortably against him, John said, "Come on. Fair's fair. I want to know whether I was an idiot not to notice sometime this past year that you might have been receptive to a polite request for a date."

"I think you would have scared me," she confessed. "I was, um, aware of your manly form when you painted my house this summer. You kept taking your shirt off, you know."

"Aha." The rumble under her ear sounded pleased.

"But, of course, my observation was entirely academic. I even tried to think of a friend who I could introduce to you."

"But you didn't." He was definitely pleased.

"No." She hadn't been able to think of anyone good enough for him. A confession she would *not* make.

"So?"

"It bothered me how much I wanted *you* to be the one who came after I found the body. And then when I came home with you, I started having—" how to put it? "—feelings that went a teeny bit beyond friendly."

"Lust," he said contentedly.

She very much feared that lust didn't cover it. *Love* came a whole lot closer.

"Maybe."

Suddenly John rolled onto his side so that he was looking down into her face, his eyes serious. "You've been keeping me awake nights."

Her pulse sped. "Have I?"

"Oh, yeah." He nuzzled her cheek. "And appearing in my dreams when I did sleep."

"A nightmare?" she whispered, just before her parted lips met his.

John kept the kiss light, teasing. "Only when I came on to you and I could see how taken aback you were. Or repulsed. That was my worst fear, you know."

She pulled back in astonishment. "That I'd be repulsed?"

"That I'd shock you." His gaze was watchful again. "We were buddies, you know. I was afraid, if I made a move…"

"You'd blow our friendship."

"Yeah."

Natalie smiled wryly. "I was afraid of the same thing, you know."

And still was, another of the many things she couldn't say.

His face cleared. "Yeah? You were?"

"Of course I was." She framed his jaw in her hands, loving the rasp of a nighttime beard against her palms. "Having you call just to talk, because *you* needed to talk, not because you were being nice to a lonely widow, was something I really looked forward to." How tepid, how euphemistic. Why not say, *I lived for your calls?*

Because he hadn't said any such thing.

He was silent for a moment. "Me, too," he said at last, and kissed her again.

This time his mouth was not only tender but hungry. Reassured, she felt the same leap of desire, so quickly fanned into life because it had been banked for so long. If she also felt an ache at the things he hadn't said and a fear for what this vulnerability could do to her, it only intensified her response.

Oh, yes. This was a risk she'd had to take.

TELEPHONES RANG; a fight broke out in the hall where a uniform was wrestling a suspect into the booking room. Swearing, a plainclothes officer jumped out of the way and spilled coffee down his shirt.

Ignoring the familiar chaos, John sat at his desk in the Major Crimes unit and brooded.

Now what?

A simple question, but one with many layers for him. Starting with, what did he do this minute? Once he decided on some strategy, he'd join Baxter at Natalie's house to finish digging through Stuart's crap in the garage. Hell, they should have volunteered to price everything for a Saturday sale while they were at it.

In the longer term, did he come clean to the department? This one made him uncomfortable, because he was an honest man but the answer was still no. He wanted to know more first. He wanted to protect Natalie Reed.

There were those who'd say he wanted to protect himself.

If he didn't go to Internal Affairs, the question *now what?* became especially relevant. Reed had been dead a year. How to figure out what he'd been thinking those last months? How to discover his partner? Where he'd stashed the goods or the bucks?

Where was he going as far as Natalie was concerned? He was risking his career to shield her. He'd taken her into his bed last night, and he wished like hell he could have her there every night.

Until death do us part.

He frowned at his computer screen, although he couldn't have said what information it displayed.

A month ago he'd still been struggling with the reluctant belief that he should have Debbie move home, hire nurses, for her sake and the kids'.

Until death do us part.

He hadn't even known he was attracted to Natalie, never mind seeing her as the person he wanted to spend the rest of his life with.

Was it too quick? Was he reacting to the stress of the circumstances? Or was he head over heels in love with a woman who in one short year had become his best friend outside his brothers?

Did Natalie feel the same? He wanted to assume she did, because last night she'd come so willingly and joyfully into his arms and his bed. But—oh, hell—times had changed. Maybe she'd seen sex as an uncomplicated pleasure with a friend.

What would she say if he went on his knees to her tonight and said, "Stay forever. Marry me?"

And what about Debbie?

John groaned and tugged at his hair.

A hand clapped him on the shoulder. "That brain giving you trouble?" asked Ryan Fairman, a good-natured detective. "I always knew it would, sooner or later. Just lookin', a man can tell."

John mock-lunged at his fellow officer, who feinted and, laughing, continued on his way.

The interruption helped. John focused on his computer screen, where he'd brought up a list of Det. Stuart Reed's arrests in the month before his death.

About all the information did was confirm what John had already remembered: while he was on a leave of absence, Stuart had paired with Geoff Baxter, whose previous partner had retired. Thus their own convenient pairing, after the funeral.

The two had had a good month, last September. At the top of the list was a rare triumph. They'd cleared a ''cold'' murder—a teenage girl who'd been abducted on her way home from high school ten years before. She'd been raped and her body dumped the same night. A tip had come in, but unlike most tips this one had panned out. The *Sentinel,* John recalled, had spread this one over the front pages, congratulating officers who never gave up on such a heinous crime. Stuart had modestly declared that this arrest was thanks to the murderer's current girlfriend, who had seen a ''souvenir'' and not been satisfied by his explanation. Nonetheless, it had involved solid police work.

''Damn it, he was a good cop,'' John muttered. ''What happened?''

Still paging down, he mulled over the one case, however, because when he thought about it, it represented Stuart Reed perfectly. He was smart, dogged, but also a publicity hound. On some level, John had always known that Reed didn't serve selflessly, that he dove into the water to save a kid's life thinking already about the headlines that would proclaim him a hero.

So, okay, he had an ego. Whose motives were unmixed? Wanting to come out looking good was a far cry from committing a brutal murder to steal and sell a drug that destroyed lives, all for money.

Maybe Lindmark's story was BS. But John's gut

said no. Stuart had changed. John had felt it. His partner had become more closed, even irritated, and a couple of times he'd said something like, "Screw the department," then given a secret smile that had unsettled John.

Oh, yeah. He'd done it. The question that mattered most wasn't where he'd stashed the money but rather who felt entitled to half of it. And how Ronald Floyd entered into the picture. A dead man couldn't broker a drug deal.

John hated even suspecting Geoff Baxter. Damn it, he'd known Geoff for years. They weren't close friends, but they ended up at the same backyard barbecues, knew each other's wives, trusted each other on the job.

Last night he'd just stopped himself from saying something to Natalie. Bad enough that he had to investigate under the table. But if he was wrong—and he hoped like hell he was—John didn't want his partner ever to know that any suspicion had even crossed his mind. Those kind of doubts weren't something a man could forgive.

Using his cell phone during the drive to Natalie's, John put out some tentative inquiries. He'd like to know how deep in debt Baxter was, and especially whether he'd bought some goodies last year without waiting for the cold cash to pay for them. Alternatively, had he been falling into debt for years? Had he taken to spending Saturday nights at the tribal casino down the road?

Or was he the stodgy guy he seemed, who put away ten percent of his paycheck, regular as clockwork, into a retirement fund?

The calls, once made, couldn't be unmade. John

only hoped he'd chosen the right people to ask. Discreet people. Any ripple would tip off a cop that he was being investigated.

Geoff was already there, pacing restlessly in the driveway. "Damn it!" he exploded. "Where the hell have you been? Doing your weekly grocery shop?"

"Just looking up Stuart's arrest records for more ideas."

Baxter gave a disgusted grunt. "How are you going to draw a line between A and B? We arrest people all the goddamn time. They don't break into our houses hunting for something the minute they get out of the pokey."

John unlocked the front door and let them into the quiet house. Already the air felt musty, as if the place had been empty for too long.

"Maybe we've been jumping to conclusions," he said mildly. "Who says he's looking for anything?"

"Huh?" Already at the door to the garage, Baxter stared at him as if he were crazy. "Why'd he come back the second time if he was done?"

"Could've left something behind the first time. Maybe he likes revisiting murder sites. Maybe he was rooting around looking for something likely to tie Natalie up with." None of which John believed, but why not play devil's advocate?

Baxter wasn't interested in any half-baked theories. Shaking his head in disgust, he headed into the garage. "You and I know there's something here."

Actually, John didn't think there was. Or else they'd already missed it, whatever it was. The dust in the back of the garage was too thick, the cobwebs weighed down by years, not months. Gray dust clung to oily parts of the carcass of a car that Stuart had apparently started to restore and then lost interest in. Most of the cartons in the depths of the garage contained the detritus from Stuart's mother, who had died ten, twelve years ago of a heart attack that was an unheeded warning to her son.

"I'll bet Stuart never looked in these," John commented after a wasted half hour. "This is minutes of garden club meetings. Can you believe it?" Muttering under his breath, he hauled the whole box out to a pile they would suggest Natalie recycle.

The middle-aged detective added another. "Tax returns from the fifties. Looks like he moved his mom's stuff here intact. Probably never had time to do anything with it."

John grunted. "He never had time to do anything with his own crap. Lucky he didn't live to an old age. He'd have been one of those coots who has to tunnel between towers of newspaper to get to the bathroom."

"Or else he'd have made a fresh start somewhere on his ill-gotten gains." Baxter's tone of irony didn't quite disguise something else. Envy? Anger? Longing?

Or, John thought ruefully, was he tuning his own ears to pick up waves that weren't there?

Instead of going back to work, Baxter blocked John's path, his arms crossed. His tone was that of somebody starting an argument. "I say we get into the safe-deposit box."

"Natalie says there's nothing unexpected there."

"Maybe her eyes aren't as sharp as ours."

John tried to hide his instinctive anger. Baxter was a cop, and they were suspicious by nature. "You mean," he said mildly, "she didn't notice half a dozen zeros in a bankbook?"

"Could be she doesn't know what a stock certificate means. Or a little, bitty key to a storage locker."

"You really think that's likely?"

Face set in pugnacious lines, Baxter said, "Could be she did see those zeroes."

John gave himself a minute, until the red haze cleared. "She's your friend, too."

"We were both friends with Stuart." The big cop shrugged. "Kind of makes you wonder how much you can trust your gut, doesn't it?"

Oh, yeah. It did. Having your judgment prove to be so wrong did set a guy to thinking. Things that weren't so pretty, like whether a cop might have murdered a man for one reason only: so that he'd have the right and even the duty to search a house for something he was personally seeking.

Something like his share of a half-a-million-dollar take. Hell, no, not his share anymore—the whole garbanzo.

But then Baxter undercut him by giving a heavy sigh and running a hand over his balding head. "What the hell am I saying? Natalie Reed? I can't see it. Tell you the truth, I don't know what Stuart did to deserve her. I always did wonder. No, I don't think she saw all those zeroes. I just figure…a fresh eye…" He grimaced.

"And you're right, too." Easy to be generous when a man felt guilty as hell. "I'm being defensive, and I know better."

His partner raised his brows. "You want to talk to her?"

"I don't think she'll have a problem with it. I'll try to set it up for tomorrow."

Baxter nodded and looked reluctantly toward the depths of the garage. "I suppose we'd better get back to it."

"Hey." John slapped him on the back. "Look at it this way. Maybe his mom had a jewelry box full of pearls and diamonds. If Stuart never looked..."

Baxter's dour face creased into what might have been the start of a grin. "What? We'll sell them and run away to Jamaica?"

"I was thinking the Riviera. Maybe the hills of Tuscany."

Det. Baxter finally did smile, a rusty twitch of the mouth. Stretching, he said, "In that case, we'd better get back to work."

HE WALKED IN THE DOOR to find his mother, both brothers, Natalie and his kids all hanging out in the kitchen. Natalie looked incredibly good in a V-necked sweater the color of a ripe Italian plum over snug jeans and clogs.

He didn't have a chance to linger on his appraisal or the faint flush that pinkened her cheeks, because his mother bent a critical look on him.

"What *have* you been in?"

Natalie made a face. "My garage, I'm afraid."

"You should be afraid," John muttered.

Connor cuffed him. "Don't talk bad to the lady."

"The lady has stolen goods in her garage." He didn't wait long enough to let her get scared. "All the records from the Port Dare Garden Club."

His mother started. "Treasurer's reports? Minutes?"

"Every one of them."

"Well." She appeared bemused. "I know there are some missing years. Nobody seemed to quite know where they'd disappeared to."

"Apparently Stuart's mother was once upon a time president. Or something. Either she absconded with the records, or she died before leaving office and nobody had the sense to reclaim them."

"Well," she said again. "I will now, I suppose."

He'd forgotten that his mother, who had taken up gardening in a big way once she had raised her boys, was also now a stalwart of the garden club. Probably running it with the proverbial iron fist inside a cute flowered ladies' gardening glove.

"I'll rescue the garden club history from the recycling bin, then." He started toward the kitchen. "What are we having for dinner?"

Hugh snapped a dish towel at him. "Get thee into the shower."

"Lasagna," Maddie said brightly. "Grandma makes the best lasagna."

"The best," Evan agreed.

"And you two won't get any if you don't set the table this minute," John's kindly mother said sharply.

Flattery got you nowhere.

He did look like hell, he saw in the mirror above his dresser. Cobwebs clung like premature graying to his hair. Dirt streaked his face and turned his forearms gray above his wrists. Like a good boy, he'd washed his hands at Natalie's house.

John stripped and showered, returning to the kitchen the minute he dressed and combed his hair.

The kids, looking subdued, were setting out hot

pads on the table. John paused to hug each of them. "Grandma in a bad mood?" he asked quietly.

Evan squirmed uneasily. "Kinda."

Maddie waited until he went back to the kitchen. "Grandma is mean to him sometimes," she said hurriedly. "I mean, he can be a brat, but this time he didn't do *anything*."

John nodded. "Thanks for telling me. We'll talk about it later, okay?"

"Okay." She cast a glance over her shoulder and raised her voice. "What do you want me to get next, Grandma?"

Having forgotten that this was family night, John had harbored hopes of having a quiet talk with Natalie this evening. Instead, he refereed arguments between his brothers, seethed as Hugh flirted with Natalie just for the hell of it, and answered Evan's seemingly endless questions about why they had to do the Pledge of Allegiance every day, and why the teacher had told a girl in his class that they couldn't talk about God in class, that religious beliefs were private.

"And when Jerome farted today, Mrs. Miller said bodily functions should be private, too," he reported. "Like, for the bathroom. But God's not for the bathroom. So why did she say…"

"Evan, you are being entirely too loud," his grandmother said, a familiar edge in her voice. "And the bathroom is hardly open for discussion at the dinner table. Now, if you'd let your elders speak…"

Seeing the way his son shrank down in his seat, John intervened, keeping his voice level with an effort. "Just about anything should be open for discussion at the dinner table. In this house, we don't believe children should be seen but not heard."

"Did I say that?" she snapped. "Only that he's dominating the conversation. I believe Connor was trying to say something."

"No hurry," John's brother said easily. "Ev, there are different kinds of privacy. Maybe Mrs. Miller should have chosen different words to make a distinction. Families have their own values. The school is trying not to influence those values. Farting, now..." He grinned at his mother.

She sighed. "This family *has* no values."

"You mean, we have no manners," Hugh suggested.

Natalie stifled a giggle.

"That, too," Mrs. McLean agreed tartly. "Natalie, how was *your* day?"

Put on the spot, Natalie told a few amusing stories from the newsroom. It was the most he heard from her. After dinner, John and his brothers cleaned up. They lingered afterward, as was their habit, although his mother left, mentioning a financial study group meeting. While John was tucking the kids in, Natalie disappeared.

"She said good night," Hugh said. He had his head in the refrigerator. "Anybody want a beer?"

"Damn," John said. "Hold on. I wanted to talk to her."

He knocked quietly on her bedroom door.

"Come in," she called.

Natalie sat in the flowered armchair, her feet tucked under her, a book open on her lap. Her shoes were on the rag rug in front of her, and her dark hair hung loose around her shoulders, fluffed as if she'd run her fingers through it. In the pool of lamplight, she looked pretty and cozy.

"You didn't have to run off," John said.

Her expression became stricken. "I'm sorry! Did it seem like I did? Oh, dear. I've just been dying to finish my book, and I thought you and your brothers would like some time to talk. Please tell them I didn't mean…"

"They didn't think anything of your saying good night." John stood just inside the room, feeling awkward. "I wanted to make sure you didn't feel…"

"I didn't."

Her very poise frustrated him. Her gaze was now pleasantly inquiring. He could have been a stranger instead of the man who had made passionate love to her the night before.

He was driven to assume a businesslike tone. "I'm wondering if Geoff and I can get into your safe-deposit box tomorrow."

Something flickered in her eyes, but she agreed without hesitation. "Of course. I think I have to open it for you, unless you have a court order. Do you want to go first thing in the morning, or at the lunch hour?"

"Morning's fine. We don't expect to find anything—"

"But you need to look, not just take my word for it. I understand." She waited, eyebrows lifted, at last saying gently, "Is there anything else?"

Talk to me, damn it.

"I was hoping to kiss you," he said gruffly.

"Oh." The exclamation came out breathlessly. Natalie jumped to her feet and rushed to him. "A kiss would be nice," she admitted, lifting her face to his.

Yeah. Nice. With his two brothers in the living

room, his children in bed upstairs, and no hope of this going anywhere.

So he kept it tender, light, a promise instead of a demand. Nice.

"Nice" was going to be a cold bedfellow tonight.

CHAPTER TWELVE

In the surreal quiet of the bank vault, the two men waited as Natalie unlocked the safe-deposit box and pulled it out. She carried it to the table, then stood back.

"Do you mind?" John asked politely.

"That's what we're here for."

She knew it wouldn't take them five minutes to look through the papers Stuart had kept here. She had wondered why he bothered with a safe-deposit box and thought of canceling it, but hadn't because of the same inertia that had kept her from making other changes this past year.

Don't make decisions too soon, everyone cautioned. They didn't know that she wasn't grieving the way they thought she was, but the shock of Stuart's sudden death had seemed to leave her with many of the traditional symptoms widows shared. Too *many* decisions to be made, maybe, and it seemed easiest to put them all off except those required for the funeral.

After all, it had been his last chance to have his name in the newspaper. Feeling the irony and even some anger, she had carefully clipped both obituary and the brief article and placed them in his album. *The End.*

The two men were huddled over the box. Geoff raised his head and said grumpily, "This is it?"

She made an apologetic gesture. "I told you there wasn't much."

"Have you taken anything out of here?"

"No...yes," Natalie corrected herself, remembering. "Foxfire's registration papers. They're in the filing cabinet now, in the study. You must have seen them."

Looking irritated, Geoff repeated, "Foxfire?"

"My horse?"

Under his breath, he muttered something no doubt better unheard, concluding with a growled, "Why the hell would anyone put an animal's papers in a safe-deposit box?"

She didn't remind him that this particular animal was worth thousands.

"Nothing else?" He sounded almost fierce. "There wasn't a key in here? Any papers you didn't understand? Something you've put out of your mind because it didn't seem important?"

John was unusually silent, letting his partner take the lead. Perhaps, she thought, because of what had happened between them. It must be terribly awkward to be investigating a woman you'd just slept with.

"Nothing," she said, holding out her hands palm up, as if to show that they were empty. "The attorney who handled the probate was with me. You can have his phone number and talk to him if you'd like, but I'm sure he didn't remove anything. We glanced through the contents, he made a few notes, and the only thing I took was Foxfire's papers. We put everything back, and I haven't had any reason to open this safe-deposit box since." Quietly she added, "I'm sorry."

Voice just as quiet, John said, "I didn't expect anything else."

A frowning Geoff Baxter, she couldn't help noticing, didn't agree.

LATE THE NEXT AFTERNOON, Natalie unlocked the front door of her house and stepped in, setting down the cat carrier but leaving the door open for John, who was following her up the walk with her suitcase. He, of course, had protested her decision to move home, but she'd been more determined, not less, because of their one night of lovemaking.

In the two days since, it had seemed impossible to snatch even a few minutes alone together, never mind hours. John was working long days on another murder investigation, as well as Ronald Floyd's. If he ever had time during the day, she didn't. And either his mother dropped the kids off by five o'clock or John picked them up on his way home. He didn't sneak downstairs to her bedroom or suggest she creep up to his, a decision she respected. She hated to think of Evan having a nightmare and discovering her in bed with his daddy.

So the time had come to put her life back on track. What would be, would be, with John. She was trying very hard to be a fatalist—or even an optimist—to combat the hollow feeling in her chest.

Alone briefly in the entry, she looked around with curious reluctance. The house, so familiar, felt alien. No wonder. It had, after all, seen intruders twice this past month, a brutal murder upstairs, a top-to-bottom search by the police, and finally the installation of a security system.

Her purse slid from her shoulder and plopped onto the carrier, startling her—and probably poor Sasha—briefly. Waiting, hesitating about stepping farther inside, Natalie had a sharp flashback to the day she had moved into this house, immediately after she and Stuart flew into SeaTac from their honeymoon in Maui. They had come straight here. All her belongings had gone into storage while they were away, and now this was home.

Stuart hadn't carried her across the threshold. After the euphoria of the honeymoon, she had felt absurdly hurt by the absence of the traditional, if silly, gesture.

"You know where everything is," he'd said over his shoulder as he went straight to the big-screen television and turned it on. He was channel surfing, one football game to another, his new wife apparently forgotten, when she quietly took her own suitcase upstairs to the master bedroom.

She'd slept here before, helped make dinner, but as a guest. Now this house was home. But it felt...not like a place she would have chosen. The sound of the commentators' voices raised in excited argument floated from the downstairs. Clearly Stuart wasn't following her up. She bit her lip, sat down on the edge of the king-size bed, and cried a few quiet tears.

Now Natalie shook her head hard to disperse the unwelcome memory. Today was different. This was just a house, and she owned it. The floor plan was identical to that of a dozen other houses in this development alone. Atmosphere, if any, came from paint and paper and wood, things that could be changed, and from the lives lived within the walls.

She *had* to come home. She couldn't afford to make mortgage payments on this house and rent an apartment, too. Besides, if she was to sell this place, it was time she got to work weeding through Stuart's things. She'd procrastinated for a year. Enough was enough.

A footstep sounded behind her. John set down her suitcase and closed the door with his shoulder. A frown drew his brows together as he watched her release Sasha from the carrier.

The cat took a wild look around and bolted for the stairs.

"She'll be okay," Natalie said aloud. As much for herself, she added, "We'll be okay."

The brief silence was thick.

"I don't like leaving you here."

"I'll be safe with the security system. Besides..." Natalie turned with a smile that cost her. "We have no reason to think whoever broke in was interested in me. You've obviously searched this place top to bottom. Why would anybody bother to break in again?"

His jaw tightened. "You were welcome at my house."

"I know I was," Natalie said quietly. "But I couldn't just stay forever." She swallowed. Oh, dear. That was exactly what she wanted to do. "It was time," she concluded with another faint smile.

"I'm going to miss you," John said in an odd voice.

"Call me." *Please.*

"Yeah. I'll do that." He reached for her suitcase. "Let me take this upstairs."

Natalie wandered into the kitchen rather than follow him. The first thing she had to do was grocery shop, she realized, after opening the refrigerator. She was glad to seize on something so practical to do.

The crime scene tape no longer barred the door to the garage. She opened it and peered in. If anything, the piles of boxes and the hulk of an MG that Stuart had thought he would restore but never got to looked more daunting. The car first, she thought. Tomorrow, she'd call around and find somebody who would haul it away for parts—assuming it had any usable ones. If not—the junkyard. That would give her room to work out there. She'd spend a whole weekend sorting the salable from stuff to go to the dump. It was still early enough in the fall that she could have a garage sale.

Last night, when she'd said there might be things she would want to keep, John had grimaced.

"Trust me. There won't be."

Closing the door firmly and locking the new dead bolt, Natalie pushed away the cloud of depression that wanted to descend.

The more of Stuart's possessions out of her hair the better. Her feelings about him were still tangled, but she knew she didn't want to keep much to remember him by.

"What are you thinking?" John had come up behind her so silently she hadn't heard his approach.

She turned with another of those determined smiles. "That I need groceries."

"You could come home with me for dinner."

Home. Oh, so easily, his house could be just that, enfolding her with a welcome she'd never found here.

But then, John hadn't asked her to stay on any basis

but as a guest, a nervous Nellie who was afraid to live in her own house alone.

"Don't be silly. I've just gotten here."

She followed him to the front door. There, he opened his arms and she went into them, for a moment gratefully resting her cheek against his chest.

"Thank you," she whispered.

He swallowed an oath and kissed her, hard and quick. An instant later, her front door opened and closed and he was gone.

Fiercely she refused to let herself cry.

Natalie waited just long enough for him to be well on his way home before following him out. She did a thorough grocery shop, then filled her evening with putting away what she'd bought, cooking dinner and returning the phone calls that had built up on her answering machine.

Only then did she go upstairs, pausing just briefly at the open door to the study, not letting herself turn her head to look for a now nonexistent stain, before continuing to her bedroom.

Sleep was slow coming, even after a plop announced Sasha's arrival. She declined to come up for a cuddle, but did deign to curl up behind Natalie's knees, a warm, comforting lump.

At John's house, Natalie had been able to avoid thinking about Stuart and her own stupidity. Now, in the bed they'd shared during almost three years of marriage, she couldn't.

How could she have deceived herself so completely?

That was what bothered her most—the idea that she could have imagined herself in love with a man who could offer one face to the world and be something

so different behind it. Did she misjudge people as
badly every day?

What if John wasn't quite what he seemed to be,
either? He'd told her that Stuart had had a partner in
crime. Perhaps John felt a financial obligation to Debbie; perhaps he *had* one Natalie didn't know about.
He could be desperate for money. Who better for Stuart to take into his confidence.

No! Her fingers clenched on her covers. She would
not believe that. Not of John, protective father and
friend, tender, passionate lover, conscientious even
toward his ex-wife.

No. Anyone but John McLean.

That insidious, internal voice, heard loudest at
night, whispered, *Yes, but you would never have believed it of Stuart. And you* married *him.*

She was able to defeat the voice more easily than
she might have expected. She knew the difference
now between a man like Stuart and one like John
McLean. When she met Stuart, she had let herself be
fooled by the exterior: the uniform and the broad
shoulders and smiling eyes and heroic record. Face
craggy rather than handsome, he'd been tall, athletic,
unarguably brave. His sense of humor was sometimes
vulgar or shocking, but she knew from friends that
hospital workers were the same. Pathos could be de-
feated only with humor. He had courted her, talked
of his exploits when she pushed, tried to make light
of them.

One night, while he was cooking dinner for them,
she had discovered the album of newspaper clippings
about him while she was browsing the shelves. He
found her looking through it.

She had been taken aback. That was a good way

to put it. It had seemed a little odd, almost childishly proud, that this big tough cop combed through newspapers for his own name, even highlighting it sometimes.

But when she looked up, he smiled crookedly. Nodding at the album, Stuart said, "That's to remind me in low moments that I can do some good."

Of course her heart melted.

More fool she.

He abandoned the facade once they were married. He'd gotten annoyed a few times that she wouldn't use her influence at the *Sentinel* to be sure he was featured in write-ups. She'd seen him throw a temper tantrum after he was dismissed in print as "a second Port Dare officer." Oh, he'd pretend to be embarrassed afterward, give a boyish grin and say, "I just like to know that somebody notices the job I do." Somewhere along the way, she looked at him in the midst of a tirade and realized he was completely self-centered.

Natalie was willing to bet that Det. John McLean didn't have an album with clippings of his own exploits.

But even knowing Stuart was egotistical, almost childishly selfish, having discovered that his interests were narrow and his observations about others cruel, she would never have imagined him a killer.

He had taken such pride in being a police officer. Not just an officer, but a detective and a hero. Knowing that he had crossed the line so completely for money made her reexamine her memories, wonder if he had ever taken pride in the job or what his badge stood for. Maybe instead the pride was all for himself, for being somebody people looked at with respect and even fear. Maybe liking to be looked at with fear had become more pleasurable. Or maybe, as John had suggested, growing anger at the city and the department had twisted his pride into vengeance.

Or maybe, ultimately, he *was* just selfish. He'd had enough of being a low-paid cop and wanted big bucks, so he felt he had the right to grab it any way he could. Which made him a psychopath. A conscienceless shell of a man who had fooled her into thinking him decent, sexy and even noble.

Curled under the covers in bed, Natalie flushed with humiliation at her own gullibility. How earnestly she had worked at her marriage, convinced she was somehow at fault when his interest waned, not understanding yet that his interest never strayed far from himself.

What kind of idiot did John think she was? Either she'd had some grain of intelligence and therefore knew her husband was a crook, or else she was naive beyond deserving sympathy. He did genuinely seem to think she hadn't known what Stuart was, which suggested that he didn't rate her intelligence very high.

So why was he interested in her?

Was he really? Or had the one night been an impulse? With kids, he couldn't possibly have much of a swinging social life. How often did he even get the chance to date? There she was, ensconced in his guest bedroom, ripe for the plucking.

Natalie threw off the covers to cool herself. The flush of humiliation spread from her cheeks to her toes. She was imagining true love, and he was scratching an itch.

Only it hadn't seemed that way.

She heard his voice, ringing with sincerity. *You're a woman of integrity. I'd trust you with my life.*

And low and gritty. *Stuart was crazy. The son of a bitch didn't deserve you.*

And he'd claimed that she had been keeping him awake nights and appearing in his dreams when he did sleep. He'd as good as admitted that he had wanted her even when she was married.

None of that sounded as if making love to her was an impulse. And it had felt…well, she wasn't that experienced, but his every touch, the groans she'd awakened, the heavy beat of his heart and the shiver of muscles, none of that had felt like a man scratching an itch.

It felt more like a man who might be falling in love along with her.

Or was she, once again, fooling herself?

Natalie flopped onto her back, moaning.

How could a woman who had made such a monumental mistake ever trust her judgment again?

What she needed to understand, she realized, was *why* she had been so gullible. Why had she needed so badly to believe that Stuart was everything he appeared to be? Why had she wanted to be married so desperately, she had closed her eyes to everything that was wrong?

And how, she thought wretchedly, shutting out the sight of the bright green numerals on her digital clock, was she ever going to get up and go to work tomorrow on so little sleep?

THE RESTAURANT WAS popular, an airy, former warehouse that now had wood floors and lush ferns enjoying the light from the glass that enclosed what had once been a shipping dock looking out over the strait. Outside, seagulls soared, and a departing ferry left a rough wake on the gray water.

John would rather have been at the local hamburger joint with his kids. Hell, he'd rather be just about anywhere else, with anyone but his mother.

Unpleasant tasks couldn't be put off forever.

The pleasantries out of the way, lunch ordered and the waitress departed, John cleared his throat. "Mom, I want to talk to you about something."

His mother raised her eyebrows. "Yes? Do you need me to take the children an extra day?"

Oh, good. Make this harder. That was the trouble with his mother. Damn it, she was always willing to help him out. She believed in family, that the members *should* be able to depend on one another. She'd been there unfailingly, in her own way, for him and his brothers. She still was.

He didn't want her ever to know how bitterly he resented the stern way she'd raised her sons. Maybe it had been necessity; it had to have been tough for her on her own—no life insurance, no marketable skills, having to work two jobs to put food on the table. No surprise that she'd needed them to grow up fast. Now he could see that maybe she hadn't had any energy left to show affection. Probably it was petty of him to wish she had been able to be softer sometimes, to let them know that she loved her boys even when they didn't live up to her expectations. Sometimes he wondered if she even remembered the woman she'd once been, the mother his childish eyes had seen.

The silence had stretched too long while he wallowed in guilt.

Irritated with himself, he thought, *Enough already!* However much he depended on his mother and respected how she'd coped after her husband's murder, he couldn't let her squelch Evan's joy and spontaneity. John didn't even fully understand why she was trying. Because Evan was a boy, and therefore required to live to a higher standard than his sister? Why was that? John's determination hardened. Was his son, too, supposed to dedicate his life to justice and protecting the innocent because of a long-ago tragedy?

She'd molded all three of her boys—screwed them up, in John's opinion, which he sometimes thought was harsh but believed nonetheless. He wasn't going to let her do the same to Evan.

"No," he said. "It's Evan I want to talk to you about."

She looked coolly back at him. "You really should be firmer with him, you know. I wouldn't say this in his hearing, but he's really become something of a brat lately."

John gritted his teeth. "In what way?"

"He interrupts constantly. You boys were taught not to interrupt adults. And the way he and Maddie bicker—"

"Maddie is the older. Why is their fighting his fault?"

"It isn't altogether, of course! Her manners lack something, too." His mother's voice softened. "I understand why you've been indulgent, considering the trauma of losing their mother the way they have. It seems to me the time has come, however…"

Levelly he said, "But I'm their father, and I don't think the time *has* come."

Her only visible reaction was a flaring of her nostrils. She waited.

"They do bicker a lot, and it is tiresome."

"I'm glad you see at least that much," she said, a snip in her voice.

He fought the anger that he knew had its roots in problems other than this one. He didn't want a rift; he just wanted to get through to her.

"What you don't seem to notice is how much they also depend on each other and how close they are, how much they care about each other." Not giving her a chance to respond, he continued, "Maddie, for example, is worried because Grandma has been so mean to Evan lately."

She jerked as if he'd struck her. Her mouth worked several times while she sought words and failed to find them.

He hadn't meant to be so blunt. Renewed guilt softened his voice. "It's pretty obvious to everyone but you how hard you've been coming down on Evan." He hesitated. "Mom, he's a little kid. A kindergartner. Suddenly you're trying to hold him to some standard of maturity that he's not even close to being at."

She found her voice. "Is it so unreasonable to expect decent manners and some help when I ask for it?"

"He's five years old, Mom."

"Hugh wasn't much older than that when his father died."

How many times had he heard that? "I know," he said, with sparse patience. "Hugh had to grow up fast. You needed him to. Evan doesn't have to."

The waitress brought salads. His mother inclined her head in regal thanks and unfolded her napkin. She did not, however, pick up her fork when the waitress left.

"I can assure you," his mother said stiffly, "that my intention was not to—"

John interrupted. "Mom, you don't have to tell me your intentions. You love the kids. You've showed that in a million ways. But it seems to me that your attitude toward Evan has been changing lately. When Maddie noticed, too, I figured we'd better talk about it."

Her chin stayed up, her gaze level. She was big on pride, something she'd drummed into her own sons. "If you feel I'm not a good influence..."

Oh, damn. "Don't be ridiculous," he said brusquely. "The kids know you love them. I just want you to go a little easier on Evan. Please. Let him be a little kid."

"Even when he's rude or quarrelsome?"

"He's a little kid. He plays with trucks! He's not ten or twelve or twenty." John hesitated. "He's more or less lost his mother, as you pointed out. He could use your affection. He needs that a lot more than discipline."

Spots of color touched her elegant cheekbones, and he realized he had—what?—embarrassed her? Angered her? As always, it was hard to tell.

After a moment, she gave her head an acknowledging dip. "Very well." She reached for her fork and uncharacteristically fumbled before picking it up, looking at it as if she had no idea what it was, and setting it back down. Still gazing down at the fork, she said stiffly, "Affection, in the way you mean, doesn't come naturally to me."

John was startled and uneasy. They never talked

about things like this. Not once, either as a teenager or an adult, had he expressed his quiet resentment, and not once in all these years had she attempted to explain why she had been something closer to a boot camp sergeant than a mother. Dipping even a toe in these waters made him shift in his seat.

"Your praise means a great deal to him. Physical affection isn't really what I'm talking about."

His mother nodded. For a moment she said nothing, her dignity intact, her carriage proud. But then she surprised him yet again.

"I've noticed how comfortable you are hugging your children. I'm well aware I wasn't demonstrative. How is it that you can be?"

Only long practice at taking the stand to be grilled by defense attorneys allowed John not to show his discomfiture.

"I've made a conscious effort," he said quietly. "And also…" He paused, briefly undecided, then gave a mental shrug. She was the one who'd opened the door. "Unlike Connor and Hugh, I remember the days before Dad died. He was…easier with touches than you were. But I remember you hugging me and kissing owies to make them better and reading to us, with all three of us squeezed up against you and draped over your shoulder. It wasn't until after—" he didn't have to say after what "—that you became more remote."

Now she did bow her head, and he was shocked to realize that he'd seen a glint of tears.

Impulsively he reached across the table. "Damn. I'm sorry, Mom."

A handclasp was beyond her, but she gave his hand

a quick, nervous pat, took a deep breath and looked up. "Those were hard days."

Explanation? Or apology?

"I'm well aware," he said. "I wasn't criticizing."

Her expression was more troubled than he remembered seeing in a woman of unshakable resolve. "I hardly knew I'd changed."

John mused, "I wonder what we'd all be like, if Dad was still with us?"

Her back straightened and her mouth firmed. "Well, he's not. Thanks to a madman who shouldn't have been in a position to hurt anyone."

She'd found a familiar chord. Any weakness was behind her. He knew what was coming next.

"You haven't arrested whoever murdered that man in Natalie's house." His mother's tone said, *Why not?*

Understanding that she was done discussing the past, John said, "No, and we're pretty much stymied. If we don't get a break soon, the case is going to end up on the back burner."

Officially, it might be in the inactive file. Unofficially was another story. He, Hugh and Connor were going to move heaven and hell if that was what it took to find out what cop had committed a brutal, drug-related murder and then been willing to kill again to get his hands on his take. But John wasn't about to tell his mother something he couldn't even tell his partner.

She sniffed. "Can you really bring yourself to tell that nice young woman she may have to live in fear from now on?"

"Live in fear?" John snorted. "*She* insisted on moving home again yesterday. Insists *my* fears are unfounded."

"Then perhaps you'd best insure that they are. Since—" her gaze was unexpectedly penetrating "—I have the feeling you're fond of Natalie."

Fond. Oh, yeah. That was one way of putting it.

"Yeah," he said. "I'm fond of her."

"As I'm sure she is of you."

"We're good friends."

His mother opened her mouth, then closed it.

"What?" he asked.

She gave a dry chuckle. "I was simply thinking better of something I was tempted to say. Since I seem not to have been doing as well as I thought I was with Maddie and Evan, I'm hardly the person to be dispensing advice."

Intrigued, he leaned forward. "Mom, asking you to go easy on Evan doesn't mean you—or your advice—aren't valuable. Spit it out."

She raised her brows at the vulgarity but gave a small nod. "Very well. It's just this—doing what you feel you must for Debbie does not mean you're still married to her."

Surprised to realize she'd noticed more undercurrents than he had guessed, John said after a moment, indirectly, "You never remarried. Or even considered it, as far as I know."

"But then, your father and I were deeply in love. As I doubt you and Debbie ever were." Apparently done with the subject, she signaled the passing waiter. "I'd like some tea now. Please do see to it that the boiling water is poured directly on the tea bag." She nodded, dismissing him. "Thank you."

Glancing regretfully at his nearly untouched lunch, John put out a hand to stop the waiter. "Coffee for me, please. Black is fine."

He might not have had a chance to eat, but he'd seen some of his mother's emotional walls crumble. No—too strong a word. Crack? Tremble, and escape unscathed? Probably the latter, but interesting nonetheless. If he wasn't imagining things, she'd expressed at least a hint of regret, a first as far as he knew.

Did that mean something to him? He didn't know. He'd have to think about it. If it turned out to mean something for Evan, that was what counted.

As for her "advice," that was something he'd have to think about, too. If his mother had taught him one thing, it was a sense of duty. It was keeping his word.

Till death do us part.

But he was grateful every time he saw Debbie that he wasn't still married to her. So maybe what he really needed to find out was whether Natalie understood that he couldn't turn his back on his ex-wife if she needed him.

Shaking his head, he thought, *Whoa.* He was making some mighty big assumptions there. Especially since Natalie had fled his house the moment that damned security system was installed. So maybe what he needed to find out first was, what did he mean to Natalie?

Trouble was, John knew that was one question he couldn't come right out and ask.

Alarm flared in his belly. Here they'd always been able to talk about anything and everything, and now when it counted, he could kiss her but he couldn't ask a straight question. Did that mean all his qualms about what would happen once he touched her had been dead-on?

CHAPTER THIRTEEN

THE COMMENTATOR GAZED solemnly at the camera. "Tonight, the only three survivors of the fatal sinking of the Greek ferry are all in critical condition at Athens hospitals. A spokesman reports that one has described a scene of utter horror..."

Click. An extremely young Alan Alda donned a surgical mask as camouflage-clad MASH staff rushed a gurney with a thrashing, bloody patient to him. "More incoming wounded," someone intoned.

Wasn't there anything *cheerful* on television anymore? Natalie wondered irritably. Click. *Sesame Street,* with puppets singing about the letter *A.*

One more click, and the TV screen went blank. So there. She didn't like to watch television anyway.

Only, the bright, flickering images and the human voices were company. She just wished they wouldn't go on and on about death and destruction.

The clock on the VCR said 7:40. Nowhere near bedtime. The kitchen was clean, the laundry done. She could sew—she'd washed the fabric Sasha had shed on, and she could cut it out. With only the pinafore finished, she needed to get moving—the wedding was fast approaching and her sister was counting on her to get her niece's dress done. But tonight she felt too restless to be careful, to concentrate.

A book, then. Except that a perusal of her shelves

didn't turn up anything that interested her. She should have gone to the library on the way home from work. Tomorrow, Natalie promised herself. She glanced disinterestedly through some catalogs that had arrived in the mail, then, caught by a photograph of a model in the kitchen, decided to bake. She could make cookies, and drop them off tomorrow at John's. For Maddie and Evan, and in thanks to him for his help.

Of course, *he* would say she was trying to even the score. Get herself out of debt.

Well, this time he was wrong. Natalie made a face. This time all she was trying to do was think of an excuse to see John.

Momentarily she paused with the cookbook in her hand. He wouldn't have to *know* why she was stopping by. He might not even be there. And it was only courteous, wasn't it, to take them something?

Why hadn't he called? He'd said he would. She sighed, looking at the clock on the stove. He might yet—he often did phone later, after the kids were in bed.

And what was wrong with her, anyway? She'd never minded living alone, either before her marriage or after. Again she made a face at her own pronouncements.

Obviously, before marrying Stuart, she hadn't been as contented as she'd thought herself, or she wouldn't have fallen so fast, so gullibly. She must have been desperate for a home, husband and children.

But she wasn't *bored.* Natalie knew that much. She could entertain herself. And since Stuart's death she had actually come to enjoy the quiet in the house. He'd almost always had the TV on when he was home, which had bugged her. He liked the canned voices. She'd come to realize he wasn't a self-sufficient man. He wanted stimulation, company, admiration. Silence drove him crazy.

Wherever he had intended to go once he ditched her, it wouldn't have been alone. Maybe he'd planned to buy a dumb, buxom blonde to gaze admiringly at him, Natalie thought spitefully, then was ashamed of herself.

The telephone stayed stubbornly silent, so she took the canisters from the cupboard and began mixing a recipe for snickerdoodles she'd never tried. The dough cooling in the freezer—why not hurry it up?—Natalie hummed quietly as she hunted for the cookie press. Above the refrigerator, maybe? Standing on a chair, she found it along with a waffle iron she never used. Maybe she should get it down and have waffles for breakfast.

The telephone shrilled and she jumped enough to almost overbalance from her precarious perch. Mumbling bad words under her breath, Natalie climbed down with the cookie press clutched in her hand and reached for the phone.

Sounding breathless, she said, ''Hello?''

''Get you from the shower?'' John asked.

To her annoyance, her heart leaped. ''No, digging something out of a cupboard.''

''Yeah? What are you up to?''

Baking cookies for you. To give me an excuse to see you.

Impossible to say.

''Oh, cleaning the kitchen,'' she lied. ''I couldn't find…a new sponge.''

''Oh, I saw 'em under the sink in the…'' He stopped and was silent for a moment. ''I guess you don't need me reminding you that I've stuck my nose in every cupboard in your house.''

He could have told her where the cookie press was.

''That's okay,'' she said. ''I want you to find out what Stuart did with the money, or who has it. And who killed that man upstairs.'' More lightly, she added, ''I just hope it wasn't too much of a shock to find out that I'm not Miss Suzie Homemaker.''

''Oh, I don't know. The number of times you've brought me cookies, I might award you the title, cobwebs behind the bookcases or not.''

Ruefully eyeing the mess she'd just made, she said, ''No more cookies. I promise.''

''You make good ones.''

''Thank you.'' She sounded as stilted as he did. It would be a cold day in hell before she took him any more.

After a moment, he said, ''You okay there alone?''

''Of course I am!'' Too much vehemence. ''I'm fine.''

''I doubt you'll be bothered. You were right. Why would anyone break in again?''

Oh, good. She could go back to her old life. No squabbling kids, no uncomfortable tension between John and his mother, no Hugh and Connor hanging around with beers in their hands, no...John.

Except, she supposed, as an occasional caller.

''You're not going to find out who killed Ronald Floyd, are you?'' she asked.

His voice became weary. ''I don't know, Natalie. I can't promise you. We need something to go on.''

She nodded, and realized he couldn't see her. ''Yes. I see.''

"My mother gave me hell for not making an arrest yet."

"I'm sorry."

"No, she was right." He sounded gruff. "I wish I could give you that, at least."

She gripped the phone with painfully tight fingers. "Please don't apologize."

Nothing but him breathing for a moment. Then, "Maddie got an A on her spelling test."

Natalie had to swallow before she could say in a semblance of a normal voice, "Tell her I said congratulations."

"Will do." Another of those awkward pauses made her wonder what he was thinking. "I'd suggest dinner tomorrow night, but I don't dare. I'm handling that homicide in Bayview."

The headline for tomorrow morning's paper was two inches high: Prominent Socialite Murdered. The newsroom had been buzzing over the story. Ronald Floyd's death had been news, primarily because he had been murdered in her house. But this killing had stunned Port Dare, because of who the victim was. Rachel Portman's husband was a wealthy businessman and school board member, while she volunteered for half a dozen causes. Their neighborhood was one of the ritziest in town, the houses all enormous fake Tudors or Italian villas or some such, the views of the Strait of Juan de Fuca and shipping traffic spectacular. If the houses had security systems, it was to protect the home owners' jewelry and top-of-the-line stereo systems and computers, not the inhabitants themselves. Murders did not happen in Bayview.

"Are you getting anywhere?"

"Yeah," he said. "Yeah, I'm afraid so."

Which meant the husband, she guessed. She knew him. He had been in a particularly foul mood last week when they discussed changing the look of his weekly advertisement.

"Oh, dear," Natalie said.

"You may say so." A muffled voice sounded in the background. "Oh, hell. Evan's calling me. Listen, we'll talk tomorrow?"

"If you have time."

"Night."

With that, he was gone. No *I miss you.* Not even a *Can we have a lunchtime tryst?* Just, *We'll talk tomorrow.*

Natalie took the cookie dough from the freezer, dumped it into the garbage beneath the sink and cleaned the kitchen.

AROUND A MOUTHFUL of French fries, Baxter argued, "He's got an alibi."

"The son of a bitch did it," John said flatly.

Monday morning, and they were sitting in the car outside the Italianate monstrosity in Bayview where Rachel Portman had been murdered as she emerged from the marble shower in the master bath Saturday morning at approximately nine o'clock. The front door had been conveniently unlocked, and some jewelry was missing from the small safe she had apparently opened in expectation of wearing a piece she kept in it. Strangely, other valuable pieces were left dumped on the dresser, as if to suggest the intruder had rushed out with only part of his booty. Her body had been discovered when she failed to show at a hospital luncheon benefit she was chairing.

This was the first time they'd been alone to discuss

the case, instead of running around interviewing everybody and his mother. Baxter had been in a hell of
a mood the past few days, sullen and snarling. John
knew his own wasn't much better. Natalie's departure
had left a hole in his life that gaped. He didn't like
her being alone, either. Whatever reason said, the
intruder-murderer was still at large, his purpose still
something of a mystery. John disliked failure, which
the lack of an arrest equated. And he hated looking
at the man beside him in the car and wondering if his
tension didn't have to do with their failure not to find
the murderer, but to find the money.

And here was a thought: what if John had been the
one to find the key while the two of them were alone
in Natalie's house? If Geoff Baxter was the one who
had killed once, would he have balked at dealing with
his partner?

John swore to himself and watched Baxter unwrap
his bacon cheeseburger. Sauce oozed as he lifted it to
his mouth. Seeming not to notice, Baxter scowled at
the windshield. "Could've hired someone."

John thrust a napkin at him and readjusted his own
thinking. "Assassins being readily available on every
street corner in Port Dare, Washington."

Geoff looked down in vague surprise and dabbed
at the sauce festooning his tie. Wadding up the napkin, he continued the argument, "How hard is it to
find some scumbag who'll do anything for a thousand
bucks?"

Hell, why not just ask for a cop? John thought
sourly.

He took a swallow of coffee. "Tricky, if you're a
prominent businessman." Damn it, he should have
gotten something to eat, too, but the fast-food burgers

hadn't appealed. He sighed. "I think he did it himself." Suddenly energized, he reached for the key in the ignition. The older crime had of necessity to be put on hold, whatever agenda he or Baxter had. For now, they might as well do more than the motions. This one they could solve. "Let's go talk to his faithful secretary again."

She was lying and he knew it. Classic story: handsome, older, well-to-do boss and the pretty twenty-something secretary who had taken to frequently traveling together. She was shocked by the murder but so far steadfast in her story: he'd been out of the office, it was true, but she had been with him. They were inspecting a building he had recently purchased near the waterfront.

John had hoped twenty-four hours of thinking it over might have shaken her. If anything, her resolve had grown more steely. Interestingly so, he thought— she was starting to get ticked that they were hassling her.

They left her house and decided to interview the husband again. John thought of himself as a patient man, but today he just wanted to make a damned arrest and go home. He could get a baby-sitter, or see if his mother would watch the kids, call Natalie and suggest...

"I wonder," Baxter said thoughtfully, "if she's really protecting Portman."

John snapped back from a fantasy that involved candlelight and Natalie's soft hand in his, her hair a dark cloud around her shoulders, lips parting... "Huh?"

Baxter sounded almost like himself. He had at least become reluctantly interested in the case. He continued his train of thought, "Maybe hubby was perfectly happy with his marriage. Maybe his girlfriend was the one who wasn't happy."

John had briefly considered the possibility Saturday, of course, and discarded it on the basis of the secretary's youth and apparent distress and shock.

Genuine, he wondered now, or shock at the very real brutality of committing a murder?

"Possible," he conceded, cursing himself for being so preoccupied with seeing his own girlfriend that he was more interested in resolution than truth.

Ralph Portman was staying at the Inn By The Sea, in a suite often used for entertaining or honeymoons. Although it was midafternoon, he answered the door in a bathrobe, his face ravaged. "Have you arrested someone?" he asked with hope.

"I'm afraid not, Mr. Portman," John said stolidly. "May we come in?"

The husband's face crumpled, and he backed away to let them in. Sobs shook him as he sank onto the chintz-covered sofa. The two cops glanced at each other. Baxter went down the hall to the bathroom and returned with tissues, which he put in the businessman's hand. John sat, too, and Baxter stood to one side, arms crossed.

Eventually Portman controlled himself, wiped his eyes, blew his nose and looked up in intense grief. "What can I do to help?"

"Tell us the truth," John said in a hard voice. "Mr. Portman, where were you Saturday morning at nine?"

Comprehension penetrated his grief only slowly. "Yesterday? You don't think...?"

"We think you're lying. That you weren't with Ms. Ryan at all."

He cried again, noisily, but eventually confessed that no, he wasn't. She was lying to protect him. He appreciated it, but he shouldn't have let her. She'd seen immediately that he might be suspected—didn't they always look at the husband?

The truth was, he and his pretty secretary had arranged for him to come to her house at a few minutes after nine. They were having an affair, he confessed.

"But, oh God, I love my wife." He stared not at them, but at the videotape he wouldn't be able to turn off: the one where he was on his way to have cheap, extramarital sex while his Rachel was being struck down. "I would never..."

"And Ms. Ryan. Was she home when you got there?"

The meaning of his question penetrated far more quickly. "You can't think..." He blundered to his feet and ran down the hall to the bathroom, where he lost everything he'd eaten that day.

When he returned, it was numbly. "No," he said. "She wasn't there. I waited quite a while, thinking she'd run out to get something. Maybe gone to the bakery, or..." He swallowed, spoke in the voice of an automaton. "We met in the parking garage at the office. She thought it was the next morning we were to...get together." Remembering, he quivered. "Yesterday. She was very sorry, she'd done some quick errands on her way in. The line at the post office was long, she said, which was why she was late. I didn't think anything of it. She'd agreed to come in on Saturday since we had a deal in the offing. Of course she had things she'd intended to do over the weekend."

"Did she seem shaken? Unlike herself?"

He frowned in concentration. "Well, a little. But that was because of the misunderstanding. She felt bad."

"What about her clothes? We saw her later, of course. I'm just wondering if you noticed anything unusual."

"Only that…" He stopped. "She had a run up her panty hose. A really bad one. I wondered, since she was doing errands anyway, why she hadn't bought new ones."

"Perhaps," John said, rising, "we had better have another talk with Ms. Ryan."

"She wouldn't have…" But his eyes showed the horror of the knowledge that she might very well have done just that. He, too, was imagining his pretty secretary rushing out of his house, stopping the car somewhere in a quiet cul-de-sac to change clothes. Swearing, perhaps, as she punctured the nylon of her hose but knowing she was already late and hoping to be in the office before her boss arrived so that she could raise her eyebrows and say, "Today? Oh, I'm so sorry! I thought…"

A stop at the post office elicited the information that, in fact, Saturday morning had been, as usual, slow. No lines. Yes, the clerk knew Ms. Ryan, she often brought over the mail from Portland, Schultz and McArdy. No, he was quite sure she hadn't been there yesterday morning.

This time, Ms. Ryan cracked. She seemed stunned that they had even considered her as a suspect. All her planning, it appeared, had been designed to point the finger at her lover if the police didn't believe in a burglary gone bad. She, too, cried.

"He was afraid to leave her," she sobbed. "We'd never have been able to be together if she didn't..."

"Die?" John suggested softly.

Her face twisted. "Yes! He didn't have the guts." She buried her face in her hands.

John reached for his handcuffs. "Melissa Ryan, I'm placing you under arrest for the murder of Rachel Portman. You have the right to remain silent..."

She went unresisting. Booking her, talking to the prosecutor and doing paperwork ate up the rest of the afternoon and a good part of the evening. John surfaced long enough to call his mother, who picked up the kids at their after-school day care and went home with them.

"Make sure they do their homework," he said unnecessarily.

When he was finally free to leave the station, feeling exhausted and somehow dirty, John still had to detour by the inn again to tell Rachel Portman's husband that his mistress was under arrest for having murdered his wife.

Portman reeled and, apparently voiceless, nodded. His eyes had a curiously blank look that John had seen before: shock and grief mixed with deep wounds dealt by the knowledge of his own culpability.

"Can I call someone for you, Mr. Portman?"

A man appeared behind him. "I'm Ralph's brother, Detective."

"Ah. Good." John watched as one of Port Dare's most prominent businessmen stumbled away. "Keep an eye on him."

"Yes." They shook hands. "I can't believe..."

Nobody ever could. John wondered if Ralph Portman would ever be able to forgive himself.

He surfaced from his brooding to realize he was driving to Natalie's house, not home. It was eight-thirty in the evening. Would she mind?

She came to the door in a pair of leggings and a baggy sweater, her hair loose and her feet bare. "John!"

"Can I come in?"

"Of course you can!" She backed up. "Is something wrong?"

"No. I just arrested..." Hell, it would be spread over the papers tomorrow. He'd already talked to a reporter from the *Sentinel* himself. "I arrested Ralph Portman's girlfriend. She apparently had more permanent arrangements in mind."

Natalie gasped. "She killed his wife? Herself?"

"All by her lonesome." He moved his shoulders restlessly.

Debbie had hated it when she knew he came home straight from a murder scene or an arrest. "I wonder what you've been touching," she had said with a shudder, eyeing his hands as if they dripped blood, as if he might smear it on her if he touched her.

Shaking away the memory, John asked, "Can we talk about something else?"

Natalie's face held quick compassion. "Of course we can. Let's go sit down. Do you want a cup of coffee? Did you have dinner?"

Dinner? He looked blankly at her. He knew he'd skipped lunch. He hadn't even been aware of dinner-time passing.

"It's not food I want," he said in a voice that sounded odd even to his ears. "Will you come here?"

She gave him a searching look but came, accepting his need to hold her in a bruisingly tight grip. He laid his cheek against her head and breathed in a flowery scent that made him picture a tropical scene: gaudy flowers and a waterfall and luxuriant vegetation. Hawaii, maybe.

She felt so damned good against him, the swell of breasts and the hair that spilled over his hands and the length of her thighs against his. She was taut in the right places, soft in the others, begging his hands to cup her buttocks and lift her.

He groaned and tugged at her hair. Natalie tipped her face up willingly and met his mouth with a fierce passion that told him she had ached these past nights for him just as he had for her.

He kissed her as if he were a starving man offered the staff of life. He wanted to block out the memory of Rachel Portman's bloody, naked body, of the vicious selfishness he'd seen, of the torment her husband would live with forever. Natalie was goodness, decency, a warm, welcoming sexuality. Plundering her mouth, he prayed she wouldn't imagine blood on his hands.

He lifted his head and said hoarsely, "I need you."

"Yes." She pressed her open mouth to his throat and murmured. "Let's go downstairs. To the guest room. So there's no ghost."

"No ghost," he agreed, and let her tug him with her.

The room was feminine, with butterflies on the wallpaper and pale blue carpet and a puffy chenille-covered comforter on a double bed. His feet would hang over.

He didn't give a damn.

Making love to her tonight was all sensation. John didn't let himself think, only feel. He skimmed the

sweater over her head to find her braless, her breasts
plump and white, the nipples puckered already. His
blood thickened and he groaned, a primal sound.
Those breasts in his hands, in his mouth, sent undi-
luted pleasure to his groin. There should be words—
but he couldn't let himself think what they should be.
She seemed not to mind, giving small gasps and mur-
murs he couldn't make out, her breath coming quickly
between parted lips, her fingernails biting into his
shoulders as he suckled her breast.

Perversely, he took his time, when all he wanted
was to bury himself in her slick warmth. She made
love to him even as he did to her, unbuttoning his
shirt so that her mouth could move hotly over his
chest, her tongue flicking the nubs of his nipples, her
fingers tracing muscles that hardened at her touch.
She tossed his tie aside and tugged his shirt from his
waistband, pushing it off his shoulders.

Into the fog of sexual hunger came the realization
that he wore a gun. Drawing ragged breaths, he pulled
back long enough to unhook the holster from his belt
and toss it aside. He tried to do it unobtrusively. The
sight of it would have killed Debbie's interest in sex.
But Natalie only reached for his belt buckle and he
groaned and pressed one of her hands to his erection.

When he kicked off his pants, he had just the presence of mind to apply protection—he'd been carrying
a condom in his wallet since the moment she'd
packed her bags. Their legs tangled, they fell onto the
bed, sinking into the thick comforter. John wrestled
his way to the top, holding back as he explored her
belly and the nest of curls and her long white thighs.
He kissed a scar on her knee, her anklebone, her
curled toes. When he moved above her, she waited

with parted legs and open arms, the welcome he'd so desperately needed. He sank home, muffling a guttural shout in the smooth skin of her throat. Her spasms tore the bonds of his restraint, and he emptied himself inside her, finding relief and oblivion.

He must have slept briefly, John realized when he surfaced. The overhead light was still on, and Natalie was curled against him, her lips parted, her breath even. He looked with pleasure at silky, pale limbs and the swell of her hip and breasts. Her dark hair tumbled across the pillow and his arm and partially hid one breast. He was getting hard again when his gaze intersected his watch.

Damn! It was nine-thirty.

He showed his teeth in a silent grimace. His mother was still with the kids after patiently spending most of her weekend with them and making sure each got to their Saturday soccer games. He'd imposed enough. He had to go.

John eased away from Natalie, watching regretfully as she stretched, murmured, sighed and snuggled into the comforter. He gently tucked it around her for warmth. He got dressed, returned the holster to the small of his back and stood above Natalie for a long moment, aching to climb back in with her and to hell with his mother and kids.

What would Natalie think when she woke up and he was gone? That he'd come for a quickie and fled into the night? He could leave her a note—but that almost seemed worse. "Thanks, I'll call," was insulting.

He couldn't remember the last time they'd talked. Really talked. After they made love the first time, life had closed in. Kids, family, work. Had she been glad to escape his house? She was nice to Maddie and Evan, but they weren't hers. Given a taste of his messy life, had she concluded she didn't want to share it?

Did she guess that he *wanted* her to share it? He sure as hell hadn't said so. And tonight, he wasn't sure he'd spoken ten words. He couldn't remember what he had or hadn't said, except, *I need you.*

He swallowed, remembering the way she had walked unhesitatingly into his arms in response.

''I love you,'' he said softly, but she slept on.

He made himself back away, step by step, until he bumped against the door frame. With one last, hungry look, he turned off the light and left, resetting her alarm system on his way out the front door.

They had to talk. She knew the burdens he carried. When he said *Marry me,* her answer would tell him whether she was willing to carry them with him.

The fact that he had no idea whether that answer would be yes or no scared him to death.

CHAPTER FOURTEEN

NATALIE AWAKENED in the middle of the night, cold. She groped for her bedding and encountered an unfamiliar texture. For a moment she went completely still as she struggled with her disorientation to remember where she was. In the pitch-dark, no digital clock offered a green glow. Her exploring fingers found a fluffy fabric covering the thick comforter.

At the same instant that she realized she was naked, Natalie remembered. Hesitantly she reached beside her and found no one. John was gone.

Finally she sat up and turned on the lamp, comforter clutched to her breast. No note, either, unless he'd left one upstairs. He must have covered her, or she wouldn't have slept this long—her internal clock told her it was the middle of the night. Since she'd also been lying atop the comforter, it was no wonder she'd eventually found her way out from under the fold he had laid over her.

She thought about going back to sleep here, but it felt so strange. And she might oversleep without her alarm clock. Eventually she pulled her baggy sweater on, turned out the lamp and made her way upstairs, turning lights on and off as she went. The neighbors would wonder, if any were awake to note her procession through the house.

Sasha sat in the middle of Natalie's bedroom floor,

eyeing her critically. The cat's cool stare made Natalie feel like some kind of floozy, creeping home in the middle of the night.

"I love him," she told the black cat, who wasn't impressed.

She brushed her teeth and her hair and slipped between cold sheets on her side of the bed. She lay very still, reaching out with her senses, wondering, if there were such a thing as a ghost, whether Stuart would be one. Did his hidden, ill-gotten money constitute the unfinished business they always said kept a soul restless?

But she had never seem him except in her memory and didn't now.

Which left her free to speculate about John. He did have children. She wasn't bothered that he'd had to slip away tonight. If only it didn't feel just a little sordid, having a man arrive at eight-thirty at night, not want to talk or even have a cup of coffee, only to have sex, then sneak out while she slept.

Would he call tomorrow?

Undoubtedly—he was gentleman enough to do at least that much. But Natalie dreaded the idea of another stilted conversation that left her lonelier than if he'd never phoned.

He wanted her, at least, and she was grateful for that much. He had seemed truly desperate for her tonight. For an instant she wondered if he had just been hungry for life-affirming sex, or for her in particular, but in her heart she knew better. All she had to do was remember the look in his eyes as he said, "I need you."

But as what? An occasional lover? A friend?

He had let her pack and leave his house with no

more than, it seemed, token arguments. He appeared often on the verge of saying things to her and then stopping himself, as if he had inner conflict. Why? she worried. Was he sorry he had ever touched her? Did he like her but not love her? Was he completely uninterested in remarrying, considering the obligation he still felt to Debbie? Or had Natalie herself frightened him, with her admitted inability to let anyone close?

She punched her pillow.

And would she be able to ask him any of these questions? Or would she, uncomfortable with emotional intimacy, be a polite, pleasant acquaintance on the phone tomorrow?

In other words, a coward?

How had it happened that they made soul-searing, glorious love but could no longer talk like the friends they'd been this past year? Why did the one mean the loss of the other?

Staring into the darkness, Natalie wondered unhappily why she couldn't have lover and friend both.

JOHN LOOKED at the telephone a dozen times that morning and thought of calling Natalie at work. But he had people wandering by his desk, and she probably did, too, assuming she was even at it. What kind of conversation would they have? He could just hear it. *How are you? Fine. And you? Did you, um, sleep well?*

He couldn't say, *You have no idea how much it meant to me when you accepted me without questions last night. When you wanted me as desperately as I wanted you.* Or, *Can you live with me, my kids and my ex-wife?*

John swore under his breath. That sounded twisted. Think of a better way to put it. *When my ex-wife calls, I have to go running.* Oh, yeah. That was really calculated to make a woman swoon with delight at the bargain she was getting. Two school-age kids, a husband who was a cop—she'd have already learned from Stuart the erratic hours and gruesome nature of the job—and a financial and emotional obligation to an invalid ex.

Put that way, he figured he might as well save his breath. Let her find a better deal.

Bleakness swept over him as he had a flash of her walking down the aisle toward another man.

One way or the other, Natalie had figured as part of his future for a long time now. It wouldn't be just the vital, loving woman he'd held in his arms last night who he would lose, but also the one person to whom he'd been able to talk about his fears and frustrations and losses.

His desk phone rang and he answered automatically, although his mind was still on Natalie. Did he have a chance with her?

"John?" his ex-wife said in her small, breathless voice.

His attention snapped into focus. "Debbie. What's up?"

"I haven't gotten my alimony check," she said timidly. "I was just wondering…"

"Jeez." He pinched the bridge of his nose. "I've been caught up in a couple of cases at work and I haven't paid my bills yet. I'm sorry. I'll get it off tomorrow."

"That's all right. I just thought…was afraid…" Tears threatened. She cried easily these days.

He couldn't blame her. "You don't have to worry. I'm not going to cut you off, I promise."

She drew a deep, shaky breath. "I'm sorry. I have too much time to worry, I guess."

Something drove John to say, "You know, I used to think about putting an addition on the house. An apartment for you, so you could see the kids all the time, be involved in their lives." He was regretting his big mouth even before he finished. What? Did he *want* to sabotage his chances with Natalie? He finished uncomfortably, "I always figured you'd say no."

"Of course I would have! Who would take care of me?" she said with sharp fear. "You're never home. I couldn't count on you. You don't understand my limitations."

"I do understand them," he said, forcing himself to be patient. He swung his chair around so that his back was to a scuffle on the other side of the squad room. "I know you'd need round-the-clock nursing care." With genuine puzzlement, he asked, "Wouldn't you like to be closer to the kids?"

"No!" she cried. He heard her tears. "No. I feel safe here. I miss them, you know I do. Sometime, when I'm in remission…but right now, I need my parents. When I call them, they're always there."

Unlike you, was the subtext. *You were never there.*

"What about a nursing home here in Port Dare?" They'd had this discussion before, but he had to try again. "Your parents could drive up a couple of times a week. It sounds like it would be good for you and Maddie and Evan if you were closer."

"What's wrong?" she asked meanly. "Are you needing someone to watch them after school?"

He never had liked this woman. John shook his head. Okay, he could live with her self-pity—he might have felt the same way dealt her cards. He hoped he would have hidden it better, especially around their children, but he could understand it.

What he didn't get was her fear of life. Fact: she had a cruel disease. But why not try to do as much as she could? It was as if she'd crawled back, if not into the womb, at least as close as she could get. She was a little girl again, and as selfish as one. She wept over Maddie and Evan, but she always thought of herself first.

He had done his best by her, but she could never resist jabs. *I couldn't count on you.*

"I don't need you for day care. You know better than that," he said evenly. "I was thinking of you."

"That's what you always say!"

He had a bad taste in his mouth. "And you just can't believe it?"

"Why didn't you think of me when we were married?"

It was a blow to the gut, considering he was thinking of asking another woman to marry him. Reeling from it, he asked, "Was I really such a bad husband?"

Debbie sniffled. "No! No, of course you weren't!"

Unkindly he figured she'd just remembered which side her bread was buttered on.

"There was just always something more important."

He glared at a sergeant trying to drop something on his desk. "You mean, my job," he said into the phone.

The sergeant retreated with his sheaf of papers.

"Yes!" Debbie exclaimed. "Do you have any idea how many dinners I threw away? How many times I cried, because you didn't come home when you'd promised to?"

"You know I can't walk away from an accident on the highway or a crime scene because it's dinnertime."

"You could have changed jobs. If you didn't have other family, I would be so frightened for Maddie and Evan. Do you ever make it to parent conferences, or…or…?"

She didn't even know what he *should* be making it to, because she hadn't paid enough attention when they talked.

"Yeah," he said. "I make it. When I can. They understand when I can't."

"Do they?" she said starkly.

Another blow, but he recovered from this one more quickly. His kids were pretty damned well adjusted given their mother's situation, if he did say so himself. They didn't seem to feel a speck of doubt about his love. They needed reassurance, sure. Kids did. They didn't need him to prove it constantly by sacrificing little bits of himself.

He gave a grunt that might have been a laugh if it had held any humor. "You don't miss me at all, do you?"

She was silent for a moment, then chose to answer indirectly. "We should never have married."

"No," he said. "We shouldn't have."

"I'm sorry," she said suddenly, wretchedly. "I blame you, but I wasn't the right wife for you, either."

"Will it bother you if I remarry?" He felt surprised

that he'd been driven to ask. It wasn't as if he could make choices based on what bothered his ex. Hell, everything bothered her.

In fact, he anticipated a sharp, self-pitying come-back. Instead, after a brief pause, his ex-wife said quietly, "No. I only wish I had the chance…"

"You'll get better," he said heartily.

"Maybe. For a little while at a time." For a moment she sounded very adult, a woman instead of a sad child. "But it would be good for Maddie and Evan to have the kind of mother I'll never be."

Stunned at her utter selflessness, he was ashamed of his earlier assessment of her character.

"If they forget me, I'll understand," she added softly, a small sniff adding to the martyrish tone.

He gave a reluctant grin at her return to form. "I won't let 'em."

She didn't ask who he was considering marrying, either from lack of interest or because the idea was mildly disturbing. He was just as glad.

John renewed his promise to send the check, reminded her that this was their Sunday to visit, and they said goodbye.

He looked at the phone and thought again of calling Natalie, but it was almost time for the press conference about the Portman murder, and the desk sergeant was circling for another try.

Later.

"Later" meant picking up his kids from after-school care. Maddie was distraught because she hadn't turned in a homework assignment that day, and she'd told Grandma last night she didn't *have* any homework, which meant she'd been able to watch TV.

"Grandma will think I was lying, but I wasn't!"
Her face was turning red. "I forgot! And Miss Miller
looked so…" She hesitated.

"Disappointed in you?"

"Yes!" Tears began to spurt.

"Well, you know what you'll be doing this evening." John glanced in the rearview mirror. Evan was
falling asleep, his cheek against the car window. It
was rare for him to need a nap anymore. "He okay?"
he asked Maddie, nodding over his shoulder.

Wiping her tears, she frowned toward her brother.
"Well…he was kinda quiet at day care. Jenny asked
if he was all right."

The teachers hadn't said anything to John. Talking
quietly to Maddie about why she hadn't kept her assignment sheet up-to-date, he parked at home and
went around to wake Evan and help him unbuckle.

He could tell the minute he opened the car door
that his son had a fever.

Evan came awake sluggishly, but when he did, his
eyes popped open. "Dad." He struggled against the
seat belt, his voice urgent. "I don't feel so good."

John got the belt unsnapped and pulled the boy out
of his booster seat and the car just in time. He threw
up his lunch on the driveway, just missing John's
shoes.

"Eew!" Maddie screeched, jumping back.

That was pretty much John's sentiment. But he was
the grown-up, so he got to clean Evan up, take his
temp and put him to bed with a bowl, then go out
and hose off the driveway.

Washing his hands at the kitchen sink, he said,
"Go see how your brother is. I'll figure something
out for dinner."

"I don't want to go near *him*."

John reached for a hand towel. "He kept you company when you had chicken pox."

"That's 'cause you wanted him to get them, too." She sighed melodramatically. "I sat with him on the day care bus. So it's probably too late anyway."

"Yup." John opened the refrigerator and scanned the contents. "Unless this virus is something you've already had."

She brightened. "You think?"

"We can hope." He popped the Tupperware top and scrutinized some leftovers his mother had deemed still edible. Another eew. Disposal fodder.

Maddie trudged out. John found a couple of microwave dinners in the freezer and a bag of frozen peas. His daughter would be perfectly happy. To think he had actually considered calling Natalie and suggesting they all go out to dinner. Here was another example of the thrills and chills she'd be taking on if she agreed to become Natalie McLean.

John had no sooner gobbled his microwave pasta than Evan threw up again. John took the opportunity to give him some liquid acetaminophen in hopes it would stay down long enough to make him feel better, which, miracle of miracles, it seemed to do. A slow, easy back rub and a few stories read aloud, and the five-year-old fell into a heavy sleep. John inspected Maddie's belated social studies project—a cardboard colonial church with steeple that would be the centerpiece of the village she'd be making during the next week—and sent her off to take a bath and get ready for bed.

Not until she was tucked in could he reach for the phone.

"Hey," he said quietly, when Natalie answered. "What's up, Sleeping Beauty?"

"Why didn't you kiss me awake?" she countered.

"You looked so peaceful. And sexy," he added, leaning back against the tiled edge to the kitchen countertop.

She didn't react to the addendum. "Did you have to get home to your kids?"

"Yeah. I'd called Mom to pick them up at day care."

"Oh."

He hated the awkwardness of the silence and the knowledge that she didn't know what to say. That *he* had destroyed the ease between them.

"I wanted to stay," he said. "But I didn't like the idea of having to call home and tell my mommy where I was."

He almost heard her shudder. "Heaven forbid. I already wonder what she thinks about me. The way I keep popping up at your breakfast table."

"Mom called you 'a nice young woman' last week. In the midst of chewing me out for failing to catch your bad guy."

"Oh, dear. I'm sorry you got a lecture because of me."

"But she does like you."

"I'm glad." Natalie sounded slightly wary.

"Damn, I wanted to see you tonight," he said explosively. "I can't tell what you're thinking when we're talking on the phone."

"My thoughts aren't that mysterious." But that hint of aloofness clung to her voice.

"No? Then what are you thinking right now?" John challenged.

Only the smallest hesitation preceded her saying, "That I wish I could see you, too. For the same reason. Because..." She stopped so fast he could almost hear the screech of brakes.

"Because?" Cordless phone to his ear, John paced across the kitchen and back. "Come on, Natalie. We've been honest with each other. Let's not stop now."

"Have we been?" She gave a small sigh. "Okay. I'm thinking that you might have called tonight just because you're a gentleman. Sneaking out in the middle of the night isn't your style."

He closed his eyes. "Having affairs isn't my style at all. You must know that's not what's going on here, Natalie."

"Then...then what *is* going on?" Pride mingled with anger—or was it fear?—in the question. "You wanted to see me tonight. Why aren't we together?"

"Evan's sick," he said bluntly. "He puked all over the driveway. I was going to call and suggest we all go out to dinner together. Not exactly a romantic date, I realize, but at least we could have talked. Instead, I took his temp, got some meds down to lower his fever, gave him a back rub, and lent my artistic aid to Maddie's social studies project, which was building a colonial era church out of cardboard." *My life in a nutshell,* he thought.

She was silent for a moment. "I know how busy you are, John. I shouldn't have even said that."

With an edge, he said, "You mean, what a goddamned mess my life is, don't you?"

"Mess?" For all the world, Natalie sounded genuinely startled. "You've got a beautiful home, a job you seem to love, incredible kids, and a great extended family. Where's the mess?''

He tamped down on soaring hope. ''Debbie…''

''Debbie?''

''You know I still feel an obligation to her.''

''Of course you do.'' Faint surprise infused her ready agreement. ''She's Maddie and Evan's mother.'' Then her tone abruptly changed. ''Oh. Are you trying to tell me you won't get seriously involved with anyone because you feel too much tied to her? If so, it's really not necessary—''

''No!'' He swore. ''No.''

''Then what?'' she asked.

He ached again to see her mobile expressions, the way her eyes darkened with emotion, the softening of her mouth just before she smiled.

''We should be having this discussion face-to-face.''

''But then,'' she pointed out tartly, ''the only time we've been face-to-face since I left your house was last night.''

He grimaced. ''And I said I didn't want to talk.''

''That was one of the things you said.''

''I need you. I meant that.''

''Yes. I noticed.''

He rubbed the back of his neck. ''Not just physically.'' His voice had roughened. ''Even last night, it was complicated. I wanted you, but mostly I needed your arms around me.''

After a moment, she said softly, ''I'm glad you came over.'' Another small silence. ''I don't think Stuart ever needed me.''

''Like I said, he was an idiot.''

Then she irked the hell out of him by saying

lightly, and not for the first time, "You're good for my ego." This seemed to be her standard line to put him at a distance by implying they were indulging in no more than a frivolous flirtation.

"Is that all I'm good for?" he asked grimly.

Tension quivered in this silence. "No." She spoke quietly. "You're good for me in every way."

Eyes closed, he leaned his forehead against the pantry door. "I love you."

Her breath rushed out, as if he'd winded her. "John?"

He unclenched his teeth. "I shouldn't have said that. Not like this. You don't have to reciprocate. I just wanted you to know. To be thinking about it. About me."

She made a sound. Was she crying? But, no. Incredulous, John realized she was laughing with an edge of hysteria.

"That was funny?"

"No, I…" She hiccuped, then giggled again. "Oh, dear. I'm sorry!"

John straightened and glared at the empty kitchen. Stiffly he said, "I'm glad I didn't show up at your door with a ring and red roses. If you think this is funny…"

"But that's just it!" Abruptly she sobered. "It's the fact that…maybe this is the only way we *can* talk. On the phone, when we can't see each other. Lately, we've been so constrained in person."

"I had a hell of a time keeping my hands off you, you know."

"But even after…"

"And then I was afraid I'd blown it. You wouldn't

meet my eyes, you wouldn't talk to *me*. I thought I'd lost your friendship.''

In a near whisper, she said, "And I thought the same.''

"I've never had a lover who was my best friend.''

"Me, either.'' Her voice became even more tremulous. "Maybe that's what love is.''

He stared out the dark window. "I miss you.''

"I have been so lonely,'' Natalie said in a rush. "I've missed you, and the kids, and...'' She broke off, her voice changed. "But then I can't help thinking that we've always been better friends on the phone than in person. Maybe we do best when we're sort of anonymous to each other. Without any attraction complicating things. And that scares me, because talking to you like this isn't enough anymore.''

"It doesn't have to be! I love it when I'm with you.'' John swore. From upstairs, Evan was calling him, in a high, panicky voice. "Damn. I've got to go. Evan's awake, and I think he must be sick to his stomach again.''

"Oh, no!'' Natalie said quickly. "I wanted to tell you something I've been thinking about Stuart.''

Taking the stairs two at a time, John didn't care about her ex-husband.

In a hurry, she said, "It's that...the only thing he bought was Foxfire. I thought he was trying to say he was sorry, or to tell me he cared. But he didn't.''

"Oh, damn!'' Even with only the light from the hall, John could see that poor Evan had thrown up all over himself and the bed.

Trying to pull his pajamas away from himself, looking so little and miserable it about broke John's heart, Evan sat in the middle of the mess crying. "I couldn't find the bowl!"

"Big guy, it's okay." John crossed the dark room and flicked on the small bedside lamp. "Hey, don't worry. We'll get you cleaned up in no time." He laid a hand on the boy's forehead, which nearly scorched him. God. Should he call the doctor? Straightening, John said into the phone, "Natalie, I've got to go. Evan's fever has skyrocketed."

"Oh, no. Okay. It's just…I was wondering if Foxfire could possibly be…" She let out a whooshing breath. "Oh, never mind. It can wait. And it's probably a wild idea anyway. Tell Evan I wish I could give him a hug. And I'll talk to you tomorrow."

"Tomorrow," he promised, and then, "Love you," but he wasn't sure she hadn't already hung up.

It was well over an hour before he'd bathed his son, changed the sheets and tucked him in.

"Don't go away, Daddy," the five-year-old begged.

John smoothed wet hair back from his hot face. "I won't go anywhere," he murmured. "You try to sleep, and I'll be here when you wake up. I promise."

He sat beside him, cooling his forehead with damp washcloths, watching him at last fall into a heavy slumber. Evan's face was flushed, his movements restless.

It was going to be a long night, John could tell. He'd leave the light on so Evan wouldn't wake up scared. If he lay down beside his son and kept the stainless steel bowl between them, maybe he could snatch a few hours of sleep between bouts. If Evan's fever climbed any more, he would call the hospital. They must have a pediatrician on duty at night.

John pulled an extra quilt over himself and stretched out next to Evan. Sleep was slow coming for him.

Maybe that's what love is.

Yeah. Maybe. If so, he was the luckiest man on earth to have found it. She hadn't said, *I love you,* but he'd swear she meant it. She didn't just miss him, she missed his kids.

He lay there trying to sleep, greedily replaying over and over every word she'd said, every peal of laughter, weighing every hesitation, every nuance.

He heard himself. *I've never had a lover who was my best friend.*

And her voice, as rich and velvety as if she lay beside him, whispering in his ear. *Me, either. Maybe that's what love is.*

He wouldn't think about her worries. Sure they'd always talked more easily on the phone. They'd been attracted to each other, and neither one had wanted to acknowledge it. There'd always been a tension in person that had bothered him. All he had to do was persuade her that it wouldn't be a problem anymore, not now that they didn't have to pretend friendship was all they felt.

It wasn't until the third time Evan awakened, endured dry heaves and finally slept again that John remembered the tail end of the conversation.

The only thing he bought was Foxfire. I thought he was trying to say he was sorry, or that he cared. But he didn't.

Abruptly wide-awake, John listened to what he hadn't let her say.

Her marriage was failing, and she knew it. Clearly Stuart had intended to leave her. But when he'd gotten his hands on big money, what had he done with it? He'd bought his wife an extravagant present.

Why?

What was it she'd said at the end? *I was wondering if Foxfire could possibly be…*

What?

Morning—and answers—seemed an eternity away.

CHAPTER FIFTEEN

HOW DUMB even to have mentioned her crazy idea to John, when she hadn't had a chance to check it out. And it probably *was* crazy.

Sure, horses were sometimes worth half a million dollars or even more. Stuart could have bought one of those, knowing full well that the average person couldn't tell the difference between a National Champion stallion and a nice Arabian. People did keep commenting on how extraordinary Foxfire was. What was it Pam Reynolds had said the other day? She'd implied that the stallion made the ten-thousand-dollar Arabian in the barn look like a plug. Stuart wouldn't have even had to hide the registration papers; *she* wouldn't recognize the name of any top Arabian horse. The breed never received the publicity that Thoroughbreds did, where everyone on the street knew the name of the Kentucky Derby or Breeders' Cup winners.

Stuart could easily have decided in a couple of months that the horse was too much for her. Or pled poverty and admitted that he shouldn't have spent so much. What could she have done?

The idea had been niggling at her for a day or two, with her trying to dismiss it. How silly to think the horse she'd taken trail riding just yesterday was a blue blood worth that kind of money!

If he was, she would lose him. Of course he would have to be sold. Probably he should be, because his value was at stud. But the desolation that gripped her even at thinking of kissing him on his soft muzzle and watching as he was loaded into a trailer was enough to make her reject the notion out of hand.

Foxfire couldn't possibly be more than he seemed.

The trouble was, she knew in her heart that he wasn't. He was exactly what he seemed. She had always known that he was magnificent, ridiculously beyond the kind of horse she'd even dared to dream of owning. He had never quite belonged in Port Dare, Washington.

Now, after hanging up the phone from her conversation with John, Natalie moved restlessly through the house checking locks and wondering how on earth she would ever sleep.

She was torn between exhilaration and depression. He loved her! But only long-distance, it seemed. Or was she being absurd?

Maybe *she* was the one who caused the strain when they were together. A telephone friendship wasn't real. It could be as intimate as she chose, because it didn't have consequences. In person, though, that was different.

But then there had been times when she felt wonderfully comfortable with him. She remembered once when he had been rebuilding her fence. Drinking lemonade, they sat on her tiny deck in the sun. He'd had his back to the house wall, his jean-clad legs stretched out on the planking. Sawdust clung to the denim and to the fine hairs on his powerful forearms. Natalie even remembered what they'd said. Debbie's diagnosis had been followed with shocking rapidity by her move into a nursing home. The kids had just moved in with him, and he'd talked about his shock and guilt. Hours somehow passed. The ice melted in their glasses and the late afternoon sun sank toward the west, casting long shadows.

That wasn't the only time. There had been others. She wished now that she had talked as much as she'd listened. Why had she left him with the illusion that her marriage to Stuart had been perfect? That she felt the grief a widow was supposed to feel?

Had she not wanted to admit her secret shame, the certainty that *she* was to blame for the failure of the marriage, for Stuart's disinterest? Or had she felt safe because John assumed she still loved her dead husband? Did being a widow, with all it implied, give her an excuse not to examine why her heart leaped when she heard John's voice on the phone or knew he was coming over?

Even while she was staying at his house, she admitted, they'd had good talks. That one night, for example, when she was in her bathrobe, or even when she finally did confess what a mistake her marriage had been.

She wished he'd told her in person that he loved her; but then he would have had to wait another day, or two days, or three, depending on how sick Evan was and whether another major case descended on his shoulders. Given a couple of days, she would have been certain he was using her, that he had only had sex with her because she was available.

And now she knew, even if she still wanted to see the truth in his eyes.

Natalie hugged herself and did a quick two-step, her stockinged feet thudding on the kitchen floor.

He loves me!

If only she were still staying at his house. She could have offered to take a shift with Evan. They could have stolen a few kisses in the hall. She could have seen him sleeping, his face younger.

She wanted to stay home tomorrow with Evan, not go to work and wonder how John was coping. She wanted to be entwined in his life.

Would he ask her to marry him? Natalie hugged herself again. *Please, please, let him ask.* Could fate possibly be that kind to her?

Oh, it was going to be a long night.

Her wanderings had brought her to Stuart's study. Natalie stood uneasily in the doorway. She'd come in here this past year because he'd always paid bills here, and so she did. Obedient to the last, she thought ruefully. The records and spare checks and whatnot were all in his ugly desk and the metal filing cabinets. She'd put the manila envelope with Foxfire's registration papers in the cabinet after she'd brought it home on impulse that day from the bank.

She didn't know what looking at them would tell her. Foxfire was only the short form of his name. His full registered name was on them. But how did you research a horse's career?

Perhaps she could call the Arabian Horse Association. They must keep records. Or at least somebody there could tell her how to find out about a particular horse. Couldn't they?

Weighted by the quiet of the house, she went to the filing cabinet and opened the drawer, grabbing the manila envelope. Hairs on her arms stood up. The study was downright creepy. Last night she'd tried to feel Stuart's ghost, but she'd been in the wrong place.

In here, in this room stamped with his personality, he'd left more tangible traces. Or perhaps Stuart wasn't the one haunting the study. A man had, after all, died violently here.

Natalie scuttled into her bedroom. She didn't lock the door. After all, she still had to turn lights out, and it wasn't as though anyone would break in. She just didn't like Stuart's study.

The phone rang as she was pulling the papers from the envelope. Her heart leaped. John might be calling again if Evan had fallen asleep.

"Natalie," Geoff Baxter said. "I hope this isn't too late for you."

She was a little ashamed of her disappointment. Geoff had been a good friend this past year, too.

"No, of course not. I heard about your big arrest yesterday."

"Yeah, that was an ugly one." He paused. "Hey, how are you?"

With her finger, she found Foxfire's registered name: Al Nahr's Foxfire. His dam and sire were listed, as were *their* dams and sires. The dam sounded Polish, and Natalie vaguely recalled that Egyptian and Polish strains had their own distinctive characteristics.

"I'm good," she said in answer to Geoff. She thumbed through the papers, found nothing—like the names of former owners—that seemed helpful. Foxfire was registered in Stuart's name, she'd noticed the day she took the papers from the bank, not hers. "I really appreciate everything you did to try to find out who broke in here."

"We'll catch him yet," he assured her.

"John doesn't sound so sure."

"Ah, hell. He's a half-empty kind of guy. Me, I'm

an optimist. Some son of a bitch knows that money is sitting around somewhere. He'll make another move.''

Anxiety quivered in her. "But he must know you've searched for it.''

He grunted. "What scares me is that he isn't going to believe *you* don't know where it is.'' When she didn't respond immediately, Geoff said, "Oh, hell. I shouldn't have said that. I might be wrong. I'd just feel better if we caught the bastard. Or, at the very least, found the damn drugs or money and publicized the fact that we have.'' He sighed. "You haven't come up with anything, I assume.''

"Actually…'' How crazy would it sound out loud?

"Actually?'' he prompted her, an electric quality of excitement changing the timbre of his voice.

"Well, I did have an idea.'' Okay, she'd sound crazy, but Geoff would appreciate the fact that she was thinking about the problem, at least.

Natalie explained.

"A four-legged animal can be worth that much money?'' He was incredulous. Before she could answer, he said, sounding thoughtful, "Yeah, of course they can be. I know racehorses are. Is that what you're thinking? He won something like the Triple Crown?''

"If he'd won the Triple Crown,'' she told him, "Foxfire would be worth more like thirty million. Arabians don't race—well, they do, but it's smaller time. Mainly, they're showed. I'm thinking…well, even a top ten stallion in the National Championship should be worth quite a bit. It's what people will pay in stud fees that makes them valuable.''

He got right to the point. "How are you going to find out what this horse is worth?"

Natalie picked up the manila envelope and peered inside. "Well, I was thinking that tomorrow..." Her breath caught when she saw that a sheet of manila, probably cut from another envelope, was taped inside. She never would have seen it if she hadn't nearly stuck her nose inside the envelope.

"What are you going to do tomorrow?" Geoff asked with an edge of impatience.

"I...hold on." Natalie set down the phone on the bed so she could use both hands. With her thumbnail she carefully peeled off the tape. It took her a moment to remove enough to see a folded sheet of paper tucked inside. She tugged it out and opened it.

"Natalie?" Geoff's voice was muffled and tiny.

The invoice dropped from her shaking hand. "Oh, my God," she whispered.

"Natalie?"

Staring in dismay at the piece of paper that would take her beloved horse from her, she picked up the phone. "Geoff?"

"You've found something."

"The receipt." Her voice squeaked. "He did, Geoff. He paid over half a million for Foxfire."

"A horse."

"He *used* me," she said bitterly. "No wonder he smirked that way."

"Smirked?"

She was raging now. "It would have served him right if I'd had Foxfire gelded without consulting him! I wish I had! I wish..."

Alarm sharpened Geoff's voice. "You didn't, did you?"

"No." Depression struck. "Oh, I wish I had. Because then he wouldn't be worth that much, and I could keep him."

"Can he be sold for as much?"

"Oh, probably. I don't know. Maybe not. Stuart didn't know anything about horses. Maybe he overpaid. But then…"

"He must have researched this before he bought. He must have been planning it for a long time." Geoff sounded steamed.

"And I was pleased and flattered, and I've loved Foxfire so much—"

He interrupted. "You know John and I are going to need to take a look at those papers and the horse both."

"Yes," she agreed dully.

"Have you said anything to him?"

"No." She'd tried, but he wasn't listening.

"Okay. Here's what we'll do. I'll rouse John in the morning, and we'll meet you at the stables. Better make it early. Eight-thirty. No, damn it. We're supposed to have breakfast with the mayor. Lucky us. Can you get there as early as seven-thirty?"

"I suppose so." John hadn't said anything about the breakfast. Natalie supposed he'd forgotten, as worried as he was about Evan.

"Bring everything with you."

"Yes," she agreed again. Maybe she should burn this envelope. Why hadn't she kept her mouth shut?

Dumb question. Because, if she had, Stuart's missing drug money would have hung over her head forever. At least now they knew. Whoever had killed Ronald Floyd and searched Stuart's study would hear, and she'd be safe.

It wasn't as though Foxfire would be killed, or even hurt. He would be sold back into the world he'd come from, a fancy stable with his own groom and a swimming pool for horses and white-boarded pastures full of shining, dainty mares there just for him. He did like mares.

After saying good-night to Geoff, Natalie turned out the lights, found Sasha and went to bed. For once the cat was willing to cuddle when Natalie needed the company instead of the other way around. Sleep was elusive, however. If her mood had been tumultuous earlier, now it was such a complex jumble, she didn't know if she was happy or sad or angry or all three at once.

Probably all three.

She must have slept, but not enough, because she could hatefully have thrown the alarm clock against the wall when it buzzed at six-fifteen. Heavy eyed, head pounding, she wondered why she'd agreed to an early meeting. Couldn't they have done this later in the day? She could have taken time off from work.

The shower and coffee almost woke her up. Anticipation at seeing John helped. She dressed in slacks, Swedish clogs and a linen-silk blend sweater that draped sublimely, then she made a full turn in front of the mirror to see the effect. Not exactly wear for the stable, but she wouldn't be there long.

She arrived to find that the broad double doors to the main barn were open, which must mean that Pam was about somewhere. A strange pickup and rented horse trailer were parked between the arena and the open doors, so maybe a new horse was arriving. Natalie didn't see either of the plain sedans that the two detectives drove. They had darn well better be here after suggesting this obscene hour of the morning.

Besides, she felt like a teenager about to have a rare chance to see her crush.

She was partway to the barn when Geoff called, "Hey."

He'd just stepped around the rented horse trailer and was looking down with distaste at his shoe. "Damn stinking..." he muttered, scraping it off on the fender.

"Where's John?"

"Huh?" He looked up. "He couldn't make it. Something about one of the kids."

Disappointment descended out of proportion to John's failure to show. "Evan was sick. Oh, dear. I hope it's just the flu."

"Can I take a look at those?" He held out a hand for the envelope.

His perusal was silent and brief. "Stuart's name is on this, not yours."

"No, but that shouldn't be a problem. I'll just need the will to show that I'm his heir."

He grunted. "Will you bring the horse out here?"

Surprised, Natalie said, "Don't you want to see him in his stall? He's...restive on a lead rope."

Geoff was sweating, which struck her as odd considering the crispness of the morning. "I don't really like horses. It's...just a thing I have." His brows lowered. "You won't tell anyone, will you?"

"Of course not."

"I just don't want to go in there."

She glanced down at her polished clogs, crisp black pants and softly draped, peach-colored sweater.

"Maybe I could get Pam."

He'd started to lean against the trailer, but he straightened quickly. "Who?"

"The stable owner. She must be around some-where."

The detective shook his head. "Let's keep this quiet for now, okay? We don't want the world to know what this damn horse is worth. Think of the security issues. And you're a lousy liar. She'll be able to tell you're making up a story about showing the horse to a friend. You can handle him, can't you?"

"Of course I can." Natalie threw up her hands. "Okay, okay."

She didn't spot Pam inside. The barn had that won-derful rich scent of hay and manure and bedding and horse that Natalie had always loved. Heads popped over stall doors as she passed, and soft whickers and jingled halters and the clunk of hooves striking thick wooden walls were the only sounds.

Foxfire was waiting, his call more ringing when he spotted her.

"Hello, beautiful," she said, putting her hands on each side of his head and resting her cheek against his elegant nose.

He tolerated the sentiment only briefly, then shook his head hard, dislodging her. "Silly," she murmured, blinking away tears. "We aren't going for a ride. I wish we were. But I will put you out in the paddock after I show you off." She clicked the braided leather lead rope to his halter and slid the bolts open so that his stall door would slide to the side.

Foxfire danced out and tossed his head so that his glorious mane flew. Usually Natalie cross-tied and saddled him here in the barn. She felt more in com-mand once she was up on his back. But he was on his best manners, following her docilely with only a few wicked snorts aimed at the horses they passed.

The parking area and arena were still deserted at this hour of the morning when she emerged with the fiery chestnut. He, of course, hunched his back and crab-hopped sideways the moment he spotted the strange trailer and man. With difficulty, Natalie clung to the heavy leather lead rope.

Geoff backed up against the trailer.

After letting Foxfire dance in a circle, she tapped his nose, settling him into a showring stance with his rear legs braced back, his neck arched so that his mane foamed over it, and his tail held high.

"Isn't he a beauty?" she asked the detective.

He'd pushed away from the trailer. "Yeah. Yeah. I guess he's something. But—damn!—a horse."

Foxfire bared his teeth and she gazed sternly at him. "Behave yourself," she told him in a low voice. "You're being admired." Over her shoulder, she reminded Geoff, "Nobody guessed."

"And nobody's going to."

Puzzled by his odd choice of words and the rich satisfaction in them, Natalie turned.

And looked into the barrel of Geoff Baxter's gun.

EVAN'S FEVER WAS DOWN by morning, maybe just because it *was* morning, but John felt confident enough to phone his mother.

She hadn't said another word about their conversation at lunch. He'd seen her be nothing but gentle with his son since. Maybe she'd understood more of what he was asking than he'd guessed.

All he wanted for his son was what he'd missed himself. It was beginning to seem that it might not be too late for that much, at least. He hoped so. Hurting her once had been hard enough, and he didn't know if he could do it again.

"I was going shopping with a friend today, but we can change our plans. What time do you need to leave?"

Unease had crawled along his skin like a too-cool breeze ever since he'd awakened. What had Natalie wanted to tell him? Why did he have this gut feeling it was important?

"As soon as possible," he told his mother.

"Lucky for you I'm an early riser," his mother said sternly. "I'll be over in a few minutes. I can have breakfast at your house."

His glance strayed to the kitchen clock. Seventwelve. Too early to call Natalie?

"To hell with it," he muttered, and dialed. Her phone rang four times, and then the answering machine kicked in. "Natalie? Call me when you get this message."

Either she wasn't up, or she was in the shower. What had he expected? For her to be waiting by the phone?

But his disquiet grew as he threw together a lunch for Maddie to take to school and set out her cereal and a glass of orange juice.

Five minutes later, he called again. "Damn it, Natalie, pick the phone up," he growled.

She didn't.

He knew she was an early riser. *Maybe not this early,* John told himself.

When he heard his mother's car crunching on the gravel, he went upstairs to kiss Evan goodbye.

"Grandma's here. She's going to call me if you feel any sicker. Okay?"

The five-year-old eyed him. "Can I watch TV?"

His revived interest was a universal sign of recovery. "Yeah." John tousled his head. "All day long, if you want."

"And Maddie has to go to school," his son said contentedly.

"But she didn't spend the night puking," John pointed out.

He left Evan mulling over whether the luxury of spending the day on the couch watching TV and having Grandma wait on him hand and foot was worth the misery that preceded it.

John gave his mother a few quick instructions and called goodbye to Maddie, who was eating her cereal and reading the back of the carton.

"Thanks, Mom," John said, giving her cheek a rare kiss.

She looked startled but not displeased as he left.

The morning was clear and breezy, ruffling the waters of the strait, which sparkled in the sunlight. He felt hyperalert this morning, like a police academy graduate turned loose for his first solo patrol. He tracked every vehicle within a mile, knew when a pedestrian stepped off the curb to cross the street behind him. Outside of Old Town, the parking lots were deserted in the strip malls, giant retailers and fast-food joints that lined the highway. Urban became country in the blink of an eye. Leaves had turned, painting the foothills with swatches of scarlet and orange and blazing gold amidst the green of cedar and fir.

The season set him to thinking about things besides what Natalie had meant to tell him last night.

Stuart Reed had died just over a year ago. Would Natalie consider that a decent interval? He wanted to marry her now, before November's first dusting of snow. She belonged in his house, in his bed. He might have been patient under other circumstances. But, given Stuart's blood-soaked legacy to her, he wanted to know she was safe. If she were his wife, under his protection, he wouldn't have to worry about her, like he had last night.

The moment he turned the corner onto her street, that worry clutched his chest and wouldn't let go. Her car was missing from her driveway. Barely seven-thirty in the morning, and she was already gone.

He pounded on her door anyway, in case her car was in the shop and she just hadn't mentioned it last night. No answer, no lights left on.

Swearing, he leaped back into his car. Why would she go into work so early? A screwup with an advertisement? But the morning paper was already out; his mother had carried his in. Breakfast with a friend? She hadn't said anything.

Why would she? he thought dourly. She hadn't yet agreed to a November wedding and the requisite requirement of filing daily schedules with each other.

A light turned red ahead for the turn onto the highway. He sat drumming his fingers on the wheel, trying to decide what to do. He didn't even know why he felt so on edge. She wasn't in danger on a bright sunny morning.

I wanted to tell you something I've been thinking about Stuart.

The light turned; traffic slowly started forward.

What if she'd discovered something? He'd cut her off. What the hell else could he have done, with Evan sitting in the middle of his own vomit, crying? But what if she was bursting to tell someone?

What if she'd called Geoff Baxter?

Uttering a vicious profanity, John reached for his cell phone.

Baxter's wife answered. When he asked for her husband, she said in surprise, "Oh, I assumed you two were together. He left early this morning. How early? To tell you the truth, I wasn't even up. It had to be six-thirty or before."

"He didn't say anything about where he was going?"

"No. Only that he'd call later. Is something wrong?" she asked timidly.

"Probably not. We just…crossed our wires."

John didn't like coincidences. Natalie, who had figured something out, had left her house unusually early this morning. As had Baxter, who had bought an RV he couldn't afford within weeks of the murdered drug dealers being found drifting on their boat. John was still waiting for more information on Baxter's finances, but the one purchase had been a red flag he'd learned about only yesterday.

Where were they? Damn it, *where?*

He drove without knowing where he was going. He was thinking hard, trying to remember every word she'd said.

Foxfire is the only thing he bought. I thought he was trying to say he was sorry, or that he cared. But he didn't.

John swore and signaled, pulling onto the shoulder of the highway.

She was right. They should have wondered a whole lot earlier why the only thing her scumbag of a husband had bought was a gift for the wife he intended to leave.

He heard her timid attempt to tell him. *I was wondering if Foxfire could possibly be...*

What?

The answer slotted into place. What she was wondering was whether the horse could possibly be worth one hell of a lot more than they'd thought.

Okay. So she'd told Baxter. Why would he be making a move? They'd have to prove the horse was a walking half mil. They'd need the papers, to make phone calls. Buyers weren't standing on every street corner for an animal worth that kind of money. There wasn't a serious Arabian farm in Port Dare. Why wouldn't Baxter wait?

Because, if he did, he'd lose his money. Once anybody but he and Natalie knew Stuart had sunk the drug money into the horse, it was as good as gone. If he could somehow persuade her to sell Foxfire first...

And then what? Keep her mouth shut.

Fear grabbed John with long white fangs.

Of course Baxter couldn't count on her to stay quiet. He'd have to get her to sign papers selling the horse to him, then dispose of her. Even then, he didn't have a chance. He must know it. But John remembered the increasingly frenzied way he had searched Natalie's house. Maybe Geoff Baxter wasn't thinking straight anymore.

Or maybe he was. What if Natalie's body wasn't found for a while? If he could spirit the damned horse away, then he could take his time finding a buyer. In the normal course of events, with Natalie missing, nobody would give a thought to her horse. If Baxter somehow compelled her to leave a note or even tell the stable owner that she was moving the horse, it wouldn't be until her body was found and a serious investigation began that somebody might question where the Arabian had gone. Even then, who would figure he might be worth serious money?

A harsh sound emerged from John's throat. Okay, he'd just made up a hell of a good story. Probably Natalie was having breakfast with a friend, and Baxter was buying his wife a surprise birthday present.

But John wanted to see the horse with his own two eyes and know that it hadn't been moved.

Then he might even get a laugh out of his own fiction.

CHAPTER SIXTEEN

"I DON'T UNDERSTAND," Natalie said stupidly.

"Half of that dumb animal's price is mine." Geoff Baxter gave an unpleasant laugh. "Now I figure all of it is mine. If Stuart wanted you to have half, he shouldn't have tried to cheat me."

Her hand slackened on the lead, and Foxfire tossed his head so that his mane flew. Heart drumming, Natalie regained a firmer grasp.

"We're friends." *Another dumb thing to say.*

So dumb, he ignored it.

"What was wrong with a bank account?" he asked.

He probably didn't want or expect an answer, but she gave one anyway. "Banks report unusually large deposits."

"If this damn horse broke his leg, it would all be gone."

Horses could be insured, she knew, but she hadn't seen any paperwork to indicate that Stuart had taken out a policy on Foxfire.

Maybe he had enjoyed gambling. No, playing with fire she thought, semihysterically.

"Load the horse," he said.

John, where are you? she thought desperately. If only he could hear her.

She swallowed. "Foxfire doesn't load easily."

His voice rose. "Walk the damned horse into the trailer. Now!"

He wouldn't risk shooting Foxfire, would he? She shortened the lead rope, backing toward the stallion. If she could get on his far side...

"Oh, no, you don't," he said sharply. "Bring him over here."

From the other end of the barn aisle, Pam Reynolds called, "Natalie? Is that you?"

Geoff's gun hand jerked. "Who is that?"

"She owns the stable."

"Tell her you're sorry, you're moving the horse. Tell her you sold him. Just get rid of her."

Natalie said in a low, urgent voice, "She'll want to help load him."

He was sweating, twitchy. "If she sees me, or you say a word to her that you shouldn't, she's dead. Don't think I'd hesitate."

Natalie took a deep breath. "It's me, Pam. Don't worry."

The older woman strode down the sawdust-covered aisle. "You're not dressed for a ride."

"No, I'm..." Foxfire danced sideways. Her arms were beginning to ache from struggling to hold him and she teetered uncomfortably on the clogs. "I meant to call you last night and forgot. I'm taking him to a place over near Stanwood for some training. I'll feel safer riding him once he's had some more schooling."

Pam Reynolds paused before she emerged from the shadowy barn. She sounded taken aback. "But you haven't said anything. I didn't know you were thinking about looking for a trainer."

Natalie stole a look at Geoff, standing so that the

trailer blocked Pam from seeing him. He held the gun pointed right at Natalie's chest. A muscle spasmed beneath one of his eyes.

Don't come out, Natalie begged her friend silently. *Please don't come out.*

Trying to sound careless, she said, "I asked if you were willing to ride him. Since you weren't..."

Pam's face became expressionless. "You did agree to give notice before you take your horse from the stable."

"I'll pay for the month."

Waggling the gun, Geoff mouthed, "Get rid of her."

"If you'll excuse me now," Natalie said. "Foxfire is getting antsy."

Pam started forward. "Let me help you load him."

"No!" Foxfire danced in another circle, rump toward the detective. Natalie thought briefly, wildly, about making a run for it, but the stallion kept going, exposing her to the line of fire. What good would it do, anyway? The farm was deserted but for the two women and the man who would hunt them down and kill them. "No," she said again. "You're upsetting him. I'll do better alone, if I just take my time."

Pam checked. "You're sure?"

"Yes." She couldn't bear it if this nice woman was gunned down in front of her because of Stuart's sins. Because *she* had made such a gross misjudgment of character and her own heart. "Please," she begged.

"If that's what you want." Creases in her forehead made Pam look older. She nodded and vanished into the barn.

"She's gone," Natalie said.

"Good for her." He jerked his head toward the trailer. "Get him in."

She was as good as dead once Foxfire was loaded and she signed—what?—some kind of note selling the horse to Geoffrey Baxter. His only chance at returning to his life with the money was for her to die.

But if she *didn't* load Foxfire, what would he do? She'd seen him already casting nervous glances toward the gravel lane leading from the main road. Other people would be arriving soon, and he knew it. Would he kill her and try to load the horse alone? What did he have to lose at this point? One way or another, he had to get rid of her.

Her mind jumped. Was he really afraid of horses, or had that been an excuse to make her bring the stallion out here?

"I'll try." She grabbed Foxfire's halter and brought the horse's head down to where she could momentarily rest her forehead against his nose. He calmed immediately. She would have said, *Be good,* but she wasn't sure she wanted him to docilely load. Natalie settled for, "I love you."

"Get on with it!" Geoff snapped behind her.

Swallowing dryly, Natalie led an immediately uneasy Foxfire toward the ramp. She had never loaded him, never seen him loaded, had no idea how he felt about travel. He rolled his eyes toward Geoff, showing the whites, and tossed his head again, almost wrenching the lead from her hand.

An idea formed. Could she fake a balk, if Foxfire started up the ramp?

Could she bring herself to use her beloved stallion as a weapon?

What choice did she have? She would not allow herself to be led to her death.

"Okay, sweetie," she murmured. "Let's go."

Her clogs clomped loudly on the wooden ramp. Foxfire shied. Backing up, feeling for footing, she pulled. Real terror grabbed her throat when he started forward. He could clatter up the ramp and be in the trailer in seconds.

He placed one hoof on the ramp, started to put his weight on it, and then thought better of it, yanking back.

Geoff swore and started forward. Foxfire reared.

"What's wrong with the goddamn horse? Isn't he trained?"

She got his feet back on the ground. Patches of sweat were forming on his flanks and his eyes were rolling.

"He doesn't know the trailer and hasn't had any reason to be loaded in one for over a year. Just…just chill!" she finally snapped.

She soothed the stallion with her voice, then tromped loudly on the ramp, creating another panic. Over and over they started, until Foxfire was bracing all four hooves at the least tug on his lead.

The whole time, she was having…flashbacks, maybe. Her life passing before her eyes. Physically she was here, struggling, sweating, seeing the chestnut hair on her slacks and sweater, feeling the ache in her arms and the tearing pain where the lead rope ripped through her palms, knowing she was likely going to die.

On another plane, she saw her stepfather's snarl, heard his cutting voice. "You ungrateful little brat."

Witnessed again Stuart's false modesty and de-

spised him for his vanity. The craggy smile was as
vivid as the dust and the braid lead tearing her hands.
"That's to remind me in low moments that I can do
some good."

And John, always John. His bare back and sweat-
dampened hair as he worked on her house. His tenderness as he talked to Evan last night. His passion-
darkened eyes and his raw voice saying, "I love you.
I've never had a lover who was my best friend."

Please let me live, she prayed. *Let me have this
chance at happiness.*

By this time, Geoff was swearing in a continuous
mumbling litany. Soon she would find out what he'd
do if she didn't—or couldn't—load the horse.

"I'm sorry, I'm sorry," she kept saying. "I'm *trying!*"

And finally, "You're going to have to help me."

She saw the whites of *his* eyes, now, and would
have given a feral smile if she weren't so scared. So
it was true that he didn't like horses. No wonder Stuart had bought one. He could be sure that his "partner" would never come to look at the pretty gift he'd
bought his wife.

"Do you think I'm that damned stupid?" he all but
screamed.

"Well, then what do you suggest?" she yelled
back.

Pam, be listening. Don't come out here. Call 911.

The easygoing, clean-cut cop she'd known was nowhere in evidence. His hair stuck out in tufts and
sweat dripped from his nose and jaw and soaked the
underarms of his sport coat. His eyes were wild, his
gun hand shaking.

"If you try anything stupid, I'll kill you," he said finally, from between gritted teeth. "Anything at all."

"Are you familiar with horses?"

"What difference does it make?"

"You'll have to push," she told him.

He swore, the obscenity losing its impact after the past five minutes—ten minutes? Twenty? She had no idea how much time had elapsed and didn't dare look at her watch.

"Push," he said.

"Yes. I'll pull, you go behind him and just lean your shoulder against his rump and push. I think that will kind of...startle him into going."

His eyes narrowed. "Horses kick."

"If they don't know you're back there." Or if they're in a fever already. "Approach him from the side, so he sees you. That's right," she said as he warily followed her instructions. "Please don't shoot him by accident."

Foxfire rolled his eyes toward the stranger who had been loitering at the edge of this scary scene. Natalie felt his gathering tension.

"Put your hand on his back. Like that," she encouraged, as though they were friends again. "Now, just move slowly around to his rear."

The tail whipped, snapping across Geoff Baxter's face and drawing another profanity from him.

He faced the horse's side, his left hand resting gingerly on Foxfire's sweat-soaked chestnut back. His gun hand dangled, the barrel pointing at the ground.

Forgive me, Foxfire.

As if all her senses were heightened, she was aware of a car turning off the road. Before Geoff could notice, she said hastily, "Okay, *now*. Push!"

As he moved, she yanked hard on the lead, letting it snap as she pulled. The already panicky stallion reared back, then felt the strange man shoving against his hock. Fury and terror bunched in his powerful back and hindquarters. He lashed out viciously.

Geoff fell back with the first kick, startled more than hurt, because he'd been standing too close for the hooves to connect. If he had thrown himself to the side, the rampaging horse would have missed him with the next wild kick.

He didn't. Steel-shod hooves crunched bone as they connected with Geoff's ribs and the arm he'd thrown up to protect himself. A shot cracked and wood splintered on the barn wall.

Dust made the air acrid as a car slid to a stop in the gravel. Natalie was transfixed by the sight of Geoff Baxter, making a horrific, guttural noise, crawling on his hands and knees in the sawdust-strewn dirt toward his gun.

Her nerveless hand dropped the lead rope. Foxfire screamed defiance and fear, bucked one more time and raced away with the leather lead flying.

Natalie sank onto the wooden ramp and watched as John McLean kicked the gun away and arrested his friend and partner.

"HOW DID YOU KNOW to come?" she asked.

She sat on the closed toilet seat in his bathroom. Crouched in front of her, John was smoothing ointment on her raw palms and reaching for a roll of gauze on the bathroom counter.

He grimaced. "You told me enough. I felt like an idiot once I thought it through. You were right. Why didn't we look at the one large expenditure we knew

Stuart had made? Especially since, given what we knew about him, it was an odd one.''

"Maybe because you didn't know it was an odd one until I admitted that our marriage had been falling apart. I should have been honest sooner.''

He squeezed her knee, his eyes vivid. "You couldn't know. How could either of us?'' He made a rough sound in his throat. "Two friends. Men I'd worked with, thought I knew inside and out. And both of them were willing to kill for money.''

Natalie had heard part of Geoff's justifications.

"We got two scumbags off the streets for good.'' Even as he was being strapped to a gurney and loaded into the ambulance that had arrived within minutes of John's call, Det. Baxter had been pleading for understanding. "What's so goddamn bad about that? So we sold the drugs. It would have hit the streets if we hadn't been there. Don't you ever want a life you can't buy with our poor excuse for a salary?''

Rage had twisted John's face, and he'd bent to look into the back of the ambulance, voice low and furious. "You would have killed Natalie so you could have some luxuries. What's so goddamn bad about that? I'll tell you...''

The two uniformed officers had pulled him back before he got his hands on Geoff again.

"What was it he wanted?'' she asked now.

"Nothing so big. That's the sad part.'' John tucked the end of the gauze bandage in and sank back on his heels. "Right after he and Stuart did the drug dealers, Geoff bought an RV. I, uh, did a financial check on him.'' He shook his head. "I didn't want to believe it. I didn't even want to put the idea in your head that he might have gone bad, so you'd look at him differently. But try as I might to deny the possibility, I couldn't help remembering that he and Stuart were partners when it happened. And damned if Baxter hadn't made the one big purchase. I don't know why the bank gave him the loan on his salary. It looks like the bank was about ready to take the RV back.''

"But Linda also had her hours cut at work this past year," Natalie remembered.

John grunted. "Maybe they could have made the payments if Linda had kept working full-time. He must have convinced her that they could. The financial picture alone, at least as much as I've discovered so far, wasn't enough to do more than make me uneasy.''

"Did he say why he killed Ronald Floyd?"

"As an excuse to search your house. Floyd was nothing to him. Another scumbag to get rid of, I guess. A fly to be swatted.''

Natalie bit her lip. "Poor Linda."

"Yeah. It's going to be a shock. I should go see her tonight.''

"Do you want me to come?"

Creases formed on his brow. "Would you?"

"Hey, she and I are in the same boat, aren't we? The shamed wives of crooks.''

He caught her wrapped hands loosely. "You don't have any reason to feel shame.''

"I was an idiot."

"No more than I was, or any of Stuart's friends."

Was it true? she wondered, feeling a peculiar little lift. Stuart Reed had fooled plenty of people besides herself. She actually hadn't known him as long as the men he'd worked with in the Port Dare P.D.

"Okay." She smiled. "*We're* idiots."

His face changed, the blue of his eyes becoming electric. "Idiots in love."

"Past or present?" she whispered.

"Oh, definitely past." His voice caressed her. "Live and learn. I know what I want now."

Natalie found it hard to breathe. "What's that?"

"You," he said simply. "Friend and lover."

"You really do mean that," she said in wonder.

"Oh, yeah." His thumbs made small circles on the backs of her wrists. "Have you figured out what *you* want?"

The time for timidity was past. "You," she said, with equal simplicity and grateful awareness of the echo. "Friend and lover."

Relief flooded his face before he shuttered it.

"You didn't know that?" Natalie asked in amazement.

"I wasn't sure."

"I've been in love with you for a long time. I just never let myself see. Maybe because I'd been so dumb about Stuart, I didn't trust my feelings. Or maybe because you were his friend, and I was always sure you were taking care of me for his sake."

"Thus the cookies," he said dryly.

She felt herself blushing, but nodded.

His voice changed, became harsh. "Do you know how scared I was this morning when I got over to your place and you were gone?"

"I thought I was meeting you." She explained that Geoff had said he'd call John, and about his lies when she arrived. "Since I knew Evan was sick, I believed him right away."

"Why wouldn't you have, since I was stupid

enough not to tell you my suspicions?" His mouth twisted. "He would have had to kill you, you know."

Mute, she nodded.

"It would have been my fault." Muscles knotted in his jaw. "I couldn't have lived with that."

"Of course you would have," she said firmly. "You have Evan and Maddie."

"*And* my mother, *and* two brothers..."

In fact, his mother was still here, and Connor was in the kitchen with her. Maddie was still at school, but Evan was watching TV in the family room. Natalie was pretty sure the packed house explained why she and John still lurked in the bathroom.

"You're not used to family hanging around," he said.

"No, but I like it." She smiled shakily. "I like them. All of them."

He swore, his hands tightening momentarily on hers before she winced and he instantly loosened his grip. "Natalie, you deserve roses and candlelight and the diamond ring I don't have, but I can't seem to make myself wait."

Her heart drummed, and her eyes burned. She couldn't cry. Not now.

"Wait?" she squeaked.

He glanced around, seeming to become aware of their surroundings. A Mickey Mouse towel hung over the shower door, and a toy submarine and a rubber shark jostled for space in a basket with a mermaid doll and pink and purple star-shaped soaps.

"At least I seem to be on my knees. I know how to do that much right."

"You've done more than that right." She had to

clear her throat. "I couldn't have survived this past year without you."

"You'd have survived today, though. You're a gutsy lady."

"You'd have still been in time, even if Foxfire hadn't decided to defend my life and honor." She smiled despite the threatening tears of emotion. "Or, more accurately, that he was definitely *not* getting into that trailer."

John's grin answered hers. "Not with some jerk shoving on his rump, anyway."

Pam and Natalie had managed to catch Foxfire, but not before he tore up and down a fence line trumpeting his presence to the grazing mares. Uninjured, he had been enjoying a special mash when Natalie left him.

Remembrance dimmed some of her joy. "I'll have to sell him, won't I?"

"Foxfire?" He looked surprised. "Assuming anybody can prove that Foxfire was bought with stolen money. It's not like anyone's putting in a claim. What you get for him would go to the victim's fund."

"He was bought with money from selling heroin. It *should* go to the victim's fund."

"Here's a suggestion." John bowed his head and kissed one of her bandaged palms. "What if we cut a deal where you put him up for stud, and the money you earn pays off what Stuart stole? I'm guessing they'd go for that."

"I...maybe." He'd given her hope. No, more than that. He'd said *we*. "We can try," she agreed. "Thank you."

"Now, can I get on with this proposal, before Evan decides he needs to use this bathroom?"

She could just picture it: John mid-proposal, his son throwing up in the toilet, John's mother hurrying to be sure he was all right, and Connor hanging out in the hall with laughter in his eyes at his brother's ineptitude.

She nodded vigorously.

"Natalie, you know cops make lousy husbands. We work bad hours, we're unreliable, we're..."

"Heroes," she finished.

"On rare occasions. Mostly, we push paper around our desks and write reports that will bore lawyers, judges and prosecutors."

Natalie studied his face, eyes that showed weariness and anguish as often as amusement and tenderness, premature creases in his forehead, jaw unshaven because he'd hurried to her rescue. "I don't mind the hours," she assured him.

"I have kids."

"I know."

"Obligations."

"I know that, too."

His gaze was dark and intense, his voice low and hoarse. "Since the day I brought you home, I've known you belong in my house, my bed, my heart. I don't like waking up and realizing you're not here."

Her own heart was near to bursting, her eyes to overflowing.

"Will you marry me?" he asked.

Tears ran down her cheeks as she laughed and exclaimed, "Of course I will!"

At the exact same moment, the doorknob rattled. "Da-ad!" a five-year-old complained.

"Use the downstairs bathroom," Dad said, just before he kissed his friend and lover and wife-to-be.

Who, grateful for his foresight in locking the bathroom door, flung her arms around his neck and kissed him back with complete trust and happiness greater than she had known possible.

* * * * *

*This isn't the end of
the McLean brothers.
Watch for Connor's story—*

THE WORD OF A CHILD

*—coming in September 2001
from Harlequin Superromance.*

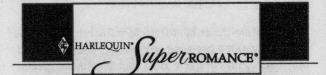

HARLEQUIN *Super*ROMANCE®

Welcome to Montana

BIG SKY COUNTRY

Home of the Rocky Mountains,
Yellowstone National Park,
slow-moving glaciers and
the spectacular Going
to the Sun Highway.

Set against this unforgettable background,
Harlequin Superromance introduces the
Maxwells of Montana—a family that's
lived and ranched here for generations.

You won't want to miss this brand-new trilogy—
three exciting romances by three of
your favorite authors.

MARRIED IN MONTANA
by Lynnette Kent on sale August 2001

A MONTANA FAMILY
by Roxanne Rustand on sale September 2001

MY MONTANA HOME
by Ellen James on sale October 2001

Available wherever Harlequin books are sold.

HARLEQUIN®
Makes any time special ®

Visit us at www.eHarlequin.com   HSRBSC

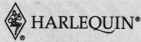

If you enjoyed what you just read,
then we've got an offer you can't resist!

Take 2 bestselling love stories FREE!
Plus get a FREE surprise gift!

*Harlequin truly does
make any time special. . . .
This year we are celebrating
weddings in style!*

A
Walk
Down
the Aisle
WEDDING CELEBRATION

To help us celebrate, we want you to tell us how wearing the Harlequin wedding gown will make your wedding day special. As the grand prize, Harlequin will offer one lucky bride the chance to **"Walk Down the Aisle"** in the Harlequin wedding gown!

There's more...

For her honeymoon, she and her groom will spend five nights at the **Hyatt Regency Maui.** As part of this five-night honeymoon at the hotel renowned for its romantic attractions, the couple will enjoy a candlelit dinner for two in Swan Court, a sunset sail on the hotel's catamaran, and duet spa treatments.

Maui • Molokai • Lanai

To enter, please write, in, 250 words or less, how wearing the Harlequin wedding gown will make your wedding day special. The entry will be judged based on its emotionally compelling nature, its originality and creativity, and its sincerity. This contest is open to Canadian and U.S. residents only and to those who are 18 years of age and older. There is no purchase necessary to enter. Void where prohibited. See further contest rules attached. Please send your entry to:

Walk Down the Aisle Contest

In Canada	In U.S.A.
P.O. Box 637	P.O. Box 9076
Fort Erie, Ontario	3010 Walden Ave.
L2A 5X3	Buffalo, NY 14269-9076

You can also enter by visiting www.eHarlequin.com
Win the Harlequin wedding gown and the vacation of a lifetime!
The deadline for entries is October 1, 2001.

HARLEQUIN®
Makes any time special ®

PHWDACONT1

HARLEQUIN WALK DOWN THE AISLE TO MAUI CONTEST 1197
OFFICIAL RULES
NO PURCHASE NECESSARY TO ENTER

1. To enter, follow directions published in the offer to which you are responding. Contest begins April 2, 2001, and ends on October 1, 2001. Method of entry may vary. Mailed entries must be postmarked by October 1, 2001, and received by October 8, 2001.

2. Contest entry may be, at times, presented via the Internet, but will be restricted solely to residents of certain geographic areas that are disclosed on the Web site. To enter via the Internet, if permissible, access the Harlequin Web site (www.eHarlequin.com) and follow the directions displayed online. Online entries must be received by 11:59 p.m. E.S.T. on October 1, 2001.

   In lieu of submitting an entry online, enter by mail by hand-printing (or typing) on an 8½" x 11" plain piece of paper, your name, address (including zip code), Contest number/name and in 250 words or fewer, why winning a Harlequin wedding dress would make your wedding day special. Mail via first-class mail to: Harlequin Walk Down the Aisle Contest 1197, (in the U.S.) P.O. Box 9076, 3010 Walden Avenue, Buffalo, NY 14269-9076, (in Canada) P.O. Box 637, Fort Erie, Ontario L2A 5X3, Canada.

   Limit one entry per person, household address and e-mail address. Online and/or mailed entries received from persons residing in geographic areas in which Internet entry is not permissible will be disqualified.

3. Contests will be judged by a panel of members of the Harlequin editorial, marketing and public relations staff based on the following criteria:
   - Originality and Creativity—50%
   - Emotionally Compelling—25%
   - Sincerity—25%

   In the event of a tie, duplicate prizes will be awarded. Decisions of the judges are final.

4. All entries become the property of Torstar Corp. and will not be returned. No responsibility is assumed for lost, late, illegible, incomplete, inaccurate, nondelivered or misdirected mail or misdirected e-mail, for technical, hardware or software failures of any kind, lost or unavailable network connections, or failed, incomplete, garbled or delayed computer transmission or any human error which may occur in the receipt or processing of the entries in this Contest.

5. Contest open only to residents of the U.S. (except Puerto Rico) and Canada, who are 18 years of age or older, and is void wherever prohibited by law; all applicable laws and regulations apply. Any litigation within the Province of Quebec respecting the conduct or organization of a publicity contest may be submitted to the Régie des alcools, des courses et des jeux for a ruling. Any litigation respecting the awarding of a prize may be submitted to the Régie des alcools, des courses et des jeux of for the purpose of helping the parties reach a settlement. Employees and immediate family members of Torstar Corp. and D. L. Blair, Inc., their affiliates, subsidiaries and all other agencies, entities and persons connected with the use, marketing or conduct of this Contest are not eligible to enter. Taxes on prizes are the sole responsibility of winners. Acceptance of any prize offered constitutes permission to use winner's name, photograph or other likeness for the purposes of advertising, trade and promotion on behalf of Torstar Corp., its affiliates and subsidiaries without further compensation to the winner, unless prohibited by law.

6. Winners will be determined no later than November 15, 2001, and will be notified by mail. Winners will be required to sign and return an Affidavit of Eligibility form within 15 days after winner notification. Noncompliance within that time period may result in disqualification and an alternative winner may be selected. Winners of trip must execute a Release of Liability prior to ticketing and must possess required travel documents (e.g. passport, photo ID) where applicable. Trip must be completed by November 2002. No substitution of prize permitted by winner. Torstar Corp. and D. L. Blair, Inc., their parents, affiliates, and subsidiaries are not responsible for errors in printing or electronic presentation of Contest, entries and/or game pieces. In the event of printing or other errors which may result in unintended prize values or duplication of prizes, all affected game pieces or entries shall be null and void. If for any reason the Internet portion of the Contest is not capable of running as planned, including infection by computer virus, bugs, tampering, unauthorized intervention, fraud, technical failures, or any other causes beyond the control of Torstar Corp. which corrupt or affect the administration, secrecy, fairness, integrity or proper conduct of the Contest, Torstar Corp. reserves the right, at its sole discretion, to disqualify any individual who tampers with the entry process and to cancel, terminate, modify or suspend the Contest or the Internet portion thereof. In the event of a dispute regarding an online entry, the entry will be deemed submitted by the authorized holder of the e-mail account submitted at the time of entry. Authorized account holder is defined as the natural person who is assigned to an e-mail address by an Internet access provider, online service provider or other organization that is responsible for arranging e-mail address for the domain associated with the submitted e-mail address. **Purchase or acceptance of a product offer does not improve your chances of winning.**

7. Prizes: (1) Grand Prize—A Harlequin wedding dress (approximate retail value: $3,500) and a 5-night/6-day honeymoon trip to Maui, HI, including round-trip air transportation provided by Maui Visitors Bureau from Los Angeles International Airport (winner is responsible for transportation to and from Los Angeles International Airport) and a Harlequin Romance Package, including hotel accomodations (double occupancy) at the Hyatt Regency Maui Resort and Spa, dinner for (2) two at Swan Court, a sunset sail on Kiele V and a spa treatment for the winner (approximate retail value: $4,000); (5) Five runner-up prizes of a $1000 gift certificate to selected retail outlets to be determined by Sponsor (retail value $1000 ea.). Prizes consist of only those items listed as part of the prize. Limit one prize per person. All prizes are valued in U.S. currency.

8. For a list of winners (available after December 17, 2001) send a self-addressed, stamped envelope to: Harlequin Walk Down Aisle Contest 1197 Winners, P.O. Box 4200 Blair, NE 68009-4200 or you may access the www.eHarlequin.com Web site through January 15, 2002.

Contest sponsored by Torstar Corp., P.O. Box 9042, Buffalo, NY 14269-9042, U.S.A.

PHWDACONT2

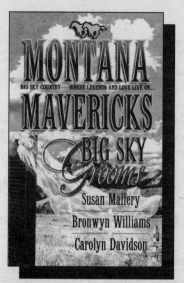

DON'T MISS OUT!

MONTANA MAVERICKS: BIG SKY GROOMS
Three brand-new historical stories about the Kincaids,
Montana's most popular family

RETURN TO WHITEHORN, MONTANA—
WHERE LEGENDS ARE BEGUN AND
LOVE LASTS FOREVER BENEATH THE BIG SKY....

Available in August 2001